Hearts Restored

It takes a child

A Relational Adventure

Cheryl Hug

Hearts Restored

-

HopeUnitingGenerations@Live.com

Hug Publishing
La Grande, Oregon

To my mother, Dorothy Pratt. Thank you, Mom, for teaching me wisdom and family. Thank you for telling me about Jesus and giving me freedom to find him for myself.

In memory of Jackie Coy, a dear friend and spiritual mother. Thank you, Jackie, for being there with open arms for me and teaching me to be childlike.

And a special thanks to Ruth Gately, who encouraged me to take real-life testimonies of healing and write this story. You are awesome and courageous, Ruth, and a great wife and mother.

Most of all, I want to thank my husband, Kent Hug, for his unending support and love. You're an inspiration to me and a great friend. You have brought me healing like no one else could. I love you!

CONTENTS

When I became a man I put away childish things, including the fear of childishness and the desire to be very grown up – C.S. Lewis

It is easy to be heavy: hard to be light. Satan fell by the force of gravity. – G.K. Chesterton

The spirit of bondage works by fear for the slave fears the rod: but love cries, Abba, Father; it disposes us to go to God, and behave ourselves towards God as children; and it gives us clear evidence of our union to God as His children, and so casts out fear. – Jonathan Edwards

Life is either a daring adventure, or nothing. – Helen Keller

Sometimes we make things too complicated when we really need to remember that the kingdom belongs to children. – Heidi Baker

Don't let what you didn't get in your childhood keep you from what God provides for His children – a perfectly faithful Father. – Bill Johnson

DAMSEL IN DISTRESS

If the Lord is with us, why has all this happened to us? Where are all the wonders that our fathers told us about?   *(Gideon)*

Am I crazy?

Her mother thought so.

"A ho dunk *ranch*? Driving a *truck*?" Her mother's eyes had rolled and the usual disapproving scowl marred her well-maintained complexion. She had wrinkled her nose in disgust. "I don't like it. Especially you hanging out with *those people* again. They fill your head with nonsense. But I suppose you don't have much choice, since you got yourself *fired* and all. Are you ever going to settle down and do something useful with your life?"

Those people were Cassie Watson, her best friend, and Cassie's family. Kristy had planned to return for her junior year at the university in another six weeks anyway. This job would provide room and board and some money to pay bills until she received her financial aid for school. It had seemed like a good idea.

But her mother had ripped into her.

"I'm not surprised you got yourself fired. You have no respect for authority."

Respect for authority?

She had never felt so yanked around. Daily, she was demeaned by lewd comments from male workers. Refusing to tolerate this is what got her fired.

But wasn't it time to stand up for herself?

To have some self-respect?

In the past, she wouldn't have complained. Old boyfriends talked the same way about her body. She had even used her body to get what she wanted. Or thought she wanted.

But she didn't want that anymore. She had changed. She was different. Cassie Watson kept telling her there was hope. And her new relationship with God convinced her she was worth more than that. Hadn't God shown her she was loved? Valuable? Precious to him? That he knew who she was and believed in her?

She wanted to be honored. Appreciated.

Loved for *herself*. Not just her body.

Was it all an impossible dream?

Things didn't look so good. She was broke. She'd been fired.

And her mother was disappointed. Probably ashamed of her.

But she couldn't please her mother anyway. Why did she keep trying? Her mother hated the Watsons because Kristy liked them. Cassie had introduced her to Jesus.

That was a threat too.

Anytime Kristy went against her mother's opinion, it was *disrespect for authority*.

She had tried to explain. To share her new faith.

It was horrible.

It always turned into a screaming match. And her sixteen-year-old brother, Toby, had taken on his usual role as "peacemaker," intervening and telling her to "calm down." Him with his cloud of depression, complete with creepy tattoos and piercings, in his usual shroud of death-décor, telling her to "get a grip?"

How humiliating!

Eastern Washington's dry hills rolled by and hot wind blew through Kristy Turner's open car windows. Late summer sun glared off the pavement and she blinked weary eyes. This was a new adventure. Shouldn't she be happy? Excited? Foreboding and rising panic was all she felt.

Who was she kidding? She was a miserable failure at being a *Christian* or sharing her faith, whatever that meant. She was a failure at *life*. How was she going to survive at the Watson ranch? With people who had it together?

And now Cassie was engaged. Their friendship would be different. The loneliness was already closing in. Why was it that every time she made a good friend they got engaged?

A warning light interrupted her thoughts.

Empty?

How long had that been on?

She was almost out of gas!

Didn't she get better mileage last time she made this trip?

Near Kennewick, she pulled off the freeway and found a gas station. Her last twenty dollars would have to do. She filled her water bottle in the bathroom and returned to the road.

Was half a tank going to get her there?

Strands of unruly hair stuck to her perspiring cheeks and forehead. Angrily, she swiped them away.

"This car is a piece of junk! The seats are splitting, the knobs on the dash are falling off, the locks stick and the air conditioner broke. It wasn't so bad it Seattle, but I can't stand in in this heat!"

She swiped the sweaty hairs away again. She couldn't get used to this tickling hair! Cutting her long, straight hair in layers around her face was a mistake. What had she been thinking?

With one hand on the wheel, she dug through her purse and grabbed a few ponytail holders. Yanking all her fly-away bangs on top of her head, she wrapped the band around it. Another band went around the rest of her straight, thick hair, lifting it off her over-heated neck.

"That's better."

She glanced at her reflection in the rear-view mirror and rolled her eyes.

Ridiculous.

Her mother's scowl reappeared in her mind, disdaining and critical eyes raking her from head to foot. "When are you going to do something with your hair? ... Who cut it like that? ... You could put on some make-up ... and lose some weight."

The comments pierced her soul. Again. Swallowing hard, she grabbed her water bottle, took a drink of the pipe-flavored water, and swiped at a stinging tear.

"Why can't she accept me the way I am? She doesn't love me. She hurts me."

The engine sputtered. Then lurched.

"No!"

Panic squeezed her chest. What was wrong?

It lurched again.

"Please Jesus!"

Stranded alongside the freeway, the stifling heat was much worse. Kristy cranked the engine, but the car refused to start. She beat on the steering wheel and then picked up her cell phone.

"Cassie! My car died!"

"Really? What's wrong with it?"

"It acts like it ran out of gas, but I just put some in. What should I do?"

"I don't know. Where are you?"

"I'm on the side of the road. On highway eighty-two. Just past Kennewick."

"Kennewick? Wait a minute. Let me check on something. I'll call back."

Silence.

"Cassie! Wait!"

The conversation was evidently over. Rolling her eyes, she flipped the phone shut. "Why does she always do that?"

Groaning, she pulled off her sandals and stuffed a sweatshirt around the seatbelt stubs. She cranked up the radio, grabbed a pillow from the overloaded backseat and shoved it against the passenger door. Stretching out on the seat, with bare feet out the opposite window, she gave in to tears.

§• ✦ •§

Billy Watson scanned the side of the freeway, squinting in the bright sunlight. Cassie said she was along here somewhere.

Topping a hill, he spotted a green Pontiac. He pulled over and parked a few car lengths behind it. Small tanned feet with red painted toenails dangled out the window. He opened the pickup door slowly, stepped to the hot pavement and quietly shut the door. Loud music vibrated through the air.

She was barely off the road, so he crept around to the passenger window, where her head lay on a pillow, eyes closed.

Was she asleep?

Probably not. Not with the music cranked up so loud.

He rapped on the windshield.

Bolting upright, her jaw dropped. She fumbled with the knob on the dash and turned down the music.

Sticking his head through the window, he grinned. "I heard there was a damsel in distress."

"Billy? What are you doing here?"

He motioned to his pick-up. "I came to the rescue on my white steed."

Her hair stuck straight up off the top of her head.

That's interesting.

"I just happened to be on my way home from Pasco. The combine broke down, so I'm on a trip for parts."

After getting past her hair-doo, he couldn't help noticing her swollen eyes and red nose. He tilted his head. "Are you okay?"

She lifted her chin. "Of course."

"If you say so." Amused, he turned away. "So what's wrong with your car?"

"I don't know."

"Pop the hood." He went to the front and lifted it. "Crank the engine!"

He chuckled. She looked funny with her hair like that. Like a little palm tree was growing on top of her head. Better yet, she reminded him of a bantam chicken, especially when she bristled and stuck her nose in the air, insisting she was okay. It didn't take a genius to tell she was not.

ᵹ❧ ❦ᵹ

Kristy made several attempts to start the engine, then Billy shouted over the hood, "Has it ever done this kind of thing before?"

"No."

He slammed it shut. "We'll find a mechanic."

Leaning out the driver's window, she squinted at him. "What do you think's wrong?"

After checking for traffic, he approached her window. "I'm not sure, but it might be the fuel pump. Did you hear any weird noises before the engine quit?"

"No."

"When was the last time you changed the fuel filter?"

She wrinkled her nose. "Fuel filter?"

He laughed. "Stay put. I'll pull in front and hook you up. We'll find some help in Umatilla."

He pulled in front of her, then backed to a short distance from her bumper and parked. From behind the seat, he produced a tow-rope, attached it to her bumper and hooked it to his hitch. A semi passed at high speed and the car shook violently. She shuddered.

He returned to the window. "Now, I'm going to take it slow. Put it in neutral and turn on your emergency blinkers. It will be harder to steer without the motor running and you have to push real hard to get any brakes, but you can do it."

The pickup moved forward slowly and jerked the car into motion. Kristy worked to keep the car a safe distance from the pickup in front of her. Her phone blared. It was probably Cassie, but she dared not answer. It took all her concentration to drive.

Finally, they exited the freeway at Umatilla and pulled into a service station. Billy went in and she punched Cassie's number.

"Why didn't you tell me?"

"Tell you what?"

"You were sending your brother?"

Cassie laughed. "You got a problem with that? I figured you were desperate. What's wrong with Billy anyway?"

"Nothing. But you could've prepared me. I'm a mess!"

"Why would you care? It's just Billy."

"Yeah, *just* Billy." Kristy glanced in the rearview mirror and gasped. "My hair!" Yanking out the top knot and pony tail, she shook it loose.

"Relax. He's a farm boy. He doesn't expect you to look like a fashion model, stranded in the middle of the desert on a hot day, wilting beside the highway."

Kristy sighed. "You could have warned me."

"Lighten up, okay?"

⚘⚘⚘

"Four hundred dollars?" Round blue eyes pooled with tears.

Billy winced. "Yeah."

"What am I going to do?" Voice catching, Kristy's chin quivered. "I need my car for school."

They were back on the freeway, headed to Wallua Crossing. The car was with the mechanic.

"I'm sorry, Kristy, but like I said, it's too late to tow your car home today. I'm not set up for it. It wouldn't be safe. If you don't want him to fix it, we'll call back and tell him. The neighbors have a trailer we could probably borrow and haul it home another day."

She sniffled. "I suppose you're right."

He glanced at her.

Thick brown hair, now liberated from the palm tree, hung around her shoulders. Freshly brushed, it gleamed in the sunshine. It was shorter than he remembered, but ... it was beautiful. He'd always secretly admired it.

She was pretty.

He shook himself and looked away.

He'd better not go there.

She must have cried off all her make-up. She looked great without it, but was not her normal, put-together self.

Two short gasps drew him to look again. Face fixed on the road, she swallowed hard, lower lip quivering.

Was she going to cry? Right here in front of him?

"Kristy, it's not just the car, is it?"

She looked out the passenger window. "You're right. It's not just the car. … It's … it's everything!"

He paused.

"When did you last eat?"

Brushing away a tear, she faced him. "Eat? I don't know. Probably last night." She turned back. "Besides, it doesn't matter. I'm not hungry. And I'm out of money."

"You haven't eaten since last night? It's almost six o'clock! And from the looks of all the stuff in that car, I'll bet you were packing all night. Well, I'm hungry and you'd feel better if you ate something. We'll stop in Pendleton. My treat."

"I can't let you do that."

"Why not?"

"Because … uh … I'm … I'm not eating."

"Not eating? Why?"

She sniffled. "I'm really confused. And I've gained weight this summer. My mother says I'm fat."

"Fat?" He scowled. "You look good to me. Besides, don't fast to lose—" Biting back his opinion, he fell silent. He studied the highway, then turned to her. "Cassie says you're going through a hard time and stressed out. Is that true?"

"Yeah."

"It sounds to me like you need comfort."

She turned to him. "You think so?"

He nodded. "I do. A little food and lots of hugs."

One eyebrow rose skeptically. "Hugs?"

"Of course. The food I can provide." He smiled crookedly. "The hugs will have to wait until we get home. Mom, Cassie and Hannah are good for that."

Kristy glanced at the side of his face. He thought she needed *hugs*? From his mother and Cassie of course. Certainly not from him. He kept his distance. As always.

Letting out a soft hiss, she looked out the passenger window. Well, she could certainly see why. He wouldn't be interested in the likes of her. Here she was bawling like a baby. He probably thought she was an idiot.

What was wrong with her?

She had a job now.

She had a plan.

She had escaped her mother's criticism.

Even though sleep deprived, broke and hungry, she should be able to keep it together better than this. But not today. She was a mess.

But it felt good to have someone help her. She had been stranded. Hadn't known what to do.

She stole a look. Lean, tanned and strong, his square jaw-line was firm. Stubborn. Like Cassie's. Full eyebrows and long dark lashes rimmed gray eyes. She'd always liked his eyes. They were … kind. And thoughtful. They made her wonder what he was thinking. A large patrician nose added to his aura of superiority. Or was it confidence? Dark curls peeked from under the rim of his ball cap. He wore a fresh T-shirt and clean, well-fitting blue jeans. His were strong, good looks. She'd always thought so, but hadn't dwelt on it. He was too old and definitely out of her league.

She twisted her lips. He would make someone a good husband. Some good church girl.

THE KNIGHT'S TOO SHINY

I will celebrate before the Lord, I will become even more undignified than this, and I will be humiliated in my own eyes.   *(King David)*

Billy leaned back in his chair and studied his dinner companion. Color had returned to her lips. Large eyes, the color of a tropical sea, searched his as she talked.

She had been hungry. Food must've helped her talk, because she was going at it with gusto, even though she was still a bit weepy. She looked so vulnerable, especially when those big eyes filled with tears. And with no make-up, she looked real young.

About twelve.

But she wasn't *shaped* like a twelve-year-old.

He looked away, suppressing a laugh.

"What's so funny?"

His face went hot, eyes darting back. "Oh, nothing. You were saying?"

"My mother. I can't seem to please her. Everything I do is wrong."

It was strange she would tell him all this, but he went with it. "Do you *want* to please her?"

Blue eyes glued to his. "I don't know. I've probably given up."

"How old are you anyway?"

"Twenty-one."

He grunted. "Sounds old enough to give up pleasing your mother."

"Then why does it hurt so much when she criticizes me?"

He didn't answer, but held her gaze.

"She got on my case yesterday when I got fired. She says I don't respect authority. And have a bad attitude."

He sighed and twirled his glass with the tips of his fingers. "Do you?"

"Do I what?"

He focused on her again. "Have a bad attitude?"

"Uh …" She sputtered. "I don't know. Maybe. I don't mean to."

"Is there something your mother did? Something you hold against her? There can be something like that behind a bad attitude."

Jaw clamping shut, Kristy blanched.

After a long awkward silence, he paid the bill, rose to his feet, reached for his ball cap and placed it on his head.

"Hey. Let's get back on the road. It's getting late."

Out of the corner of his eye, Billy studied her profile. Whatever he said sure shut her up. His mouth twisted in a sardonic smile. He had a knack of doing that with girls. She hadn't said anything for a good ten minutes.

Eyes returning to the road, he scanned the rugged forest lining the freeway. A picture flashed through his mind of her in church the spring before. She had seemed so happy then. Care-free. Singing out and really enjoying her new faith.

Where was her smile now? He'd like to see it again. And her voice. She had a great voice. Had she stopped singing? She had seemed so happy when she sang.

He stole a glance. Smooth and flawless skin. A small upturned nose. Soft, pouty lips.

She was quite a looker. Not a model type, but cute. Real cute. She was even cute earlier with that silly palm tree on top of her head.

The thick woods thinned and Billy drove down into the small town of Wallua Crossing. The vast, round valley lay beyond, distant mountains glowing in the setting sun.

He exhaled. Home. The Valley of Peace. There was peace here. Peace he could feel as he descended into the valley.

Glancing over to his sleeping companion, a wave of tenderness swept over him. "Lord," he prayed softly. "Is this lust? Something about her stirs me. Or is it because I just decided I need a wife?"

He studied her face, now peaceful in sleep, dark lashes fanning her flushed cheeks. His eyes traced her curled form, then settled on petite bare feet, lying against his jeaned thigh. She had hugged the door most of the trip, but now asleep, didn't seem to mind touching him.

With her feet, anyway.

She was exhausted and hurting. He knew how these things went. It was *God* she needed.

"Give her peace, Father," he whispered. "And heal her heart."

⇔ ‣ • ‣ ⇔

"Hey Kristy." Billy patted her foot.

She shook herself from a deep sleep. Curled on the pickup seat, she lay with a pillow under her head. Puzzled, she stared at it. Did she put it there? She blushed and sat up, rubbing bleary eyes. Her lack of sleep must have caught up with her.

"I thought you might like to know we're getting close to home. You've been asleep for most of an hour," Billy said, turning off the highway onto a gravel road.

Grabbing her purse, she pulled out a brush and undid her mussed ponytail. Curious, she paused, turning to him. "Did you put that pillow under my head?"

Billy smiled. "Yeah. It was quite a trick. You didn't look comfortable with your neck all crooked, so I grabbed it from your stuff behind the seat. I stopped for a second in town and thought you'd wake up, but you were really out of it."

Blushing again, she shook her freshly brushed hair and wetted her lips. "Thanks." She smiled self-consciously. "I guess I was pretty tired."

Soon they arrived. Nestled in the trees on the side of the mountain, the Watson ranch overlooked the large valley, glowing under a rising bright moon.

Billy pulled up to the lighted front porch. "I'll take in your bags, but then I'm off to the shop to unload these parts." He opened the door and started pulling duffle bags out of the bed of the pickup.

Circling the truck to stand beside him, she looked up and frowned. She'd forgotten how tall he was. He made her feel like a little kid.

He grabbed the bags and they headed for the front door. She turned to him. "Thanks, Billy. I really appreciate your help."

Flashing her a lopsided grin, his eyes twinkled. "Any time."

Cassie burst out the door, rushed off the porch and greeted her with a warm embrace. "Kristy! You made it!"

Cassie's mother, Linda, stood in the doorway, with her younger sister, Hannah. "Welcome to Watsonville!" Both reached out to receive her with enthusiastic hugs.

※ ⁂ ※

Bright moonlight shone through the open bedroom window as Cassie and Kristy lay in the queen-sized bed. A warm breeze blew over them and Cassie chattered. It was late, but the summer events and new engagement had her buzzing with excitement. She paused.

Kristy was quiet.

"Kristy, are you still awake?"

"Yeah, I'm awake."

"Sorry for dominating the conversation, but I'm so excited. And so happy to have you here."

"It's okay."

"I know you're hurting. Want to talk about it?"

"Mom and I had a big fight yesterday. And another this morning. She didn't want me to come. I tried to explain. I tried to explain a lot of things.

"Cassie, I don't know what to do. I can't get along with my mother. I want to honor her and make things better, but I can't. Aren't these things supposed to get fixed when you accept Jesus? It's not as if she doesn't believe in God. She always took us to church. Why won't she listen to me? Why does she get so offended? It seems like she hates me."

Heavy silence ensued.

"Billy says I probably have hidden resentment."

Cassie lifted her head off the pillow. "You talked to Billy?"

Kristy harrumphed. "How could I not? He comes upon me unannounced. I looked like a mussed, crying toddler, my eyes swollen and my nose running. My bangs were even tied up on top of my head! I tried to fake it, but I was so tired and obviously a mess. I just went with it. Besides, I couldn't help but answer his questions. I just poured out the whole story."

"That's interesting. Billy usually stays away from such personal subjects with girls. … Do you have something against your mother?"

Kristy hesitated. "There is something. But I'm not ready to talk about it. I've tried to forgive her."

"You don't *try* to forgive. You just do it."

"Cassie!" Kristy groaned, then sat up in bed and folded her legs. "Both you and your brother are about as sensitive and tactful as your father's prize bull!"

"Oh. Sorry. Go ahead."

After recollecting her thoughts, Kristy went on. "My mother doesn't accept me. I've always felt that way. Like it's painful for her to be with me. It seems my very existence pains her. … And she resents any close relationships I have with other people."

"You told me about this. Too bad your father isn't around."

Groaning, Kristy dropped down and rolled away from Cassie.

Heavy silence returned.

Cassie sighed.

Her thoughts traveled back to a conversation she and Kristy had the spring before in their shared apartment.

Also late at night.

Also when Kristy was upset about her mother.

"Tell me about your father, Kristy," she had said.

Kristy stiffened on the couch, turning away. In a small voice, she had said toward the wall, "He left ten years ago. I haven't seen him since."

"What happened?"

"Mom says they had a fight. They'd been fighting a lot before he left. He was gone a lot. Worked a lot."

"Were you close?"

"I thought we were. He always told me I was special. I guess I wasn't that special. Since he never came back."

"Did he send child support for you and Toby?"

"No. We moved to Seattle not too long after he left." Her voice grew quiet. "According to Mom, he doesn't want anything to do with us."

Cassie frowned. "I'm so sorry, Kristy. That would be tough. I don't know what I'd do without my father. He's always there for me when Mom gets exasperated. Daddies are good for that."

"Evidently mine isn't."

"Do you know where he is?"

"No."

"Do you pray for him?"

"Sometimes. But it hurts to even think of him. He betrayed me. I also feel bad for Toby. He seems so lost."

In the dark silence of the bedroom, Cassie wondered if she should have returned to the awkward and painful subject. Kristy always clammed up when she asked about her father.

Kristy sniffled beside her.

"I'm sorry I brought him up, Kristy."

"It's okay."

Cassie sat up and grabbed her friend's hand. "God will have to make up the difference. Father, your word says you're a father to the fatherless. Be a father for Kristy. We don't know what's happened to Kristy's father, but would you touch him right now? Draw him to you and back to his children. They need his love."

Kristy sat back up in bed, grabbed a box of Kleenex, and blew her nose.

Suddenly, Cassie had an idea. She rolled off the bed, scampered to the door, flipped on the light and rummaged through the closet.

Kristy squinted in the bright light. "What are you doing?"

"Getting my shoes."

"Shoes?"

"Yeah. It's too heavy in here. We've got to do something about that."

"What?"

"Get your shoes on."

Cassie disappeared out the door and returned with two towels.

Rising from the bed, Kristy blinked hard and slid her feet into sandals. "Why the towels?"

"You'll see. Just be quiet. Follow me."

Looking down at her pajama top and shorts, she whispered, "Like this?"

Cassie smiled. "That's part of the adventure. Look at me!"

Giggling softly, they slipped out the door.

Tiptoeing down the hallway, Kristy whispered, "Where are we going?"

"Shh… You'll see."

Soon they were out the back door and into the yard with a full moon brightening the dark landscape. "Where are you taking me?"

Cassie giggled. "We're on an adventure. Trust me, you'll get some relief from your pain."

Kristy followed her crazy friend through the backyard and onto a dirt path. Soon they were in a moonlit pasture and climbing a hill into the woods. It was dark. And Cassie strode through the trees waving the flashlight. Like a lunatic.

She stumbled on a rock. "Ouch! Cassie, this is ridiculous! Wait up! What are we doing? Going on a midnight hike or something?"

Cassie stopped in the path and waited. "Something like that."

"How much further?"

"Not much. It's just ahead."

After rounding a bend, they came into a clearing and she heard the sound of running water. The path led up a grassy knoll that overlooked a glassy pond, shimmering in the bright moonlight.

"Wow! I didn't know this was here."

"Yeah. It's nice and private. Hidden in the trees like this. Daddy built it when I was little, for irrigation and watering the cattle. It's fed from a spring up the hill." Cassie stopped, set the towels on a large log, and pulled off her pajama top.

"Cassie! What are you doing?"

Cassie laughed. "Something I should do more often." Slipping out of her shoes, she pulled off her shorts. "Going skinny-dipping! The water's great this time of year."

Amazed, Kristy watched the moonlight shine off her crazy friend's backside. Cassie hurried to the edge of the pool and dove in.

"Cassie!"

Cassie surfaced and shook her head of loose hair, sending water splashing. "Come on! Jump in! The water's perfect."

Kristy backed up.

"Can't you swim?"

"Of course. I love to swim."

"Then what are you waiting for? A written invitation?"

Kristy laughed. "You're crazy! But here I come!" Pulling off her clothing and leaving it in a rumpled pile beside Cassie's, she crossed over to the edge and hesitated. "Is it deep over here? Can I dive?"

"It's deep enough. And smooth on the bottom. Just dive shallow."

Soon the two were racing through the water. They splashed each other, giggling and laughing. "It feels good, doesn't it?" Cassie asked, treading water.

"Yes, it does. How often do you do this?"

"I used to do it a lot. But lately I've been preoccupied. Not in a bad way or anything."

"It's Jeff, isn't it?"

"Yeah. He'll be here in the morning. He comes every weekend, you know."

"You told me." Kristy giggled. "I feel like a kid again."

"That's the idea."

Kristy took a breath and plunged under the water.

♺♻

"Hey Kristy! Rise and shine!" Cassie stood by the bed, already fully dressed. "We're canning applesauce and freezing green beans today. Mom wants to get an early start."

Kristy popped up. "What time is it?"

"Oh, seven or so."

"How long have you been up?"

"Not long. Don't worry, I didn't have the heart to wake you. Come on down." Cassie disappeared out the door.

Kristy rolled out of bed, threw on her clothes and ran to the bathroom to run a brush through her mop of hair. Pond water didn't exactly condition it, but she'd have to take care of it later. She pulled it back in the usual shaggy pony-tail.

The whole day was spent in the kitchen with Linda, Cassie and Hannah. Kristy was hesitant at first, not knowing much about food preservation or cooking for a large family, but Linda was a great teacher, encouraging her graciously. They chatted happily and even though she worked hard, Kristy enjoyed herself. The camaraderie of the girls was somehow relaxing and refreshing. She dropped into bed that night exhausted, but happy.

Saturday dawned bright and sunny. Kristy continued helping Cassie and Hannah with chores. Laundry, cleaning, cooking, and food preservation. There seemed an endless supply of work in this place. The guys only came in for meals. They were still hard at work getting the combine fixed.

That night she and Cassie were finishing up the dishes in the kitchen when a warm familiar baritone, accompanied by guitar strumming, drifted in from the living room.

> *I will worship …*
> *With all of my heart …*
> *I will praise you …*
> *With all of my strength …*

Kristy stopped to listen. "That's one of my favorites."

Linda smiled. "Go join him, Kristy. I'll finish up here."

She smiled. "Thanks." She crept into the living room and sat, suddenly shy.

On the couch, Billy sang with his guitar, a pile of papers on the floor. His back towards her, he hadn't seen her. When she sang the echo, Billy turned and flashed her a smile.

> *I will seek you … I will seek you*
> *All of my days … All of my days*
> *I will follow … I will follow*
> *All of your ways … All your ways …*[1]

The song ended and he winked. "That sounds good. This next one is new. Come closer, so you can see the words."

After several songs, Kristy looked up. The whole family had entered the room. They gradually took seats and joined them for a few more songs. Peace filled the air, warming her heart.

Billy turned to her. "Hey, Kristy. How about singing with me at church tomorrow?"

"Uh …" She swallowed. "I don't think so. … But maybe next week. We'll see."

"That's too bad, but suit yourself."

❧ ❦ ❧

Trailing after Cassie and Jeff, Kristy entered Fishtrap Family Fellowship. Soft music played as she settled in a chair next to Cassie.

Cindy Harding approached, reached out, and gave her a hug.

"Kristy! What brings you back so early?"

Cassie piped in. "She's working for Dad. We needed some help."

"I wanted to spend some time on the ranch anyway."

"Are you enjoying yourself?" Cindy asked.

Kristy smiled. "Yes. Very much."

They were interrupted by Billy, who called them to order. Cindy returned to sit beside her husband and Kristy looked up to the platform, where he stood with his guitar and read from his Bible.

> *"Praise the Lord, my soul; all my inmost being, praise his holy name. Praise the Lord, my soul, and forget not all his benefits—who forgives all your sins and heals all your diseases, who redeems your life from the pit and crowns you with love and compassion, who satisfies your desires with good things so that your youth is renewed like the eagle's."*

He started to pray and she bowed her head. When she raised her eyes, a young woman had stepped up beside him, holding a microphone.

Kristy's jaw dropped. She was gorgeous. Tall and willowy, with short, fashionable hair, she looked like a sophisticated movie star. Burning jealousy threatened, but she tamped it down. She frowned. When she refused to sing with Billy, she didn't know he would ask *her*. He could've told her.

When the girl opened her mouth, Kristy was dumbfounded. She had a beautiful voice. A clear, well-pitched soprano.

She elbowed Cassie and whispered in her ear, "Who's that?"

"Marcel Peterson."

"Does she sing with him all the time?"

Cassie shrugged. "Once in a while."

"Where was she last spring?"

"Visiting her father."

Billy hit the front of his guitar, strummed one loud, single chord and belted out.

> *I will dance, I will sing*

To be mad, for my King
Nothing else is hindering
There's passion in my soul!
I'll become,
Even more undignified than this! ... [2]

Drums rolled and Billy began dancing with his guitar. People came out of their seats and danced in the front and side aisles. Kristy gazed around the room, recoiling.

She'd forgotten how it was around here. This stuff always made her uncomfortable. Dropping back into her chair, she studied the faces of the dancers. Everyone was smiling and laughing. Some, like herself, chose to sit, but most were older people or visitors. She looked again at the laughing group, Ben, Linda, Jeff, Cassie, Joey and Hannah among them.

Pain throbbed in her soul.

Could she ever be that free?

It just wasn't in her.

She shook herself. In the face of the rising festive atmosphere, a sadness engulfed her.

Eventually, Billy and the others left the front and Pastor Evan rose to speak.

"In Luke chapter ten, Jesus sends out the seventy-two. He tells them to *heal the sick and tell them 'The kingdom of God has come near to you.'* When they come back, listen to what happens."

"*The seventy-two returned with joy and said, 'Lord, even the demons submit to us in your name.'*

"*Then Jesus replied, 'I saw Satan fall like lightning from heaven. I have given you authority to trample on snakes and scorpions and to overcome all the power of the enemy...'*

"*Then Jesus, full of joy through the Holy Spirit, said, 'I praise you, Father, Lord of heaven and earth, because you have hidden these things from the wise and learned, and revealed them to little children. Yes, Father, for this is what you were pleased to do.'*

"The seventy-two brought the kingdom of God to those cities and Jesus saw Satan fall like lightning from heaven. They disrupted the demonic powers in the heavenly realms.

Who did this? Jesus was thrilled to say that it wasn't wise and learned people, but *little children*. People who have made themselves little children. Children can enter the kingdom and children can move in power. Jesus was over-joyed about this truth.

"Today we have a special treat. My nephew, Joshua, is visiting and I've asked him to share something."

A young man, about twenty, rose from his seat and stepped up to the stage. Kristy had never seen him before. He looked like any ordinary guy she would see at school. He took the microphone.

"Okay, so I've been learning to hang out and have fun with Jesus, right? So, I work at Wendy's, at the drive up window. This group of guys pulls up and I notice the guy has his arm in a sling. I tell him Jesus likes to heal and ask if I can pray for him. He shrugs and says, 'Sure, go ahead.' I just say a simple prayer like, "The kingdom of God is here. Thank you Jesus that you love to heal people. Come, Holy Spirit. Heal his arm."

"Well, the guy's eyes get big. He starts pulling at the sling. He says his arm's getting hot. He grabs the hamburgers from me and speeds away, screeching his tires. A while later, he comes into the place asking for me. I come out to the cash registers and he doesn't have the sling on. He pulls me out the door to the parking lot and tells me I have to pray for his buddy. He opens the back door to his car and there's this guy with a splint on his leg. He says his knee is like, messed up. I put my hands on him and thanked Papa for heaven on earth. I commanded the pain to leave and the healing to come.

"Pretty soon the guy jumps out of the car and starts hopping around cussing, yelling and pulling off his splint. He says his leg is 'burning up.'"

Laughing and clapping interrupted him, but he continued.

"I told him to try out his leg. See what happened. Pretty soon he's sprinting around the parking lot whooping and hollering. The next thing I know, he opens his trunk and pulls out a pile of drugs and stuff and dumps them at my feet.

He says, "I'm done with this stuff! ... To make a long story short, the guy got saved! ..."

By this time the whole church was on their feet, cheering and laughing. Kristy remained seated. He was healed? A desire rose in her. She wanted to do that too. But could she? How? The whole thing confused her. She just couldn't picture herself that free. Taking that kind of risk.

Smiling, the pastor called the people to order and motioned for Joshua to take his seat.

"Joshua positioned himself as a child and demonic powers fell that day. It sounds like fun, doesn't it? It takes a child. The heart of a child is not far from the Creator. It's still full of trust, wonder, vulnerability and joy.

"But becoming childlike doesn't appeal to most of us. Parents hurt us. Friends hurt us. We failed, and instead of celebrating our risk and encouraging us, leaders berated and hurt us. But look what can happen if we put that behind us and take Jesus's challenge to change, become a child and enter the Kingdom! ..."

Kristy stared at him.

"Some of you had a very short childhood. You learned early to be independent, to be afraid, to quit trusting, never take a risk. You lost your sense of awe and wonder. You had to understand everything and be in control.

Do you think a little child feels comfortable when he first learns to walk? Or climb? Or play ball? Or read? No, he falls down repeatedly. He fails repeatedly. But he keeps on trying and taking the risks ..."

She shifted in her seat.

"As children, we don't have to prove we're important or that we're mature. We don't have to understand everything or be in control. We just trust our daddy that he loves us, hears us and will teach us. We receive love. We receive instruction. We have fun. We take risks. ..."

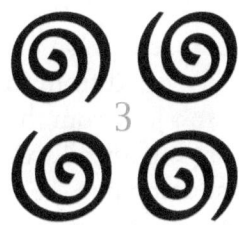

THE KNIGHT'S TOO ROUGH

Listen, O daughter ... Forget your people and your father's house. The king is enthralled with your beauty.
(King David)

Kristy shifted down and turned the huge empty truck into the cut field. Bouncing across the stubble, she spied Billy at the other end, sitting in his combine, waiting. Was his bin full? Already? She had to wait in line to dump her load. It must have taken longer than she thought.

Billy opened the door and scowled. Jerking his arm around, he motioned to Kristy from his high perch.

"Hey! Pull up closer! No! That way!"

"I'm trying!" she yelled, but the two massive engines drowned out her voice. Head turned away, Billy was concentrating on positioning the discharge auger. He jerked up a palm, motioned her to halt and gave a curt nod. The huge augers started running, more noise filling the dusty air.

Perspiration beading on her forehead, she grabbed the water bottle.

Nothing to it? Right, Cassie. This truck is huge!

And where was the gentle Billy who put the pillow under her head when she was sleeping? Or the singing angel?

Nowhere to be seen.

After two long, hot days, she wasn't sure she was getting the hang of it. Every time Billy yelled from that combine, she broke out in a sweat. And it wasn't just from the heat.

At first she thought driving for Billy would be fun, but he was a different person on that combine.

All business.

Kristy reflected on the last five days. For the most part, she was enjoying herself here with the Watson's. Cassie's parents, Ben and Linda, were different. It was obvious they loved each other. Their love spread through the whole household. There was security here. And peace.

Cassie and she had some great talks, late into the night. They'd even visited the pond again, for another midnight swim. It was so good to be back with her friend. But Cassie was preoccupied much of the time. With Jeff.

She had never seen Jeff so happy. He was beaming. Every spare moment was spent with Cassie, usually holding her hand. They were planning a December wedding and Cassie had asked her to be the maid of honor.

Maid of honor? Her? It seemed Linda and Hannah were excited about it. Hannah wasn't the least bit worried about her taking this place of honor, and was content to be a bridesmaid. It was to be a simple wedding, with the two of them and a cousin attending Cassie. Cassie's two brothers and Sam Wallace would be groomsmen for Jeff.

Billy was right. His sisters and mother were good for hugs. And those hugs were seeping into her soul.

However, Billy kept his distance.

It was better that way.

He could be kind. Like he had been after he rescued her on the freeway. But that messed with her too. Cassie said it was because she'd always dated jerks. That she was comfortable with jerks.

She was probably right.

Billy was a Christian. He was kind because he was supposed to be. It was nothing personal.

But he had been so tender in the pickup. She felt something different from him.

Cared for.

Her mouth twisted. That was then. Now that he was back home and hard at work, she didn't exist. She was nothing but a hired hand.

And a green one.

That irritated him.

He hadn't paid much attention to her, except in asking her to sing with him. That had been fun. She had really missed singing. It was like she forgot how for a while. Now it was all coming back. But she couldn't lead with him at church. Not yet.

Maybe next week.

But maybe not.

Her chin lifted.

He could ask Marcel. She was a good church girl.

ॐ ॐ ॐ

"Ben," Linda said, approaching the bed. "Have you been praying for your son?"

"Which one?"

"Billy."

"Not recently. Why?"

She pulled back the covers and crawled in, cuddling into the crook of his arm. He flipped the light off and turned to her. Sighing, he pulled her against him. A long day of hard work had left them both tired.

"He acts a little uncomfortable with Kristy here," Linda said.

"Do you think he's interested in her?"

"I don't know, but something's going on. He's unusually quiet, and thoughtful. I've caught him staring a few times. I think

33

he's attracted to her."

"She's a pretty girl. He's a guy."

"I think this is more than a casual interest, Ben. Billy isn't like that. He's usually so distant with girls. I've never seen him like this. With Jeff and Cassie so absorbed in each other, he's a bit lonely. Could we pray for him?"

Ben began, "Father, protect Billy. Give him wisdom in this situation. Also, comfort Kristy."

Linda added, "Help me to reach her, Lord. She's amazing, but she puts up so many walls. ... Show me how to love her."

Soft snoring sounded from Ben's limp and relaxed form. She smiled. "Excuse him, Lord, he's out."

&❧ ❧&

Billy entered the kitchen for breakfast and found Kristy helping Cassie put food on the table. He pulled out a chair. "Hey Kristy, tomorrow's Sunday. Would you like to go get your car after church?"

Kristy had already told the mechanic she would come and get her car. Billy and Joey had offered to replace the fuel pump in the shop, if she wasn't in a hurry. She didn't have the four hundred dollars, anyway. As it was, it was a stretch to come up with the money to buy the new part.

Surprised, Kristy looked at him. "You'll take me?"

He smiled. "Sure. Did you think I'd offer to fix your car if I hadn't planned to help you get it here? The Johnson's said I could borrow their trailer."

Kristy blushed. "Sure. I guess I never thought about how you would take me to get it."

"We'll take my pick-up. If we leave right after church, there should be plenty of daylight." He smiled again, but the others came in and he dropped the subject.

The next afternoon, they started down the freeway and he gazed at her sideways. "You're awfully quiet."

"I am? Sorry."

"Sorry? I wasn't scolding you. Are you okay?"

"I'm fine. It's just an adjustment for me, working on a ranch."

"Do you like it?"

She shrugged. "Some parts are great. It's beautiful. And I really like cooking and canning with the girls."

"But driving the truck in the hot dusty field is not your favorite thing?"

A smile tugged at her lips. "Right."

His eyes shone with a teasing light. "Even when you're driving that truck for me?"

She glanced down at her fingernails and didn't smile back. "Not really."

"Not really?" He laughed nervously. "My ego just took a whipping!"

She looked out the window.

It was a good time to change the subject.

They were crossing the Blue Mountains again and large fir trees lined the road. This had to be near the famous Oregon Trail and she forced her thoughts in that direction, imagining what it would be like to cross this rough terrain in a covered wagon.

"The old Oregon trail was through here, wasn't it?"

He grunted in assent, but didn't take the bait.

Apparently lost in thought, Billy didn't break the long silence. This was awkward.

She shifted in the seat. "You didn't have to take me back, you know. You've already done quite a bit for me."

He turned to study her curiously, then wagged his head, smirking. "I wouldn't have missed it. This gives me a chance to spend time with a beautiful woman."

She gasped. "Billy!"

"What?"

"Don't!"

"Don't what?"

"Don't flirt with me."

"Why not? You are a beautiful woman. What's wrong with me saying so?"

Without thinking, Kristy blurted out, "Guys who tell me that always want something. So what do you want?"

"Whoa! What brought that on?"

She turned away.

Billy turned back to the road.

A few moments later he responded, eyes fixed on the freeway. "Somebody must have really hurt you."

Her jaw clamped. "Yep."

After another long pause, Billy turned to her. "Kristy." Gentleness laced his voice. "Not all men come to take. Some come to restore."

ᏰᏰ Ᏸ Ᏸ ᏰᏰ

Bleep, bleep, bleep ... The continuous high-pitched sound pierced James Turner's consciousness. Constant throbbing in his forehead and back were forcing him out of a black fog.

The fog closed in again, pulling him back into oblivion. He stirred and moaned, fighting to regain his last thought. The terrible throbbing returned. When he tried to turn his head, he realized he was restrained.

"Thank God! ... Jim! Wake up!"

His eyes opened. In a dimly lit room, the smiling face of Barry Smith, his boss and friend, leaned over him. "Welcome back to the land of the living!"

The soft click of an I. V. pump accentuated the quiet of the room. Pain radiated outward from the middle of his back. Restrained in a hammock-type bed, James couldn't turn or lift his head. His eyes roamed his immediate surroundings. His left arm was strapped to an arm board and a blood pressure cuff enclosed the biceps of his other arm. It began to inflate. Looking down, he noticed both legs bound in ace wraps. A strange sensation gripped him and he tried to move his toes. Nothing.

Panic overtook him.

"What happened? Where am I?" he said. He tried to lift his head and sharp pain stabbed his upper body. He grimaced.

Barry placed a hand on his forehead. "Stay down, Jim. Relax.

36

You're in the hospital. You've been in a car accident. It's a wonder you weren't killed. If you had a look at that car of yours, you'd have to admit someone was watching out for you."

Memories returned and he closed his eyes. A red Camaro careening out of nowhere. Head on, slamming into him. An explosion. Darkness. Pain.

Then the old sadness and weight of guilt returned. He groaned, throwing his right arm, the only thing free, over his eyes.

A nurse appeared, a grim smile on her face. "Hey, you're awake. How are you doing?"

He groaned again. "I was going to ask you that. What happened to my legs?" he asked, peering at her from under his forearm.

Her dark eyes traveled to Barry and they exchanged looks. "Both legs are broken. There's a place in your back that's broken too. We're still unsure of the lasting damage. We were waiting for you to regain consciousness and stabilize before operating."

She took hold of his big toe. "Can you feel anything down there? Can you move your toes?"

James frowned. "No. I don't feel a thing. And I can't move either. That's not good, is it?"

UP THE MOUNTAIN

*Unless you change and become like little children, you will
never enter the kingdom of heaven.*   *(Jesus Christ)*

Billy awoke to smacking on his bedroom window. Rain? He leapt
out of bed and went to look out. A good one. They wouldn't be
back on the combines until Monday, at the earliest. This could
be their chance to go to the mountains.

After breakfast, he approached his father. "Dad, if we left
early tomorrow, we could be back at work by Monday morning.
It will take at least that long for the grain to dry, anyway. This is
the best time of year for camping in the high lakes."

His father hesitated. "It's a pretty busy time to take off. Who
were you thinking of taking?"

"Jeff and Joey want to go and I thought we could take Cassie,
Hannah and Kristy. I could borrow backpacks for them from
Fred. It would be a good break for all of us and lots of fun. I
haven't asked the girls yet. Thought I'd run it by you first."

From his recliner, his father laid the newspaper in his lap and
peered over his reading glasses. It had been a full two weeks since

Kristy arrived and there was a good week left of harvesting. "Well, I appreciate that, but you want to take the whole crew?"

Billy nodded.

Returning to the paper, he turned a page and scanned its contents. "Thanks for warning me. I'll think on it."

"Think fast, okay? We have a lot of work to do to get ready. I want to leave real early in the morning."

Newspaper now in his lap, his father gave him his full attention. "Backpacking, huh? No horses? You think they'll go for this?"

"Like I said, I already asked Jeff. He's game. Kristy's afraid of horses, so I don't think she'll mind leaving them home. It's only for three days. We'll have to miss church on Sunday, but I'm sure I can get Sam to fill in for me."

Eyeing him warily, his father asked, "Do you really think Cassie and Kristy would be interested?"

Billy shrugged. "If they don't want to go, we'll make it a male bonding time. Jeff and Joey are excited about it."

"Let me talk to your mother. She might have something in mind for the girls this weekend."

෴ ⁂ ෴

"Backpacking? Me? I don't know," Kristy said. "I'm not sure I could do it."

"Why not, Kristy?" Cassie and Hannah stood in Cassie's bedroom, pleading. "It'll be fine. The guys will help us. It's hard, but really fun. And it's so beautiful up there," Cassie said.

"But it's raining."

"Ah ... by the time we get up there, the weather will be back to sunny. It changes real fast this time of year. They say it's supposed to be sunny tomorrow," Hannah said.

"With scattered showers," Kristy interjected.

"Oh, we won't melt!" Cassie said. "Come on. It's our chance for some fun. Where's your sense of adventure?"

"I don't even have a backpack."

"We don't either," Hannah said. "Billy says he can borrow

some."

"Oh, all right."

Hannah squealed. "Yes!" Pumping her fist in the air, she ran from the room.

Late that evening, Kristy stuffed a small stack of clothes and personal items in her pack. Billy divided supplies into piles to go in each pack, making sure to give lighter loads to the girls. Jeff looked up from fitting Cassie with a backpack, adjusting straps. "Where's the food?"

Cassie removed the pack and waved her hand. "It's all on the table. Kristy and I did the shopping this afternoon."

Protesting groans soon came from the kitchen.

"Cassie!"

Jeff wasn't happy.

Kristy looked over to her companion, who ignored the protests, busy stuffing her pack.

Jeff emerged from the kitchen with Billy at his heels, both scowling and weighing cans in their palms. "Cassie? Did you pick out this food?"

She continued working. "Kristy and I. Why?"

"It weighs a ton!" Billy said.

Cassie didn't look up, but remained concentrated on her task, shrugging. "Well, how were we to know? We've never shopped for a backpacking trip before."

"But you've been camping. And you've been hiking. I thought you'd know to shop for something light. You could've asked." Jeff frowned at her, then the can in his hand.

Cassie exhaled sharply and eyes flashing, gave Jeff her attention. "I did ask. I asked you before I left, remember? You said, 'whatever! Just get something to fill us up!'"

Kristy stared at them both, wide eyed.

So this is what Cassie meant when she said they fight.

"I was just finishing up an account when you called. I didn't have time to give you details."

"You could have asked me!" Billy interjected.

Kristy backed up, but Cassie stood her ground. "You weren't even here before we left. I recall you told us to 'just take care of it!'"

Kristy took in the chaotic sight. Various items were scattered over the living room in haphazard piles. It was late and the rest of the family had gone to bed. Her eyes returned to Cassie, holding off two stubborn and opinionated men. Face flushed and strained, her friend ran her fingers through dark curls.

Two against one. It wasn't fair.

Kristy stepped forward, straightened to her full five-foot-five inches and stared straight into Billy's frustrated face. "You said to take care of it, so we did!"

All three stared at her, like she just dropped in from another planet. Billy recovered first. "You stay out of this. It doesn't concern you," he said.

"What do you mean it doesn't concern me? I helped her make the menu and do the shopping!"

He turned away, rolling his eyes. "But you don't know anything about camping."

"How were we to know you had opinions about this? Are we supposed to read your minds?"

Billy turned back to her. "I thought you could figure it out. It was *backpack* food we wanted. We're not road camping. We're. Going. Backpacking."

Face flushing, she glared at him. "So you think we're stupid?"

Eyes wide, Cassie and Jeff looked at each other.

Jeff stepped between them. "Uh … Billy. Back off." Then turning to her, he said, "Kristy. It's okay. We'll get by. It's okay."

"Come on Kristy. Let's take a break." Cassie took hold of her arm and pulled her toward the stairway.

Leading her upstairs, Cassie entered the bedroom. Closing the door behind them, she shoved her into the corner chair. "Kristy, it's okay. Calm down."

"I don't want to go." Kristy's voice caught and she brushed

away tears. "You guys can go without me."

"It'll be okay. You'll see. They're just tired and grumpy. It's been a long day. We're all tired."

"Billy didn't have to insult me. He does the same thing when I'm driving truck. He treats me like a stupid slave if I don't read his mind."

"Have you told him?"

"No."

"Well, tell him. He won't know how you feel unless you say something. Is that why you've been so quiet lately? You're upset with Billy? You'd better tell him."

"But I can't tell him. He might get the wrong idea."

"Wrong idea?"

She lifted her chin. "Yeah. He might think I care what he thinks. You know. Too much."

Cassie rolled her eyes. "Whatever. You think too much, Kristy. If you feel it, just tell him. It'll work out. Trust God."

"Trust God? I trust God. It's Billy I don't trust."

"What did he do to lose your trust?"

A soft knock sounded on the door.

"Come in," Cassie said.

The two offenders entered. Looking sheepish, Jeff began. "Uh, we were talking and we thought we should apologize. The food's okay. We'll make do."

Billy crossed over to the chair. "Kristy, I'm sorry I got so worked up. It's no big deal. It's only three days. We'll spread the weight around." He extended his hand. "Friends?"

Kristy took it, not meeting his eyes. "Yeah. Friends."

Billy stood looking down at her. Head tilted, he peered into her averted face.

Jeff appealed to Cassie. "We could really use your help down there. We have a bit more work to do. If we all pitch in, we might get to bed sometime tonight."

꿍 ❦

Kristy couldn't sleep. Knowing she had only four hours didn't help. But mostly it was the scrape with Billy.

What had gotten into her?

She actually yelled at him.

He probably wouldn't want anything to do with her now.

But he made her mad.

To admit to him she was upset about how he treats her? Just the thought of it put her in a panic.

He apologized.

She had to give him credit for that. He'd looked like a little boy when he came into the room. Gone was the confident swagger and know-it-all attitude.

Maybe he did care what she felt.

But was he *interested* in her?

She was crazy to even consider such a thing.

❧ ❦ ❧ ❦

"You don't have to stay back here with me. I'm slow, but I'll get there."

Kristy and Billy were climbing a steep part of the trail and she was lagging behind. Every step required an act of determination. The others had gone ahead, but Billy refused to leave her.

Billy stopped in the trail ahead and turned. "Do you really want me to leave you alone?"

Kristy huffed and puffed. Breathless, she smiled sheepishly, face flushed and hot. She stopped and wiped her brow. "Not really. It's kind of scary being alone. Who knows if I'll ever catch up?"

He let out a sigh, meeting her eyes. "Kristy, I'm really sorry about last night."

She clamped her jaw and strode past him. "It's okay."

"No it isn't. I was a jerk. Will you forgive me?"

She continued trudging up the hill, thumbs yanking at the shoulder straps of her pack.

"Yeah, I forgive you. You already said you were sorry, remember?"

"Yeah, but you're still upset. I wanted to hear you tell me you

43

forgive me. There's something to that." He chuckled, close behind her. "It's easy to say you're sorry. We're all 'sorry' critters."

"I'm not really upset."

"Then why are you avoiding me?"

She continued forcing one foot in front of the other, determined to move forward, trudging up the trail.

"Kristy?"

"Fear, I guess."

"Fear?"

"Yeah. I'm not used to this."

"Used to what?"

"Arguing. ... Well, arguing and then still being okay. It scares me."

"Why's that?"

"In my family, a fight means ... Well ... we don't ever really solve it. Sometimes there's icicles in the air for weeks. Even years." She stopped in the trail, breathing hard.

"I guess that would be tough. But I was proud of you last night."

"Proud of me?"

"Yeah. You got right in my face. It gave me hope."

"Hope for what?"

"For us. That we could be friends. You have some fight in you."

She turned to continue her trek. "Oh, I have fight all right. There's a lot of fight in there. And anger. It scares me sometimes."

Why was she telling him this?

The two trudged up the steep trail and Kristy stopped again, breathing hard.

Billy stayed behind, maintaining silence. Finally he spoke. "Relax, okay? I'll be okay with your anger. It's not me you're mad at anyway. It's all the other jerks that hurt you. Right? I want to get to know you. Can you try to relax?"

He wanted to get to know her?

Smiling slightly, she wiped perspiration from her forehead with the back of her hand.

"Okay, I'll try."

Billy smiled. Reaching forward, he extended his water bottle. "Want a drink?"

She took it and gulped down a few swallows, sinking down to sit on a nearby rock. "I'm bushed. Working in fast food and driving truck didn't get me in shape for all this."

He examined her pack, testing its weight. "It seems light enough. You'll make it." He grinned. "You're doing great. You want a granola bar? It might help."

After a snack and short rest, he urged her on.

They rounded a bend and came to a large green meadow. A rippling creek wound through it, clear as glass. "This is beautiful!" Kristy said. "And look! The trail has leveled off. It looks easier from here."

Billy flashed her a smile and stepped up to stand beside her. "This is one of my favorite places. It's easier hiking here, but a few miles down the trail there's a bit more climbing. Don't worry though, the worst is behind us."

They pressed on. Rugged mountains with jagged peaks rose on either side of the high meadow. Small, twisted trees lined the trail. Kristy breathed in the clean, fresh air. Sun shone on crystal clear, running water in the creek. She smiled back at Billy.

His face fell and he stopped. "Hey! Did you put on sunscreen? You look pink!"

"No."

"You didn't?" He yanked off his pack and set it on a flat rock, shuffling through one of the side pockets. "I told you to do that before we left. Your skin is fair and the sun is murder up here. Your shoulders and face look bad already." He looked at her, as if seeing her for the first time. "Shorts and tank top with no sunscreen?"

"I..."

He held a large tube in his hand. "Come here."

She hesitated.

He pulled her towards him and turned her around, taking hold of her backpack and pulling it from her shoulders. "Unbuckle."

She obeyed and he lifted it from her back. He began applying the lotion to her shoulders and arms, while she stood dumbfounded. Coming to her senses, she pulled back and shoved him away. "Don't! I'll do it myself, thank you!"

Handing her the lotion, he said, "Don't forget your face. Here, take my hat." He placed his ball cap on her head, bringing the bill down to shade her eyes and nose. "You really shouldn't get any more sun on your face. Didn't you bring a hat?"

"I think it's in the bottom of my pack."

"What good is it going to do you in your pack? This is when you need it! Give me that stuff when you're done, okay?"

Rolling her eyes and heaving a sigh, Kristy set her jaw. Finished with the lotion, she plopped the tube into his outstretched palm.

After applying a generous amount to his tanned face and the back of his neck, he returned the tube to his backpack and held up her pack. "Here. We'd better get going. We're falling behind."

Hiking again, she remained silent, pursing her lips as she followed his lead. She lengthened her strides, trying to keep up. The old bossy Billy was back. It was like he was a sergeant in the army and she his only clueless soldier. She winced. Her heel was getting sore. What she would do for a good soak in the creek. But no way was she going to mention it.

Half an hour later, they rounded a bend in the trail and distant laughter floated toward them on the fresh mountain breeze, along with playful voices and splashing water. The rest of the group were playing in a clear pool near the trail.

Cassie and Jeff frolicked on the water's edge, laughing and splashing. Joey glided through the water, bolted out on the other side and shook himself. "Brrr ... It's cold! But it sure feels good!"

"Hey, you guys! You finally caught up!" It was Hannah.

Squinting in the mountain sunshine, she sat on a rock, soaking her feet.

෪෨➤෧෪෨

After resting for a bit, the group was off. They stopped for lunch in a grassy spot near the creek. The packs remounted, they regrouped and Billy and Jeff went ahead, followed by Hannah and Joey. Cassie and Kristy brought up the rear.

Kristy limped along behind Cassie, both feet burning, but especially the heel of her right foot. "How far do you think we've come?" she asked Cassie's back.

"I'd say around five miles," Cassie answered.

Kristy squinted, looking up at the hills in front of them. "How far to Mirror Lake?"

"About two miles. The guys went ahead with Joey and Hannah to find a camp spot. Maybe they'll have something cooking when we get there." She smiled over her shoulder. "I doubt they'll complain about those cans of chili tonight. We'll all be mighty glad to see them."

"My feet are killing me!"

Cassie stopped and turned. "Blisters?"

"Yeah. Both heels when we stopped to swim. Now I'm sure they busted. The right one's really burning."

"You're limping. Why didn't you say something? We should put some moleskin on those."

"I wasn't going to say anything. Not when Billy was around. He already chewed me out for not wearing sun-screen."

Cassie laughed. "Don't take it so hard. He's just bossy. Used to running a crew. Mr. Practical." She sat down on a log by the trail and squirmed out of her backpack. "Sit down. I'll see what I can do with your feet."

While Kristy took off her shoes, Cassie dug in her pack for the first-aid kit. "So, how are the two of you getting along? I noticed he stayed back with you."

"Okay, I guess. He wants me to relax. Says he wants to get to know me better."

47

Cassie turned to her. "He said that?"

"Yeah. Why?"

She pulled out the moleskin and a small pair of scissors. "He never pays attention to girls. But it seems different with you. He shows a little interest."

Pulling off her socks, Kristy said, "You think so? He didn't have any trouble asking *Marcel* to sing with him."

Cassie examined her blisters, laughing. "This is better than I thought. You're jealous!"

"I am not!"

"Sounds like it to me," she said, clipping at the moleskin.

"I doubt he's really interested in me anyway. I'm not his type. I'm a city girl with a history, who's afraid of horses. He's a farm boy. Pure as the driven snow. With no plans to get off the farm."

Cassie looked up. "How do you know his plans? Did you talk about that too?"

"No."

"Well, Jeff told me Billy said he wished you were older. I've never heard him say anything like that about a girl."

Kristy winced while Cassie placed the moleskins on her heels. She remained silent.

He wished she was older?

Of course to him she was just a kid.

A smile teased her dry lips.

Why would he say that?

By the time they arrived at the lake, Kristy could hardly put one foot in front of the other. Joey and Hannah were watching for them and directed them to the campsite, but remained down at the lake, exploring. When Kristy stumbled into camp behind Cassie, Billy and Jeff had two tents up and a fire going. Jeff rose from a log, greeted Cassie with a smile and helped her out of her pack. Kristy sank to the log and stretched out her legs. She couldn't move another inch.

Billy meandered towards her, smiling widely. "Hey! You made

it. Here, let me take your pack. Unbuckle." She complied and he pulled it off.

Pointing up an incline, he directed her to a level spot with a tent, hidden in the trees. "We set you up over there. Do you want me to unroll your sleeping bag and put it in your tent? Then you can lie down and rest."

"Sure. That would be nice." She looked up at the darkening sky. "What time do you think it is?"

"Probably about eight. Hey, where are those cans of chili?"

Cassie and Kristy looked at each other.

They giggled.

ON THE MOUNTAIN

Kristy rolled over and groaned. The skin on her shoulders
burned. Her stiff, sore muscles screamed and she scooted to the
left to avoid the rock that protruded from the tent floor,
tormenting her right hip.

People considered this fun?

Poking her head out of the warm sleeping bag, the frigid air
assaulted her burning face. It was cold! Dim light shone through
the thin material of the worn tent. Cassie and Hannah were
curled in their bags, sound asleep.

She had to pee! She'd waited as long as she dared. Pulling
herself upright, she tried to untangle her feet from the twisted
bag. Rummaging around the crowded tent, she recovered her
shoes, loosened the laces, and struggled into them. Grabbing
her jacket, she groaned again, trying to find the arm holes.

She could barely move.

Scooting out the low door, she stood gingerly on sore limbs, then stumbled up the path.

She felt like a piece of hammered round steak as she limped along, returning to the tent. First they beat her up. Then they fried her in the sun. Then they froze her. All in preparation to be offered as a tasty feast for the mosquitoes! Shivering, she giggled, pulled off her shoes and crawled into the bag.

Later, after the others had crawled out, Kristy lay resting alone, unwilling to move. Thudding boots outside the tent stopped next to her head.

"Hey Kristy! Are you ever getting up?" It was Billy.

She moaned.

"If you don't start moving, rigor mortis will set in!" He laughed. "We have some hot breakfast out here waiting for you. There's pancakes, eggs and bacon. Don't you smell it? It's time to enjoy some of that heavy food we lugged up here."

Groaning, she sat up and winced at the pain in her legs and calves. She wasn't sleeping anyway.

"I'm coming," she said.

ॐ ॐ ॐ

On a rock overlooking the still, clear water, Kristy sat. Mirror Lake was well named. Smooth and clear as glass, it reflected the puffy white clouds, deep blue sky, surrounding granite peaks and twisted pines.

It was quiet here. A quiet you could feel. Time alone that morning in the fresh air, beauty, and solace of the mountains had left her feeling refreshed. Soul-wise.

Her body was another matter.

After lunch, everyone had scattered. Hannah and Joey were on a hike to a nearby lake. They had invited her, but she thought they were crazy. A hike? After a day like yesterday?

And Jeff and Cassie. Who knew where they were?

There was definitely something about this place. As sore and exhausted as she felt, she couldn't help appreciating its beauty. And the stars last night! She had never seen so many stars! She was looking forward to another evening. Maybe she wouldn't be so exhausted. Raising her eyes to the sky, she frowned. Clouds were rolling in. Dark clouds.

She looked at Billy, who was fishing not far away. Now she could see why he was addicted to these mountains. Shod in an old pair of flip-flops, she grimaced in pain and limped over the rocky path toward him.

"Are you catching anything?"

Reeling in the line, he rose to his feet and flashed her a smile. "No. It's not the best time to fish, but I'm heading over there." He motioned across the lake. "I have my eye on the pool below that big flat rock. You want to come with me? It's deeper there and looks like a good place for fish to hang out."

She wrinkled her sunburned nose. "All the way over there? My feet are sore."

His eyes went to her feet. "Blisters?"

"Yeah. And sore muscles."

He smiled down at her. "It takes some getting used to. We covered a lot of miles yesterday. You're green, but you're a good sport." He looked down at her feet again and scowled. "Flip-flops?"

"I couldn't bear those dirty shoes today. They rub my blisters."

"Come with me. I'll take it slow."

They made their way on the rough path toward his rock in silence. After casting his line, he settled himself on the flat granite surface with knees drawn to his chest and elbows resting on them.

"Wow! You can see the fish down there!"

"Yeah. The problem is, they can see you too." Chuckling, he patted the place beside him. "Sit. Tell me what's on your mind."

With great care, she lowered herself and stared out over the lake. "Not much."

"You said you hadn't heard God in a while. This is a good place to hear him. Have you yet?"

"No, but I feel refreshed."

"Being refreshed is part of hearing God. The mountains are good for that."

Easy silence enveloped them, each enjoying the quiet stillness of the fresh mountain air. He recast his line and squatted.

"I have trouble hearing God."

She gulped. Why was she telling him this?

"When was the last time you heard him speak to you?"

"I'm not sure. Probably when I was in church last spring."

"What did he say?"

"He loved me."

"Do you believe it?"

"I suppose so. But I've had a pretty rough summer. ... I'm so confused. ... I feel like a failure. ... I haven't felt his presence much."

He looked at her sideways. "Do you think if you had a little girl that was confused, that you'd love her any less?"

She laughed nervously. "No, but I'm sure he's disappointed in me. I can't do anything right."

"So you can't do anything right. Nothing surprises him. And if you or I had a child that couldn't do anything right, we wouldn't love them any less, would we? He's got much better love than us. He's a good father."

Billy tugged his line, then stood to reel it in. He cast it in a different direction and squatted, eyes scanning the still lake. "If he told you he loved you now, would you believe him?"

She bit her lip. "I'm not sure."

"Maybe that's why you're not hearing him. All this beauty speaks of his love. But if you won't believe what he wants to say, how will you hear him say it?"

"I suppose you're right, but I do want to know what he wants me to do. I would believe that. Why won't he tell me?"

His eyes pierced hers again. "You really want to know what I think?"

Her heart pounded. "Well, yes. Or I wouldn't have asked."

He laughed softly. "God doesn't want to tell you what to do. He wants relationship. You're not a slave. You want orders so you can accomplish something important. God doesn't need our great accomplishments. They might impress you, but not him. He knows you're a needy child. And won't admit it."

"What?"

He continued to reel in his line. "Are you trying to prove yourself by performance? That will never happen. You're already okay. You're Daddy's little girl and he loves you."

Something about this whole conversation irritated her. Frowning, she rose on shaky legs.

He stopped reeling and grabbed her pant-leg. "Hey! What's wrong? Don't just walk away. Remember I told you to relax. It's okay. Tell me what you're thinking."

She heaved a sigh. Pursing her lips, she blurted out, "I'm no one's 'little girl!' I'm twenty-one years old and have paid my own way since I was sixteen. I've worked, bought my own food, clothes and paid rent for five years. Before that, I practically raised my little brother and myself. Since my father left, I have no desire to be anyone's 'little girl!' It offends me that you would talk to me like this. Are you Daddy's 'little boy?'"

He laughed. "Of course I am. Do you think it's any easier for me?" He kept hold of her pant-leg, peering up at her. His face sobered. "Okay, maybe it is easier for me. Come on. Sit back down and talk to me."

She set her jaw. "Okay."

She sat.

A long silence separated them. He cast the line again. "Have you listened to the sermons the last few weeks at church?"

She folded her arms. "Yeah, but I didn't like them."

Turning, his gray eyes studied her upturned face. He smiled knowingly. "Now we're making progress."

She frowned. Tiny drops of rain fell on her arms, but she didn't pay them notice.

Sobering, he continued, "Listen, Kristy. The reason God asks you to become a child is for relationship. He wants to be your father. He wants to connect to you as his daughter. That won't happen unless you become a child again." He paused and studied her face. "There is a child in there, not far below the surface. Isn't there? You don't have to prove anything or try to fool anyone, Kristy. You don't fool me. Or much of anyone else."

"I'm not trying to fool anyone!"

Turning away, he rose and cast his line again, then squatted down next to her, eyes fixed on the lake. A small smile played on his lips. "You're not? Then why so prickly and defensive? Are you afraid I'm going to think you're immature? Or unsophisticated? Or weak? Or insignificant? Or maybe you're trying to prove your significance to yourself?"

Groaning, she rose to her feet.

He grabbed her pant leg, but she shook him off.

"This conversation is over."

He looked up then, gray eyes dark and surprisingly tender. Her defenses began to plummet, but she looked away, regaining her composure.

"Okay. We'll talk about something else."

Just then, thunder rolled and the tiny raindrops were fat.

"On second thought, we'd better get back to camp. And fast." He stood to reel in his line.

Kristy limped to the path.

He sure had nerve.

Sharp pain shot through her toe and she stumbled.

"Ouch!" Stopping in the path, she raised her foot to examine the damage. Her big toe was skinned, oozing blood and throbbing. She grimaced, grabbed it, and waited for the pain to subside.

Boots thudded on the path behind her. Without warning, strong hands took hold of her waist and lifted her off the ground. An arm went under her knees, pulling her against a damp shirt. Billy turned, cradling her in his arms. "Grab my pole, would you?"

"Put me down!"

He grinned. "You look like you need a lift. It's going to be slow-going in those flip-flops."

Something warm and pleasant stirred within her as he pressed her against his hard chest, but a part of her recoiled.

It won. She struggled, pushing against him. "Billy! Put me down! Now!"

He returned her to her feet. "Okay! I just thought I'd help you practice being a kid. It's not so bad, you know."

He grabbed his pole and hurried around her, loping down the trail.

She stumbled again. "Billy! Slow down! Please!"

Stopping in the path, he turned. "How about a piggy-back ride? Would that be acceptable? We're going to get soaked!"

She struggled toward him on the rocky path, wincing. "Okay."

He backtracked, bent his knees and offered his back. When she was settled there, he grabbed his pole and began to run. "Hold on!"

The rain was coming down hard when they reached the campsite. After gathering up scattered clothes and supplies, adjusting the girl's tent the best they could to keep out the fast accumulating water and retrieving warm clothing, they put the backpacks inside the guy's tent and crawled in, leaving muddy shoes by the door.

"Your tent isn't doing too well. It's been one for a while. If the rain doesn't let up soon, you may have wet sleeping bags," he said.

"That doesn't sound t ... too good."

"Hey, you look cold."

"I am cold. My sweatshirt and coat are damp. They were hanging on a tree."

"Here. Borrow mine." He retrieved a sweatshirt from his pack, helped her out of hers and put his over her head. After changing into a dry flannel shirt, he settled next to her, put an arm around her shoulders and pulled her close. Willing at first, she snuggled into his side, warmth seeping into her body and soul. She stayed put for what seemed a long interval, but soon stiffened and pushed him away.

He sighed. "Sorry. I was just trying to help. … I thought … Oh well, it doesn't matter. … I grabbed a deck of cards out of my pack. How about a game?"

Halfway through the game, the sound of running and laughing came from outside the tent. Billy looked up from his cards. "There they are. I'll bet they're soaked."

Jeff and Joey soon invaded their small space. Arms and legs flew as wet clothing was replaced and adjustments made. Soon they were joined by Cassie and Hannah, who had also done their best to get dry.

Boom! Lightning flashed.

Kristy jumped. It was loud!

Thunder rumbled and cracked. Lightning flashed again and water poured off the tent roof.

Cassie laughed. "Let's play another game of cards!"

When the rain let up, Kristy and Billy cooked a pot of boxed macaroni and cheese over a small propane stove outside the door. Though it was a bit chewy, there were no complaints. They licked the pan clean. Carrot sticks and granola bars completed the meal.

Huddled tight with flashlights, they played and talked until well after dark.

"Our tent is leaking and the sleeping bags are soaked!" Hannah said, ducking in after an exploratory mission to the girl's quarters. Kristy's pack is wet, too! What are we going to do?"

Glancing in the rearview mirror, Billy drove the van down the highway toward home. Jeff sat in the back seat with Cassie against his shoulder, both fast asleep. Joey and Hannah, in the middle captain seats, were also out. Next to him, Kristy slept, leaning against the door.

She was a trouper.

But he could have made sure they were more prepared for rain.

The night before they zipped two wet sleeping bags together for the girls, and spread the other on top. That way they could cuddle together and keep warm. It was Cassie's suggestion and they took it, not knowing what else to do.

He had been worried about Kristy and the possibility of hypothermia. He shouldn't have let her help prepare dinner outside the tent door. She was already damp from rain and shivering. Thanks to that leaky, old tent, everything she had was wet. But she had insisted, saying she was fine. When the night turned colder, her wet clothes took their toll. Clad in his sweatshirt and damp jeans, he left her in the tent with the others, while he and Jeff braved the rainstorm and prepared the girl's bed.

They could have switched with the girls, but he, Jeff and Joey wouldn't have fit in a pair of small, wet sleeping bags zipped together in the smaller tent.

Considering the whole thing an adventure, Cassie wasn't fazed. But he couldn't sleep and had come out to check on them in the middle of the night. After he asked if there was anything he could do, they laughed.

"Which one of us do you want to switch with?" Kristy asked, giggling with the others. "We're fine." In the morning, they were all laughing, so they must've been alright. They said it was like sleeping on a wet sponge, but body heat had warmed the water and they were okay.

It was a rough night, but wasn't as cold as the night before, due to the cloudy sky. By morning, they were eager to leave. After wringing out sleeping bags and wet clothes in drizzling rain, they shook off the tents and packed them up the best they could. Without the heavy food, it should've been a lighter load coming out. But with everything wet, probably not. At least it was downhill and hiking kept them warm.

He examined Kristy's sleeping form. She had been sore, blistered, sunburned, soaked, cold, and mosquito-bitten. He had scolded and hassled her, but she hadn't complained. Sunburned face peaceful, her breathing was deep and even.

She's beautiful, Father. But I don't know what to think. Maybe I should back off. I don't know why I'm compelled to hassle her. I don't think she appreciates my probing questions.

Or sermons.

What should I do?

Do you like her?

There are things about her I like. But is this going to work? I can't reach her.

Kristy stirred and straightened, stretching and yawning. "Are we close to home?"

"About fifteen minutes."

⬦⬦ ⬦ ⬦⬦

"So, how was the camping trip?" Ben asked that evening. The bedraggled group had gathered around the dinner table. Having just arrived home, they drug themselves to the table after laying all the wet camping gear out to dry in the shop. They hadn't had a chance to shower and change, but they were hungry.

Joey brightened. "It was great! We hiked, fished, explored, ate chewy macaroni and got real wet!"

"Yeah. It was great until it rained," Billy said.

Elbowing his younger sister, Joey laughed. "Then all the girls had to sleep together naked. To survive!"

"We were not naked! We had our T-shirts and underwear on!" Hannah said, indignant. Raucous laughter rang around the dinner table.

"You told me Cassie made you take off your clothes." Joey said, a glint in his eye.

"Just our wet jeans and sweatshirts. It worked well. That way there wasn't much wet cloth to keep us from one another's warm skin. We didn't freeze. We were quite warm." Hannah giggled.

Jeff laughed under his breath. "I think this is more

59

information than I want to know."

Cassie elbowed him in the ribs. "Whenever I had to move, there was a body part in the way and a warm wet sponge underneath. I just adjusted my dreams. I was on a very crowded beach in Florida and the tide was coming in."

"The problem was, I kept waking up tangled in Kristy's arms and legs. She's like an octopus." Hannah said, smiling widely.

"I wasn't even sleeping next to you. That was Cassie. She was in the middle." Kristy said.

"I think Cassie was on top of me most of the night. At least I think it was her. An elbow kept squishing my nose. I couldn't even breathe!"

Laughter broke out again.

Cassie turned to Kristy. "It's still sore where you clobbered me in the jaw."

"I had to itch the mosquito bite on my forehead. It was driving me crazy."

"Billy was worried about them," Joey said. "He even went to check on them in the middle of the night."

"But I'll bet Jeff slept like a log," Cassie said.

Jeff chuckled. "I did. Knowing Cassie, I'm sure if there was a problem, our cozy little tent would've been invaded big time." He dodged a kick from under the table.

"Ouch! What was I supposed to do about it? Even if I was really magnanimous, I wasn't going to offer to switch with one of you."

Kristy was laughing so hard she couldn't eat. The whole table was cracking up until they couldn't sit straight. She thought her sides would burst. But she wasn't the only one with tears of mirth running down her cheeks. Billy was doubled over, about to fall off his chair.

She would sleep well tonight.

෨ ❦ ෨

Two days later, Kristy was back in the grain truck. That trip was no vacation. It was a lesson in survival. But she'd never forget it. The new experiences. The camaraderie. And most of all … Billy.

"Jesus, the more I'm around him, the more I realize how wonderful he is, even if he is bossy and opinionated. But why is he paying attention to me? He's right about so many things, but I don't want to be his project. What does he want from me? I tried asking, but he thinks I'm suspicious and hurt. He's right, but would he ever really consider me seriously?"

There was something so comforting about it when he put his arm around her in that tent. She had almost abandoned her resolve, but she couldn't bear the thought of falling for another guy and having it not work out. Her heart was shattered. He didn't understand. From what she'd gathered, he'd never even had a girlfriend. He didn't have a clue what he was getting into.

He said he could handle her anger. She wasn't so sure.

And … relax?

Tears threatened and her head bowed.

"Oh, Jesus! Help me!"

Billy was right. She was trying to prove something. She wanted to be important. Significant.

"I'm so confused. I need love, but I'm afraid of it." She wanted to relax, but she just couldn't.

She looked up. "Lord, you know what I've done."

Someone like Billy would never want her. She'd just get hurt again. Hot tears streamed down her face. Eyes squeezed shut, she covered her face with her hands.

"Oh my God! I need a daddy. Father, please be my father. Forgive me for trying to do things myself and resisting your request to be a child! Forgive me for my pride. I'm not good at this child business. Would you help me? Would you take me as your little girl?"

Voice catching, she continued, "Would you accept me, knowing what I've done? I don't want to be a child again, but I don't have much choice. I can't go on like this. I can't do this without you." She wiped away tears.

Kristy.

A still small voice entered her conscious mind. She sniffled, head raising.

I accept you. … I never rejected you.

"I'm afraid. Will you protect me?"

Love always protects.

"Thank you, Father."

Suddenly she was aware of loud thrashing. Billy was coming. She looked at her streaked face in the rearview mirror. Tears had turned the dust to mud.

She laughed. "Oh, well. If I'm going to be a child, I just as well look the part." She turned the key and shifted into gear. "Back to work."

⁊❧⸱⸱⸱❧⁊

James pulled up to the small brick house of his best friend. A white picket fence surrounded the front yard. He threw it into park and jumped out, seething with rage.

He knew it! They were in there. Together.

I'll kill him.

Opening the gate, he stepped into the front yard and a voice arrested him.

Vengeance is mine, I will repay.

James awoke with a start, perspiration beading his brow. Soft morning light shone through the window. He was again aware of the rehabilitation center's bleak surroundings.

He could not shut down his racing and tormented thoughts. He groaned. After ten years it shouldn't hurt so bad, but it felt like just yesterday. If God hadn't spoken to him, he would have killed him.

He looked down at his numb legs, dead toes sticking out of the ends of long casts. He was going crazy doing nothing. All he could think about was Patricia, Kristy and Toby. And his failures. He should've found his kids by now. But it had been too long. They would hate him.

And Pat. She didn't want to see him. Of what use would he

be? He was a cripple! He was pathetic!

Kristy would be grown by now. A young woman.

A wistful smile made it to his lips. She was such a cute little thing. She'd be beautiful now. They must be okay or Pat would've contacted him. All she had to do was ask Sally. Sally knew where he was.

Throbbing in his back refocused him. Paralyzed? What more could go wrong?

God, if there was one, must hate him. Not only was he a miserable failure, but now he had to sit around and think about it. How could he keep going? He growled, pulling himself up in bed with the trapeze hanging on the bed frame. He pushed the call button for the nurse.

The door opened and his friend Barry peeked his head through. "You rang?" He grinned, entering the room. "Good morning."

James frowned. "Get the nurse to bring me a pain pill, would you? And could you get me a piece of toast or something?"

His friend smiled. "Coming right up." He turned and left the room.

Barry came to visit every morning. James was so depressed, he doubted he would be alive but for his friend's constant devotion.

Except for his preaching, he had to be the best friend anybody could ever have.

But God would never take him back now. He had to be a great disappointment. It was too late. He was too far gone. Barry kept saying God loved him. But he didn't think so. He might love others, but not him.

Barry said God wanted to heal him. Why would he want to do that? Besides, who ever heard of someone paralyzed getting healed? That just didn't happen.

CLOSE, BUT NOT TOO CLOSE

Let the little children come to me, and do not hinder them,
for the kingdom of heaven belongs to such as these.
(Jesus Christ)

Amazing love,
How can it be?
That you my king should die for me?
Amazing love,
I know it's true ... [3]

Billy sang from the couch, strumming his guitar and Kristy harmonized beside him. He glanced her way. She was relaxing. Returning his smile, her blue eyes sparkled.

He stopped. "Hey. Would you sing with me tomorrow at church?"

Her jaw clamped. "You don't need me. You have Marcel." Then, looking down, she blushed.

Billy frowned. "I *have* Marcel?"

Shrugging, she lifted her red face to his. "You sounded great together a few weeks ago. She has a beautiful voice. You don't need me."

Billy searched her blue eyes before she averted her gaze.

Laying his guitar aside, he rose. "You and I need to talk. Let's go for a walk." She didn't resist, so he led her out the front door and around to the back of the house. Side by side they wandered out toward the pasture, in silence. Chirping crickets in the tall, dry grass and croaking bullfrogs from the nearby pond, danced through the warm summer breeze, while the sun blazed over the dry golden fields.

He finally spoke. "There's nothing between Marcel and me."

"She likes you."

His head jerked toward her. "So, maybe she does. I've always thought of her as a younger sister."

"That's not how she thinks of you," she said, avoiding his gaze. "Everyone knows she's in love with you."

He groaned, rolling his eyes. "Marcel's not my type."

"Why not? She's a good church girl."

Halting, his eyes pierced hers. "Good church girl? What's that supposed to mean?"

"She comes from a good family and has always been good, hasn't she?"

"Maybe. But I doubt it." Hands in his pockets, he turned his face to the horizon.

"Why?"

He kicked at a rock with his boot. "Nothing against Marcel, but I would rather do my own pursuing. She doesn't leave room for that."

"You asked her to sing with you. Did you not?"

"Sort of ... but you wouldn't do it. You were my first choice. She makes me uncomfortable." He turned to her. "Could you sing with me tomorrow? Maybe? ... Why not try it?"

"I'm a mess and I don't want to be a hypocrite."

"You aren't making a statement of personal perfection. Do you think you have to have it all together to lead people in worship?"

She shrugged. "Probably not. I'm in a better place than I was a few weeks ago."

"I thought you looked better."

"I'm a lot happier. God's been talking to me."

He smiled. "That's great! I've been praying for you."

They wandered to the pasture fence where his horse, Blackfoot trotted over to greet them. He petted Blackfoot's velvety muzzle.

Smiling, he turned to her. "I'm sorry if I come on too strong, Kristy, but I can't resist the challenge." He winked. The horse nudged his shoulder, begging more and he laughed. "Hey, big fella."

Rigid and suddenly quiet, he noted that she had backed up. Puzzled, he was about to ask what was wrong when he remembered. "Oh. I forgot. You don't like horses."

"Uh … I think I'll go back—" She turned to leave.

He grabbed her arm. "Wait."

She looked at his hand, then his face.

He pulled away, blushing beneath his tan. "Sorry. I was wondering … Cassie's going to be busy the next few months with school and getting ready for her wedding. She had mentioned maybe you'd like some riding lessons. I'd like to teach you. I thought maybe we could start real slow … from the beginning. There's no reason to be afraid, you know."

Kristy's blue eyes widened and she stared at him. "Uh … I don't know … Just thinking about it freaks me out. I'm a real chicken."

"I promise to be gentle. I won't have you do anything unless you agree you're ready."

Letting out a long breath, she relented. "O … kay."

He smiled triumphantly. "Good. We'll start tomorrow, after church."

※ ❧ ❧ ❧

A few days later, his mother stood beside him, looking down

to where he knelt, repairing a picnic table. She continued her job of laying out paper plates and utensils on another table.

"Billy. How do you feel about Kristy?"

The grain was cut and the family was preparing for their annual neighborhood celebration. Everyone was busy setting things up. As usual, Grandpa and Grandma Watson came to help. Grandma was in the kitchen cooking and the others were cleaning and setting up the yard and pasture for games. All the neighbors from the surrounding area were invited. Linda took the opportune time alone with Billy to approach the subject.

He cleared his throat and looked down, feigning concentration on his project. "Why do you ask?"

"Is she the kind of girl you want to marry?"

He looked up. "Mom, I know what you're getting at. I've thought about this and prayed about it. Why do you think I haven't ever had a girlfriend? I analyze everything." He glanced at the pasture, where Kristy helped Cassie set up a baseball diamond.

"Yes, I think I could marry someone like her. She's sweet. She loves Jesus. There's nothing fake about her." He turned back. "I like her. I won't hurt her if I can help it, Mom. Don't worry." He smiled. "She's beautiful. And there's something about her—"

"Billy!" His father came around the house. "Are you done here?" He nodded. "Will you go help your brother set up the barbeques in back?"

"Sure, Dad." Billy jumped up and hurried off.

Linda heaved a sigh, eyes filling.

"Is something the matter?" Ben asked.

"I'm fine." She turned to go into the house.

"Linda." He took hold of her hand, causing her to stop. "Wait. Are those tears?" He lifted a finger, wiping one away.

"I'll be okay." She looked away. "I know you're busy."

"Hey. People aren't supposed to arrive for an hour. We're caught up and have lots of help. I'll tell Mom we're taking a walk." He hurried inside.

A few minutes later, hand in hand, the two walked out toward the stock pond. Linda poured out her worries.

"Don't you like Kristy?" he asked.

"It's not that. I like her well enough. It's just that she reminds me of myself at that age."

He stopped and turned to her. "And that's bad? We survived. In fact, God has blessed us." He gave her a crooked smile. "I think Billy has great taste in women."

Linda smiled, lifting moist eyes to his. "I'm just afraid he'll get his heart broken."

He let out a short laugh. "Now you know how I felt about Cassie and Jeff," he said. "Linda, he will get his heart broken. If not now, then sometime. People do when they take the risk to care. It seems to be a part of life and love. But God heals the broken heart. We can trust him that it'll all turn out well. Billy belongs to God. Remember? We gave him to God a long time ago."

She sniffled. "I know. But it's hard to watch."

"Come here." Enfolding her in his arms, he bent his head and said into her ear, "You're a great mother, and you've done a great job convincing him he's a man. I've done what I can to teach him to be one. We're both proud of him. We have to let him go, Sweetheart. It's time. He'll be fine."

"We've made mistakes, but you're right. ...Thank you, Honey," she said into his shirt. Pulling back, her arms encircled his neck and she raised her lips to his.

⁊ ⟩ ⟨⁊

"The four of them look like they have fun together," Grandma Watson observed, sitting in a lawn chair with Grandpa, Ben, Linda, and a few lingering neighbors. They remained on the lawn, watching the baseball game in the field across the fence.

"Which four?" Ben asked.

"Billy, Cassie, Jeff and Kristy," she said.

"They're quite a group," Grandpa said. "And it looks to me like Billy's sweet on that little filly."

Kristy was up to bat. Pony-tail protruding out the back of a ball cap, she had taken her stand, bat positioned in the air. Jeff was pitching.

"Hey, batter, batter, batter!" Joey chanted from first base.

"Come on, Kristy! Show'em your stuff!" It was Billy, leading off on third base, ready to score.

The ball left the pitcher and Kristy nailed it. Cheering erupted from the other players and the spectators on the lawn. "Run, Kristy! Run!"

Billy slid dramatically into home plate. He sprang up from the dust and cheered, arms raised in the air. "Way to go, Kristy! We're ahead!" Kristy stood brushing off her jeans at second base, where she had landed safe.

Ben smiled. "What makes you so sure about that, Dad?"

"I wasn't born yesterday. I saw that same spark in your eye twenty-seven years ago."

"You think I don't have it now?" He grabbed Linda's hand, brown eyes teasing.

His father chuckled. "I'd say there's some banked coals there, burning slow and steady."

The ball collided with the bat again and Hannah raced to first, reaching the base just as the ball hit the glove of Terry Simpson, a boy from a neighboring ranch. He tagged her. "Gotcha!"

"Tie goes to the runner!" she exclaimed, brown eyes indignant. "I was safe and you know it!" She shoved him, he lost his balance and fell dramatically to the ground.

"Hey, cool down, sis!" Cassie said, trotting over from the sidelines. "It's okay."

"No! It's not okay! He did that to me last time!"

Jeff ambled over from the pitcher's mound, noting Hannah's teary eyes. "I think she's right, Buster. Let's give her this one, okay?"

Sixteen-year-old Terry rose to his feet, brushing dust off his jeans. Wide-eyed, his hands spread dramatically. "I was only teasing! What's with her?"

"Things are getting a little tense out there, Honey. Why don't we call them in for a glass of punch?" Linda asked, coming up beside Ben's lawn chair.

Ben agreed. "As soon as this inning's over, we'll suggest a break."

They came in from the field a few minutes later, Billy at Kristy's side. "You scored again. Where did you learn to play baseball like that?"

She flashed him a smile, eyes shadowed under the bill of a ball cap. "School and the neighborhood park."

"You're good at it."

"Thanks. Hannah was pretty intense out there. Is she okay?"

"Yeah, she's okay. She has a thing about Terry. Doesn't appreciate his teasing. Joey and Terry are pals. She doesn't appreciate that either."

❧❦❧❦❧

"Take it slow and easy now. Remember, he wants to be your friend. Don't be afraid." Kristy let Billy's crooning voice soothe her on this, the third official riding lesson.

"I got you. Don't be afraid."

It had been a week since they started, but both she and Billy had been busy, he with plowing and she with getting ready for school. Kristy and Cassie were planning on rooming together in town until the wedding in December. They had made arrangements to rent a small apartment.

Billy helped her up in the saddle for the first time. She adjusted herself. "I guess this isn't so bad," she said. He led Blackfoot around the corral, while she sat holding tightly to the saddle horn.

"Of course it isn't. Why were you so afraid of him, anyway?"

"I'm not sure. As long as I can remember, I've been afraid of horses."

"Well it's time to get over it. You're doing fine. Are you ready to take a ride with me?"

"A ride? Where?"

"Oh, just around the pasture. I'll ride Ginger. I promise we'll only walk them. Here are the reins."

Panic rose as she stared at the offered reins. "Yes. But alone?" Shaking her head, she pushed them away. "I don't think I'm ready for that. What if he runs away with me?"

"I don't think he'd do that. He can tell you're a novice, but he's a pretty well-behaved horse."

"Still—"

"Okay, listen. How about me getting up behind you? That way you can get the feel of how it's done."

She smiled. "That would be better."

Swinging up behind the saddle, he pulled her close. "Lean against me. Then you can feel what I'm doing."

He started out of the corral, toward the pasture, teaching her little tips. "You've got to let him know whose master. Take a strong lead. If you're nervous, don't let him know. Fake it. Sit up straight and take charge."

It was sure better than being on the horse alone. The warmth of his strong torso pressed against her back. Electricity pulsated through her.

Yes. Much better.

"If you want him to go faster, squeeze your heels into him. When he trots, squeeze your thighs against him and put your weight on the stirrups. It's a much smoother ride. You want me to show you?"

"No. Not today."

"Okay. … Not today."

※ ❧ ❧ ※

The large truck was loaded with seed for fall planting and Billy rode beside his father in the cab. Fresh morning air blew through the open windows, crisp and cool.

"It's starting to feel like fall," Billy said.

"Yeah … So, how's it going with Kristy?" his father asked.

"Good."

"You're not very talkative about it."

He reddened. "No, I'm not."

"How are the riding lessons going? I noticed you had her on Blackfoot this last week. That's progress."

He smiled. "Yeah. She's doing all right."

"She'll be gone next week. How do you feel about that?"

He shrugged. "All right, I guess. She's not that far away. Only thirty minutes."

"Dad, how do you get someone to open up? The most transparent I've seen her was on our way home from Kennewick, after I picked her up when her car broke down. But then she clammed up. There's only been a few times since that she's told me much."

"Have you asked her about it?"

"Not recently. Since we got back from the backpacking trip, I've avoided certain topics when I see she's nervous."

"Are you getting attached to her?"

"I'm attracted to her, but how can you fall for someone you don't know? I worry that she's falling for me. I'm frustrated because I don't want to lead her on and then change my mind. I want her to tell me who she is. What if she never does?"

"I think she will, but ask God."

"He seems to be encouraging me."

"Then don't give up. It'll work out."

§◦➋◦◖❀◦

Father of creation,
Unfold your sovereign plan.
Raise up a chosen generation,
Who will march through the land.
All of creation is longing
For your unveiling of power.
Would you release your anointing?
Oh God, let this be the hour.[4]

Pastor Evan rose to his feet and opened his Bible.

"'You were taught, with regard to your former way of life, to put off

your old self ... to be made new in the attitude of your minds and to put on the new self ... Therefore each of you must put off falsehood and speak truthfully to your neighbor ... Be imitators of God, therefore as dearly loved children ... For you were once darkness, but now you are light in the Lord. Live as children of the light ...'

"We are dearly loved children. Children of light. We no longer walk in darkness. Dearly loved children are not ashamed. They don't hide things. They are transparent. Open books.

He chuckled and read more.

'For if we walk in the light, as he himself is in the light, we have fellowship with one another and the blood of Jesus, his Son, purifies us from all sin. ...'

Kristy squirmed in her chair, then rose to go to the bathroom. She wasn't feeling it. Dearly loved child?

I'm not a dearly loved child. Never have been.

She couldn't be transparent. She couldn't live "in the light." That's just how it was.

She stopped just short of the door when she heard Pastor Evan say, "Karen, would you come now and share your story?"

She turned to see a lady from the church step up on the stage.

"Evan asked me to share what has happened in my life the last few years. As many of you know, for many reasons, I was hesitant to share myself with others. You see, I wasn't used to a culture of honor, identity and authenticity. I came from a church that was more of an orphanage, a culture of 'suck up, buck up and cover up.'

"At one of our Women's Advances, they were washing each other's feet. I wanted to run. Someone made a comment about my legs and how they were so soft. That did it. You see, I have very little hair and have never shaved my legs. I was self-conscious about it and escaped to hide in the back room. When Gloria came to find me, I asked to leave.

"Soon I was surrounded by women, all loving me, reassuring me, and telling me their stories. It melted my heart. For the first time, I allowed myself to open up to women. My husband and I were having problems at the time and I was hurting and frustrated, but didn't dare tell anyone at church. Until then.

"That was the beginning of my healing. Both my husband and I have changed and we are now happier than ever, but it started that night up at the lake. After that, I had sisters and mothers. They helped me through the healing. My life has never been the same."

She stepped down and headed for her seat. Pastor Evan stood.

"James says, *'Confess your sins to each other and pray for each other that you might be healed.'* The 'sin' is not just what we've done, but what we have believed about God, ourselves and others. Believe you are a dearly loved child and bring your stuff to the light. It will be taken care of so easily ..."

Kristy glanced at Billy, sitting in the back row. Pleading gray eyes pierced her soul.

She hurried out the door. Why did they have to talk about this? She wasn't ready. She felt so foolish that day with Billy, driving back from Seattle. She had told herself she would never tell more.

But it was risky for Karen too. Kristy knew what she was talking about when she described a culture of "suck up, buck up, and cover up." It was all she'd ever known. But was God calling her to something else?

Karen said that healing was on the other side. Could she dare step out?

"Father, you know what I've done. And you know who I am. You know how I feel."

What are you afraid of?

CLOSER

*The Spirit himself testifies with our spirit that we are
God's children.* *(Apostle Paul)*

Billy slid out from under the car and pointed. "Hand me a wrench, would you?"

Although a bright September afternoon, Billy and Kristy were not outside enjoying it. She and Cassie were due to move into their apartment the next day and she was helping Billy finish repairing her car. A week earlier, Joey helped Billy remove the gas tank and replace the fuel pump. He had left the reinstallation of the gas tank to Billy.

Kristy hurried over to the workbench and picked up a wrench. "This one?"

"Just bring that whole set in the blue case."

She laid it down on the cement, and after grabbing one, he again disappeared under the car.

"How's it going?"

"It's going. We should have her up and running soon."

"I really appreciate this, Billy. I don't know what I would've done without your help."

Billy's laugh echoed from under the car. "I don't either. You're blessed. Daddy takes care of his little girl."

Swallowing, Kristy kept silent.

His head emerged. "You don't like that subject, do you?"

"What subject?"

"Daddy."

Kristy forced her eyes to meet his. She willed herself to speak. "No, I don't."

Caster wheels squeaked and he disappeared again, rolling beneath the vehicle. "Tell me about your Daddy."

Heart pounding, she lifted her gaze to the ceiling and took a cleansing breath.

She could do this.

"My father left when I was eleven years old."

"Ten years ago?"

"Right."

His muffled voice came again from under the car. "Go on. Tell me about it. From the beginning. Were you close?"

A scratch in her car caught her attention and she flicked at the green paint.

"I *thought* we were close. He was very affectionate. He used to hug me and kiss me a lot. He called me his princess."

Her voice caught. "But I didn't connect well with my mother. She was distant, even when I was small. I envisioned her as a brick wall. Hard, unyielding … cold.

"Not too long ago I told her I felt this when I was little. She said she had to be that way with me because I was so stubborn and strong willed. She said I wouldn't listen to her."

The wheels squeaked on the creeper. Billy appeared again. "Remember, I asked about your *father*. Let's stick to him, okay?"

Kristy leaned against the car and sighed, folding her arms and looking away.

She continued, "I used to stay up late sometimes, waiting for him to come home from work. He was home late a lot. I longed for him. I would sneak quietly out of bed when my mother wasn't watching and come to him. He would lift me up, hold me in his arms and carry me back to bed. It was our little ritual. Mom said it was dumb and I needed my sleep. When he carried me to my bedroom, he would lay me on the bed, kiss me on the cheek and cover me with blankets. Then he'd kiss me again, whispering to me how special I was."

"You were blessed to have a father like that." He was watching her. At some point, he had rolled out from under the car. "It's no wonder you have such a great capacity to love. You were loved."

She looked at him. "You think so?"

"I do."

Moisture brimming in her eyes, Kristy blushed. Billy was still lying on the creeper, studying her.

"Get back to work, would you? We'll be here all day."

With squeaking wheels, he disappeared under the car. "Tell me more. What happened?"

"When I was five years old, my brother was born. Things got bad for me then. Mom seemed to lavish all her attention on him. He could do no wrong. I did everything wrong.

"Dad used to come home from work and I could hear her complaining about me. He did spank me sometimes, but I think it was just to please her. He tried to make her happy, but I don't remember her ever being happy. She was frustrated with me and she never hugged or kissed me. I wanted something from her. Anything."

Billy cleared his throat. "Back to Daddy."

She rolled her eyes. "I'm trying. ... Dad and Mom fought a lot. They always had some kind of bad attitude towards each other. So it was Mom and Toby against Daddy and me for a while. Until ..." She paused.

"Until?"

"Late one night I woke up when he came home. He was really angry. Mom and Dad were both good church members. Up to then, as far as I knew, he never lifted his hand to hurt her, or her him. They never cussed. We attended church regularly and Mom was a leader. Most of her friends were from church."

"That night, he cussed. It scared me. He threw things and yelled. I remember lying in bed, trembling. In the middle of the night, he came into my room, bent over and kissed me on the top of the head." Her voice caught. "He said 'Goodbye, Sweetie' and crept away. ... I pretended to be asleep. The front door closed and that was the last I heard of him.

"There are so many times I wish I had not faked sleep that night. I wish I'd had the courage to ask him what happened and where he was going, but I didn't want him to know I'd heard him cussing and throwing things. I was afraid."

Billy emerged from under the car and rose to his feet. He sighed. "Before we test this thing out, would you take a walk with me? There's not many sunny days left 'til winter." He crossed over to the door, removed his coveralls and hung them on a hook. He turned to her.

"Are you coming?"

Silent, they meandered toward the pasture.

Scruffy, the family's border-collie, followed, eager for attention. Billy bent to scratch his ears. "Hey boy. Leave us alone awhile, okay? Go home." He pointed toward the house.

After the dog scampered away, tail between his legs, Billy grabbed her hand and turned up the hill. After a few minutes of silence, he asked, "So, what happened then?"

Kristy dragged in a breath. "The next morning Mom was a mess. Her eyes were swollen and she said she was sick. But I knew better.

"Dad didn't return. A week later, we were moving to Seattle. Mom said he wasn't coming back and she needed to find a job to support us.

"I was devastated." She halted.

They were at the edge of the pond.

His warm hand squeezed hers. "Continue."

Forcing the words out, she continued, "I begged her not to leave, but she wouldn't listen. She was determined. Her parents and all her family lived there in Meridian, so I was surprised, but after two months, we were in Seattle, beginning a new life without dad. She went back to her maiden name. I became the housekeeper and babysitter and she worked."

He sat on a log beside the pool and pulled her down to sit beside him. "Did you ever find out what happened?"

"Mom refuses to talk about it. I quit trying to get any information out of her."

"How about your grandparents? Did you try them?"

"I didn't see much of them after that. They visited a few times in Seattle, but never mentioned it. It wasn't like your family. Nobody talked about anything uncomfortable. Mom wasn't real close with her parents, anyway. But I think they owned the mortgage on the house, since I overheard her talking with them on the phone. She hasn't told me much."

"How about your father's parents? Aunts? Uncles?"

"Dad's parents died when I was real young. There was Aunt Sally, Dad's older sister. I think she might know something, but I don't really know her. She lives in California."

Billy squeezed her hand again. "I have a feeling about this."

"You have a *feeling*? What do you think I've been living with for the last ten years? Too many feelings." She sniffed. "I used to be desperate for information, but now after so long, I'm afraid to find out the truth. Why hasn't he found me? Mom must be right. He doesn't want anything to do with me." A tear escaped down her cheek.

He placed his arm around her shoulders and pulled her close. "The truth will set you free," he whispered into her ear. For once, she didn't resist his affections, but welcomed the embrace. He held her close, while she shuddered and trembled, breathing in deep gasps.

"Billy, I'm scared," she said into his shirt. "Really scared. There's so much you don't know about me, so much I've hidden from everyone. Even myself." She pulled back, wiping her face on her sleeve.

"This morning at church God told me to start telling the truth. He said I won't have real relationships unless I do. He wants me to have them. But I'm afraid."

Gray eyes pierced hers. "What are you afraid of?"

"I'm not sure. More pain, I guess. I might fall apart."

"It's okay to fall apart. How can God heal you unless you're broken?"

"I already feel something breaking inside me. It started when I told God I would be a child again."

A gentle smile crossed his face. "I'm glad to hear it."

"Billy. Promise me something. Please. I feel like I'm going to crack. I'm afraid of what I'll do or say. Promise me that whatever happens, you won't hate me."

"Hate you? I could never hate you."

"You say that now, but please. Promise me."

"Okay. I promise. I'll never hate you. Now, promise me something, will you?"

"What?"

"Go with me to the Prayer Room on Friday nights. Starting with this Friday. They pray for healing. Commit yourself to doing it, okay? No matter what happens. Even with the two of us."

She hesitated. "Okay. ... I'll go. No matter what."

Friday evening, Billy pulled into Kristy's apartment parking lot. Shutting his eyes, he leaned back in the seat and let the fall breeze blow through the open pickup window.

"Father. Help. Touch Kristy tonight. Only you can heal her heart. I had no idea what she'd gone through. She's your special little girl." He smiled. "And a beautiful woman."

"Billy!" He jumped at the sound of Kristy's voice at his ear. "I've been waiting for you in front. You didn't see me?" She walked around to the passenger side and let herself in.

He flashed a smile. "No. I didn't see you." Turning on the

ignition, he backed out of the parking lot. "But hey. It's good to see you. I really missed you this last week. I'm used to having you around."

She smiled. He drank in her shining hair and sparkling blue eyes. Dressed in a long blue knit top with short capped sleeves, her soft curves caught his casual glance. He looked again. Her soft, smooth feet were in leather sandals and her toenails painted a dark pink.

He swallowed. "How was school?"

"Good. I don't think it'll be too hard this term."

His eyes fixed ahead. "What are you studying, anyway?"

She laughed, removing her white sweatshirt from one shoulder and tying it around both. "What do you think? Psychology!"

Letting loose a short, hearty laugh, he quipped, "From my experience, most girls are born studying psychology."

She smiled graciously, absorbing his attempt at humor. "Did *you* finish college?"

"Yeah."

"What was your major?"

"Business."

Looking at him curiously, she ventured, "What do you plan to do with it?"

"I'm going to start my own business someday. Maybe soon. Meanwhile, I am learning some other things. How have you been this week?"

"Good!"

৬৩ ৩ ৫৬৩

Kristy was glad this wasn't her first time to visit the Prayer Room. At least she knew what to expect. But it wasn't going to be the same going with Billy as it was with Cassie.

She and Cassie had been to the Prayer Room several times the spring before. This was where she had her first encounter with Jesus. Young people had been gathering there for over a year now, calling out to God for a move of the Spirit. A flutter of anticipation surged though her and she drew in a long breath.

Billy opened the door and stood aside to let her pass. They entered a large coatroom. Music played from within. She hung up her sweatshirt and took off her sandals. He removed his shoes.

"Here goes," he said, smiling down at her. He opened the door.

It was as she remembered. The walls were covered with murals, Bible verses and prayer requests. A large scroll lay on the floor, covered in scripture verses, revelations and encouraging words. A communion table with crackers and grape juice was set up in the corner and a large rugged cross stood behind it. Flasks of oil and lit candles lay on another table. Pillows scattered the carpeted floor. Young adults and teenagers dispersed about the room, worshiping. Some stood. Some knelt. Some lay on the floor. Others sat.

Matt Spalding, a slightly built young man with fiery eyes reached out his hand to greet Billy. "It's great to have you back!" he said, smiling and shaking Billy's hand. Soon he was hugging him fiercely and both growled playfully.

Matt's gaze flew to Kristy and he extended his hand. "Hey. I recognize you. You've been here before, right?"

Smiling, Billy introduced her, "This is Kristy. She was here quite a few times last spring."

"Oh, yeah. You came with Cassie, didn't you?"

She nodded.

"We're just getting started. Come in and make yourself comfortable."

Healing words
You speak the healing words
Healing words
Set me free ...[5]

Kristy sat beside Billy on the carpet, eyes shut and singing with all her heart. Feeling desperate, she lay face down. "Lord, please give me healing words," she prayed softly. "I need them."

Suddenly, she heard a soft chuckle. Lifting her head, she saw a young man lying on his back near her, eyes closed, smiling from ear to ear. Earlier, he had appeared somber and sad. She was sure she'd seen tears in his eyes. Now he shook with mirth.

Giggling came from another corner and she turned her head to see a young girl on the floor, eyes shut, breaking out in laughter. Matt, of all people, joined in. What was happening? Soon many in the room laughed along. In awe and curiosity she watched them, uncomfortable, but drawn to the strange behavior. This had happened a few times last spring. What were they laughing at? It just didn't seem right for them to do this at a prayer meeting.

Someone nudged her. She looked into a pair of fiery green eyes. A slight girl, about sixteen, with short blonde hair, bent over her, grinning. Clearing her throat, she blushed. "Excuse me, but I had a vision when you came in the door. I don't know you, but God won't leave me alone about it. Do you want me to tell you what I saw?"

Kristy rose to her feet, eyes wide. Billy stood beside her and offered his hand. Grabbing it, she held on tight. "Sure. What was it?"

"I saw you by a pool at night. A full moon was shining off the water. A friend was treading water in the pool, urging you to come in. You hesitated, but then threw off your clothes and dove in. You laughed and splashed, playing in the water."

Kristy's stared at her.

The girl grinned again. "I think God was saying that the pool is his love. The light of the moon is revelation. If you dive in and be immersed in his love, he will give you more revelation. And the clothes—they were past ways of thinking. Fear, shame and performance were three things I saw written on them. He wants to restore all things in your life and give you new ways of thinking."

In shock, Kristy clung to Billy's hand.

The girl turned curious. "Does that mean anything to you?"

She nodded.

Smiling, the girl turned and left.

Billy studied her face. "Are you all right?"

She sighed. "I think so."

"Do you want to leave? It's late enough."

"I think so."

A short while later, he parked his pickup and turned to her. "Do you want to talk about it? You looked like you'd seen a ghost."

She hadn't spoken a word since they'd left the Prayer Room.

"It happened," she said, still staring ahead.

"What happened?"

"The pool. In the middle of the night. Out on the ranch."

"What are you talking about?"

"When I first got there. Cassie took me up to the pond a couple of times in the middle of the night. We swam."

He chuckled. "You mean Cassie took you on a couple of her moonlight skinny-dipping adventures?"

Kristy's head jerked toward him. "You know about those?"

Bursting forth with a hearty laugh, he slapped his knee. "That sounds just like God! He's speaking to you." He turned to her. "Yes, I know about Cassie's midnight skinny-dipping. When she was younger, we were pretty close. She told me everything. She hasn't shared those kinds of things for quite some time, but every once in a while I've seen signs. Bare footprints in the mud. An item of clothing left behind on the log. You know, that sort of thing."

Kristy buried her hot face it in her hands. "I didn't know you knew. How embarrassing!"

Placing a warm hand on her shoulder, he sobered. "Kristy, it's okay. I promise I won't spy on you and Cassie at midnight. I think it's wonderful that God spoke to you like that. I am honored that you shared it with me."

After a short silence, she sighed. "Sorry. I'm just not used to telling people such personal stuff. But I'm glad you were with me tonight. I was scared. I didn't know what she'd say. You know, I had just finished asking God to give me healing words. I had no idea ... So how do I immerse myself in his love?"

He withdrew his hand and placed it on the steering wheel.

"For me, it means I keep believing he loves me. I take every chance to thank him for it. I stay in his presence, worship him and share with him. I keep receiving love from others as if it was coming straight from him. It is, you know."

Kristy reached across the gap separating them in the pickup, squeezing his hand. "Thank you for taking me tonight."

"Hey. I'll walk you to the door."

"You don't have to."

"Don't you want me to?"

She shrugged. "It would be alright. ... I guess."

He chuckled. "What would my sister say if she saw you coming in the door unescorted?" Then he pointed across the parking lot to a blue Chevy pickup. "And it looks like Jeff's here with her tonight. I would never hear the end of it if I didn't mind my manners."

She laughed. "Okay then."

⸺ ⸎ ⸺

James Turner sat in the recliner looking out the window into the courtyard, his useless legs elevated before him.

A scene came to mind. The last time he saw Patricia. In a fit of rage, he had cursed and thrown things.

He was still angry. Just thinking about it infuriated him. They ruined his family. They ruined everything.

He stayed away from home afterwards, unable to trust himself to go back. Word had come to him she was frightened of his violent outbursts and seeking a divorce. Devastated by discovering his wife's affair with his best friend, and not knowing where else to turn, he had gone to see the pastor of their church.

"Pastor, don't you think something should be done about

this?"

"About what?"

"Will and Pat?"

"Look, just because you're angry and can't patch it up with Pat doesn't mean you have to ruin another marriage as well. Will is back with his wife. He's getting counseling from me. What do you want? Revenge?"

"No. It's just that Will is a deacon. Don't you think that the church should know about this?"

"What do you want me to do, ruin the church too? There are a lot of people to think about here. A lot of damage could be done."

James had argued, but to no avail. Angry and frustrated, he did something he hadn't done for years. He left the state and went on a drinking binge. Three days later, he was picked up for drunk driving in Oregon and soon he lost his career as a policeman.

A buddy from work served him divorce papers, which he signed without contest. He couldn't bear the shame. Unemployed, he was now a marked man, with a record and no means to support his broken family. By the time he returned home, Patricia had taken the kids and moved, and no one would tell him where.

He could've kept trying to find them, but didn't have the heart.

Ruined and devastated, he moved to Florida to start over. As far from Meridian, Idaho as he could get. Barry had given him a job as a car salesman seven years ago. He was the only friend he had.

The door opened and his friend stepped in with a tray and a smile. "Here." He laid the tray on the bedside table and wheeled it over to him. "Hey. What's going through that head of yours today?"

"Nothing. Just remembering stuff."

"You don't look happy."

"I'm not."

"You could be."

"You keep saying that. Would you leave it alone? I told you how I lost my family. Now I can't walk. I can't even perform normal body functions. I'm a miserable excuse for a human being. Sometimes I think you're here just to add to my misery."

Barry smiled. "You're a miracle waiting to happen. Jesus is the Healer and the Savior. He wants to restore you. He loves you."

James threw a pillow at him. "Get out!"

TOO CLOSE?

*Now if we are children, then we are heirs. Heirs of God
and co-heirs with Christ ...* (Apostle Paul)

"Stop!! Stop!! Whoa!" A horse galloped past the shop's open
door. "Whoa! ... Help! Somebody help!"

It was Kristy.

Covered with grease, Billy dropped the tire iron and sprinted
outside.

Ginger ran through the apple orchard, Kristy barely hanging
on to the saddle, dodging limbs. Clearly out of control, she
appeared to be scared out of her mind. The horse tore through
the trees, abruptly turning at the back fence.

He flew through the gate and ran toward them. "Take
authority! Kristy! You've got to take authority!"

Was she going to be impaled or hit by one of the branches?

"Pull back on the reins! Turn her head!"

The horse flew past, reached the gate and stopped. Then it
ambled towards him, avoiding his eyes. Kristy slid off, trembling.

He grabbed the reins. "What are you doing on Ginger? She's

different than Blackfoot! She senses you're a novice and takes advantage! Do you want to get yourself killed?"

Kristy's pale face stared at him, wide-eyed. "I —"

"Where's Cassie? ..." He examined the crooked saddle. "Did you saddle her too?"

She nodded.

"I told you I'd help you in an *hour*. Can't you follow instructions?"

Kristy's face reddened. "No! I can't follow instructions." She turned to leave.

He grabbed her arm. "Oh no, you don't. You're not leaving yet."

She pulled out of his greasy grasp, eyes blazing. "I *am* leaving. Now. And I'm not taking any more riding lessons from *you*!"

He followed her through the gate and on toward the house. In a few quick steps, he caught her arm again and turned her toward him. "Look, Kristy, I was teaching you to ride. We made an agreement and you jumped the gun."

"Well, you're not teaching me to ride anymore. I don't like being yelled at!"

"So you do have a problem with authority, like your mother said. Did it ever occur to you that I yelled at you because I was afraid you'd get hurt?"

Blue eyes flashed fire. "Well, don't worry about me anymore, okay? I'm *not* your responsibility!"

She pulled out of his grasp and made a sour face.

"Wait a minute, Kristy."

"I'm tired of you ordering me around. Just when I think you're starting to be nice, you start yelling again and treating me like a stupid child! You did it on the hike, remember? And you did it while I was driving truck for you. You ordered me around like a slave." She swiped away angry tears. "Now you're starting to do it with riding lessons. I don't know why I agreed to this. I don't even *like* you!"

He froze and watched her march toward the house. Then, as

if she just remembered, she turned around and headed toward her car.

"Kristy!"

"Don't '*Kristy*' me! The name is Kirsten! … Kirsten Turner!" Jumping in the car, she sped down the driveway.

Heart sinking, he stared after her.

"That's that, I guess," came his father's voice, startling him. Billy turned to see him standing not far behind with Jeff, both in dirty coveralls.

"How long have you been standing here?"

"Long enough. Don't you think you were a bit hard on her? About the horse, I mean. I remember when you first started to ride. Granted you were a lot younger, but I recall—"

"I know … I know!"

Stepping up, his father inspected the horse, standing docile beside him. He examined the crooked saddle. "That's not too bad of a saddle job for the first time, Son. You must be a pretty fair teacher. Just the fact that she took the initiative and saddled up a different horse shows she's gotten over her fear. Yup, you must be a pretty good teacher. It's too bad—"

"Okay, Dad! You made your point."

Smiling, his father turned to leave.

"It was your comment about her mother. That's what did it," Jeff said soberly. "Trust me, that's what did it." He turned to follow Ben back to the shop, wagging his head.

Billy led Ginger back to the barn. "Stupid horse!" he said under his breath. "I should have blamed you from the beginning."

Sighing, he removed the saddle and hung it up. He brushed her down, contemplating the confrontation with Kristy.

Her name is Kirsten?

It would've been nice if she'd have told him her real name. He hadn't even known her name! He put up the curry comb and leaned on the stall door, gazing at the horse.

"Thanks for your part in making a fool of me, horse." Ginger nudged him with her muzzle. "And don't try playing innocent with me. You planned this all along, didn't you? You, with your sweet nature and all. You're a phony! Underneath that front lies a vengeful beast who has always wanted to get back at me for the pranks I played on that little sister of mine. Your true love."

After a long silence, Billy left the stall. He hesitated at the barn door. "It's probably just as well. As much as I like Kristy, I have to admit, she's too fragile for me. I'm like a bull in a china shop around her. I'm always offending her.

"I didn't even know till today that she felt that way when she was driving truck for me. I must be self-deluded." He looked up, jaw set. "But I refuse to walk on eggshells around her, afraid I might not breathe right. I'm just a farm boy!"

He raised his voice a few octaves, wagging his head from side to side. "I don't even like you!" He mimicked. "Well, I'm glad I found out before—"

Wincing, he closed his eyes and hung his head.

"It's too late. I care about her. Fragile or not."

⊱♦⊰⊱♦⊰

Hot tears clung to Kristy's eyelashes, blurring her vision. She swiped them away with her sleeve, but they kept coming, pooling and rolling down her cheeks. The heavy weight on her chest caused her to gasp for breath. Seeing a turnout in the road, she pulled over and gave in to raging emotions. She pounded on the steering wheel. "Oh, God! Why does he yell at me like that? I was horrified! And right in front of his father and Jeff!"

"This kind of stuff is always happening. And I can't believe what I said to him. I dumped the whole load. I'm so embarrassed. ... What must they think?" She folded her arms, lower lip trembling. "I'm not going to church tomorrow. I can't face him. Or them. I'm sure *Marcel* would be glad to sing for me!"

"God, he can't be right for me. I told him all that stuff. ... I took a risk like you wanted. Even with the horse. And now this! He just isn't safe." Her head dropped on the steering wheel and she sobbed.

Billy scanned the Prayer Room that Friday night.

Come on, Kristy. You promised.

It was one thing for her to refuse to answer his phone calls, but quite another for her to break a promise. He heaved a sigh. "Father, take care of her. I don't know what else to do." Entering into worship, he began to sing, closing his eyes. Soon he was aware of a male voice beside him.

Opening his eyes, he caught a wink from Jeff and a motion across the room. There was Kristy, with Cassie, kneeling and praying. He smiled.

> *Your deep, deep love*
> *Washes over me*
> *Your deep, deep love*
> *Fills my every need.*
> *Oh I long to hear*
> *Your voice call out my name*
> *It draws me to your deep, deep love.[6]*

Cassie entered the apartment living room just as Kristy arrived back from class. She walked up and looked straight into her eyes. "Kristy, my family knows what happened. They know you're not sick. They know why you didn't come to church the last few weeks. You can't keep ignoring him. You can't keep this up forever. I'm getting married in a month and you're the maid of honor. He's the best man. You have to talk to him."

Kristy threw her books down and dove for the couch, burying her face in the cushions, hair falling loosely around her head.

"I don't want to," she said, voice muffled.

Cassie went over to her friend and knelt on the carpet. "The whole family even sides with you and knows it was his fault. How could you have it any better than that? Why don't you just forgive him?"

Kristy set her jaw. Her face lifted to meet Cassie's eyes. "I don't know. It may take a while. He hurt me."

Cassie grabbed her hand. "Kristy, please don't go there. I can see the tormentors already at work. It will only get worse."

"Tormentors? What are you talking about?"

"There's a story that Jesus told. It's about this guy who owed a large debt to the King. He was forgiven. Then he turned around and refused to forgive some poor guy for a small amount of money owed to him. He demanded payment in full. The King was not pleased and put him in prison to be tormented until the debt was paid. ... Please, don't do this."

Kristy's eyes widened. "I remember that story from Sunday School. What kind of tormentors are you talking about?"

"You know. You're afraid to go to church. Your joy is gone. You're angry all the time. You mope around here pretending there's nothing wrong. Bob's asking you out again and you're actually considering it. You're more miserable than before you came to Jesus."

Staring at her, Kristy's eyes filled. "You're right, but Cassie, you don't understand. With Billy there's more to it. It's not just that he hurt me. He scares me."

Cassie blinked. "Why's that?"

"If I forgive him, we'll continue getting closer. And I know if he really knew me, he wouldn't want me. I can't be hurt like that again."

Cassie smiled knowingly. "So you guys are getting close and you're afraid."

Kristy groaned. "Yes, I'm afraid. I have issues. And pouring my heart out to some guy is too risky."

"Then why are you considering going out with Bob?"

"That's different. He's safe."

"Safe? How?"

"I wouldn't even be tempted to tell him that kind of stuff."

Cassie harrumphed. "That doesn't make sense."

Kristy smiled crookedly. "Who says we're talking *sense*?"

Cassie reached for her hand and squeezed it. "You need to

talk to someone, Kristy."

"I know."

"Why don't we pray about this?" She bowed her head. "Father, help Kristy find someone that can help her heal. Show her where she can go and give her the courage to do it."

Kristy looked up. "In the meantime, what should I do about Billy?"

Cassie rose from her knees and let out a long breath, blowing hair out of her face. Brown eyes bored into Kristy's. "You don't have to take riding lessons from him. You don't have to sing with him. If you want to avoid him, that's okay. Tell him you need your space. Dump him! But please. Forgive him."

Kristy sighed. "Okay. Next time he calls, I'll talk to him."

❧ ❧ ❧

"I'm really sorry, Kristy. I was wrong. Will you forgive me?"

"I forgive you," Kristy said into the phone.

He sighed. "Thanks. It was totally out of line for me to mention your mother. It just slipped out in the heat of the moment. I ... I didn't really want to hurt you."

"It's okay. I forgive you."

"Can I pick you up for prayer tonight?"

"Uh... Not tonight. I'll go with Cassie."

Silence.

"Are you coming out for a riding lesson tomorrow?"

Silence.

"Kristy?"

"I ... uh ... don't think that would be a good idea."

"Okay then ... I get it."

"Thanks Billy."

"Will you continue to keep your promise to me? Go to the Prayer Room? I plan on keeping mine to you."

"I will."

"Good bye, Kirsten. Kirsten Turner."

A short giggle escaped, then she choked on an unexpected emotion.

"Good bye."

6♦❩-❨♦6♦

Kristy woke to a cold cloudy morning. At the thought of the day ahead, her heart filled with dread.

Her research paper was due tomorrow.

Maybe if she skipped class and worked real hard on it all day, she could pull it off. She groaned, pulling the covers over her head. "Father, you know where my head's at lately. I'm losing interest in this stuff. My heart's hurting. I want to follow *you*. I want to heal." She jerked the covers down.

Maybe if she read the Bible it would help.

Sitting up, she grabbed her Bible from the bedside stand and it fell open to Matthew five. Skimming down the chapter, she read aloud some underlined portions. *Blessed are the poor in spirit, for theirs is the kingdom of heaven … Unless your righteousness surpasses that of the Pharisees and the teachers of the law, you will certainly not enter the kingdom of heaven … If someone strikes you on the right cheek, turn to him the other also. … Love your enemies …*

Letting out a tortured groan, she turned to another book. Her eyes fell on Ephesians 4:2. *Be completely humble and gentle; be patient, bearing with one another in love.*

Slamming the Bible shut, she returned it to where it was and sunk back in the bed. "Why is it like this when I read the Bible? It makes me feel like more of a failure. Lord, I can't do this—"

6♦❩-❨♦6♦

Linda studied her oldest son from across the room. Face sober, he strummed his guitar in a melancholy tune. Where was his smile? He didn't seem himself lately.

It had to be this thing with Kristy.

"Billy, are you okay?" she asked.

He stopped strumming and looked up, twisting his lips. "No. Not really. People keep asking me that. … Am I supposed to fake it?"

"Nobody's asking you to fake it."

"Well, at least I found out something through this whole experience with Kristy."

"What's that?"

"I have a heart. I've always wondered if I did. Now I know I do, because it's hurting in there."

"I'm sorry."

"Jeff says she's too fragile for me. Somehow that doesn't give me much comfort. I'll get over it. ... I suppose."

His mother rose and crossed over to him. Placing an arm around his shoulders, she bent and kissed his brow. "Well, I think you're wonderful."

He smiled sadly, meeting her eyes. "Thanks Mom."

Laying aside his guitar, he leaned back on the couch. "Mom, why is it that the girls that like me, I don't like? I have to go and fall for one that doesn't want me. Why's that?"

"I don't know, Honey."

"Most girls irritate me. For instance, Marcel. The last few weeks she's noticed the vacancy on the worship team and has been more than willing to stand in for Kristy. She's a good-looking girl with a beautiful voice." He glanced out the window. "And Kristy says she likes me. The fact that she follows me around and bats her eyelashes should give me a clue, but she bugs me." His eyes returned to his mother. "I try to be nice, but—"

Linda laughed and ran her hand through his dark hair. "Don't worry, Honey. God has someone for you."

ᔥᔡ ᔤ ᔥᔡ

A knock sounded on James Turner's door. "Come in!" he called.

Barry strode in, three young men trailing close behind.

James sat up. He recognized them. They were from Barry's church. They had been at the car dealership a few times, talking excitedly with Barry of miracles and healings. He couldn't help being curious, but he hadn't taken them seriously. They could believe what they wanted to believe. It didn't have much to do with him.

The four surrounded the bed. "James, I want you to meet Rob, Luke and P.J.," Barry said. "P.J. here, just got back from Africa. He witnessed someone come back from the dead."

James shrugged.

The three were very young, probably early twenties.

Barry announced, "James, we're here on a mission."

He looked up. "What kind of mission?"

"Another resurrection."

Standing around his bed, the four of them grinned.

James looked at each beaming face. "What are you talking about?"

Determination lined Barry's face.

"We're talking about you. Your soul and your legs. It's time for a healing and a resurrection. We're here to call it forth. Do we have your permission? Are you willing? Or do you want us to wait until you're clear dead? Then call you back?"

James was stunned. Barry was serious! He thought back to his past conversations with him.

Did he really believe this stuff?

He looked at his legs, now stretched out before him, numb and lifeless. What did he have to lose? There wasn't much chance of them coming back to life on their own.

"Are you guys going to get loud?"

Barry laughed. "Of course. ... What are you worried about? What people think?"

"I ... uh ... Okay, go ahead. Whatever."

Cheering broke out and Barry turned to shut the door. They began to march around the room, singing and praising God. They passed a Bible around and went about praying and boldly proclaiming scripture verses with his name inserted in them.

"Thank you, Father, for heaven. Thank you for invading this earth, bringing your Kingdom and doing your will."

"The Kingdom of God has come to this room. Jesus, the Healer, is here to heal James, deliver James and save James."

... You disciplined him like an unruly calf, and he has been

disciplined. Restore him, and he will return, because you are the LORD his God. …"

"I have surely heard James Turner's moaning: …"

"The Lord declares, 'Is not James my dear son, the child in whom I delight? … my heart yearns for him; I have great compassion for him, declares the LORD.'"

"… I have seen James's ways, but I will heal him; I will guide him and restore comfort to him."

Scriptures came, over and over. Then more came, filling the room.

Barry's voice boomed. "Spinal cord! Nerves! Be healed! Be totally restored!"

"Amen!" A chorus of male voices cheered. "Let it be so!"

"Healing and salvation, come!"

"Amen!"

"By the authority you have given me, Father, let it come! We receive it!"

"Amen!"

"Let it come!"

"There's no paralysis in the Kingdom!"

They began to sing.

> *I need you Jesus, come to my rescue*
> *Where else would I go?*
> *There's no other name by which I am saved*
> *Capture me with grace.*
> *I will follow you …*[7]

James looked down at his feet. Nothing. But something was happening.

Was that *hope* he felt? Rising within him?

Tears rolled down his face. "I need you, Lord. Help me! My life is yours. Forgive me for turning away. I don't understand why all this has happened to me, but I'm yours now. Whatever's left of me. I have nowhere else to turn. I'll do whatever you say."

THE WORD COMES

*... if indeed we share in his sufferings in order that we
may also share in his glory.*   (Apostle Paul)

Ben Watson leaned back in his chair. Thanksgiving was one of his favorite days. Most were finished eating, but the family lingered at the long table, chatting and enjoying the good will that was theirs. His heart swelled. The whole family was there, with Grandma and Grandpa Watson and a few others. His eyes finally rested on Billy, who sat at his side, unusually sober.

Having Kristy with them didn't help his mood. He hadn't said a word the whole meal. But then, he might have been silent anyway. It was not uncommon the last few weeks. Kristy didn't look happy either. They were civil, but it was tense between them. He glanced at Linda, who talked in low tones with Molly, Jeff's Mother. She raised her eyes. Then, biting her lip, her gaze darted from Billy to Kristy and then back to him. Raising his eyebrows, he gave her a resigned smile.

Billy sprang out of his seat. "Hey Joey. Want to shoot some hoops with me? The weather's not too bad tonight."

"Sure. Jeff, do you want to come too?" Joey asked, pulling on the sleeve next to him.

Ben chuckled. Jeff didn't notice the tugging, as he was deeply absorbed with Cassie. With their wedding only two weeks away, he didn't notice much of anything but her.

"Jeff?" Joey persisted.

Jeff shook himself and turned. "What? … Oh, hoops? Sure. I'll be out in a minute."

"I'll come out for a bit, too," Ben said, scooting out his chair.

The three left the table and headed for the utility room to get sweatshirts and coats. They were soon joined by Jeff. The air was clear and crisp. Ambling out to their makeshift court behind the barn, Ben addressed his oldest son. "Is it that bad?"

Billy frowned. "What?"

"Kristy."

He grimaced. "It's just hard. I'll get over it. I'm really happy for Jeff and Cassie, but …" He looked ahead to where Joey was already shooting baskets. "It could be worse… I just thought—"

"Stuff like this is never easy, Son. I'm proud of how you've handled yourself. God will bless you in time with a good woman."

Billy twisted his lips. "Yeah, I'll try to remember that."

༄ ༄ ༄

At the sink, Linda Watson stood washing pots and pans while Kristy scurried behind her, putting left-overs in dishes, clearing counters and wiping up messes. Cassie had already left for the living room, discussing wedding plans with Molly.

She took a breath.

"Are you okay, Kristy?"

Kristy froze. "What do you mean?"

"You look sad."

Blushing, Kristy continued wiping the counters. She bit her lip. "I suppose I am."

Linda looked up at her. "Want to talk about it?"

Kristy turned her back, busying herself with a dirty spot on the counter. "I … don't know. It's kind of personal. It's awkward with me and Billy. "

Linda turned to meet her eyes. "You can leave Billy out of this, Sweetie," she said gently. "There's something else bothering you. It's been weighing on your mind a long time."

Kristy's blue eyes went wide. "I ... Did Cassie talk to you?"

"No. But I can see the weight on your shoulders. I understand more than you realize. You remind me of myself when I was your age. If you ever get the courage to talk, I'm available." She crossed over and enfolded her in a determined hug.

Kristy swallowed, going stiff. "Thank you Linda, I'll keep that in mind."

Linda leaned back and smiled into her blue eyes, holding her by the upper arms. "You do that."

δ❧ ❧δ

Billy glanced across the Prayer Room, watching Kristy worship. Eyes closed and hands raised, tears flowed as she sang.

> *I call out to you, again and again*
> *You are my rock in times of trouble*
> *You lift me up, when I fall down*
> *All through the storm*
> *Your love is the anchor*
> *My hope is in you alone*[8]

He sighed.

Jeff and Cassie hadn't come. Probably getting ready for the fast approaching wedding. She had come alone. It was admirable of her to keep her promise, but he didn't know it would be like this. It was difficult to see her hurting, knowing she wanted him to keep his distance. But it did look like she was calling out to God. He was who she needed.

He bowed his head. "Father, make her happy. I want her to be happy. Whatever it takes. She loves you and needs you. Show her your love," he whispered.

Opening his Bible, Pastor Evan began, "Dearly beloved, we are gathered here to join this man and this woman in holy matrimony… "

Standing beside Jeff, Billy's mind wandered.

It was happening. His beautiful, feisty sister was marrying his best friend.

He took in their beaming faces. Cassie wore a simple white gown, dark curls piled on her head, cascading down around smooth cheeks and a wide smile. Large brown eyes glowed with love's fire as she gazed into the eyes of her bridegroom.

Dressed in a black tuxedo with a dark red boutonniere, Jeff stood straight and tall, blue eyes fixed on hers, shining with adoration and affection.

He was a lucky guy.

And Cassie had never looked so beautiful.

Billy smiled. "Father, bless them," he whispered. Then smirking, he continued, "And bless me with the good woman Dad says you'll send me in your good time."

His eyes lifted to Hannah, standing opposite him between Kristy and his cousin Katie, all wearing dark green satin formals.

His baby sister was growing up.

Thick blonde curls, pinned on top of her head, and skillfully applied make-up, made her young face appear more sophisticated. Beautiful, but solemn, her usual sunny and carefree disposition was missing.

Then his gaze rested on Kristy's vulnerable face. Their eyes met briefly before she looked away and he took in the whole picture. She, Katie and Hannah each carried a single long-stemmed red rose, cradled in their right arms and Kristy now held Cassie's bridal bouquet with the other hand. Large blue eyes shone with longing as she stood caught up in the ceremony. Shining brown hair cascaded down in loose waves onto smooth, creamy shoulders. The pastor's voice faded as Billy stared, transfixed.

She was beautiful.

That's her.

Billy blinked.

What?

That's her.

No. It can't be her.

It's her.

But she doesn't even like me. She made it quite clear.

"The rings please."

Kristy's blue eyes rose to his. He gulped, continuing to stare.

"Billy ... The rings please."

Joey's elbow struck him in the ribs.

He startled.

"Oh."

Chuckling rippled through the audience.

Everyone was looking at him. Embarrassed, he fumbled through his pocket, produced the desired jewelry and dropped it into the outstretched palm of his soon-to-be brother-in-law.

Eyes wide, he found Kristy's gaze again and grinned. She blushed.

Smiling, he chuckled at himself. He must have looked like a deer in the headlights. He sure wasn't expecting that from God. A thrill spread through his whole being. Hope rose to the point a joyous laugh burst forth and he was barely able to stifle it. Thank God all the attention was on Cassie and Jeff.

༄ ❦ ༄

Later, Billy stood next to Kristy in the dim light of the reception hall, watching his sister dance in the arms of her beloved Jeff. For them, there was no one else present. Soon Jeff brought Cassie over and gave her to her father. He then crossed over to his mother. The two couples danced, smiling and whispering in each other's ears. The music changed.

Billy held out a hand to Kristy.

"May I have this dance?" She nodded, eyes fixed on his hand. Heart pounding, he pulled her into his arms and held her loosely, swaying to the music. Couples crowded the floor. He continued to hold her cautiously, afraid she'd bolt.

What should he do now?

Lord, help me.

"Excuse me. Can I cut in?" It was Marcel, tapping on Kristy's bare shoulder.

She was stunning. Her tall, slender figure, sleek in a black formal. Green eyes sparkled and shiny red lips parted into a full smile, revealing straight white teeth.

Jaw dropping, he froze.

As if on cue, Kristy pulled away. "Oh ... of course," she said, retreating from the floor.

He stiffened and frowned, eyes fixed on Kristy, as she hurried from the room. Where was she going?

Marcel's arms went around his neck. "It was a beautiful wedding," a syrupy voice said. Her lithe frame leaned a little too close. "You know who I thought was the best-looking man up front, don't you?" She smiled and eager green eyes peered at him from under long, heavily blackened lashes.

Mouth set, he stiffened. Struggling to control rising anger, he politely placed one hand at her waist and pushed her to an arm's length from his body.

຺຺ ໑ ໄ຺

In the bathroom, Kristy stood at the mirror, dabbing at running mascara. She sniffled. "I'm a mess." Was she losing it? Whenever she got around Billy, it happened. It was getting worse—

Shuffling caught her attention.

A whimper in one of the bathroom stalls.

Then a sigh.

Was it a child?

She bent to examine the feet under the stall door. Two small buckled and shiny black shoes with white anklets paced in front of the toilet. The whimpering intensified and increased in volume.

Kristy knocked on the door. "Who's in there? Are you okay?"

The pacing stopped.

Slowly, the stall door opened and a pony-tailed blonde head peeked out, eyes swollen and red. A girl about five or six looked up, large hazel eyes brimming with tears.

"Are you all right?"

She sniffled, shaking her head.

"Want to talk about it?"

The little blonde head nodded again, ponytails wagging and ribbons loosening. One of them was hanging entirely undone.

"How about we sit over there?" She motioned to a small couch and chair in the corner, with a lamp table.

Kristy took hold of her hand, led her to the chair, sat and pulled the little girl onto her lap. "What's your name?"

"Kelly."

"That's a nice name. I'm Kristy. Can I retie your hair ribbons for you?"

Kelly nodded.

"Where's your mommy, Kelly?"

A small finger rose to point to the main room.

"What's wrong?"

Kelly's pink lips turned down and her chin quivered. "My … daddy … left us last week. Mommy's real sad, but tries to be happy. … I just can't be happy." Large tears rolled down her cheeks.

Kristy hugged her. "That's sad. I know how you feel. My daddy did that when I was a little girl."

Her tearful eyes widened. "Really?"

She nodded.

"What did you do?"

"I cried. Like you're doing."

"You did?"

"I did. I didn't know what else to do. It hurt real bad. I wish I would have known about Jesus then. He could have helped me feel better."

"Jesus?" Kelly shook her head. "Jesus can't help anybody. I saw a picture of him. He's sick."

Surprised, Kristy looked down at her. "Sick?"

"Yeah. He is real sad. He was bleeding and hanging on a cross."

"Honey, Jesus isn't sick. That picture was when he died on the cross, but he isn't there anymore. He died on that cross, but three days later, on Easter morning, God raised him from the dead. He's alive. He can see you and hear you praying. He's very powerful and wants to help you. He loves you."

"Really?" A spark of hope lit the little girl's countenance. "Do you think he could help Mommy and Daddy?"

"Of course. You want to pray right now?"

Kelly nodded. She folded her hands and tucked her chin. "Hey Jesus. This is Kelly. Can you hear me talking to you? My heart is sad and I need help. Will you help me not be sad and will you help my mommy and daddy love each other?"

She looked up. "Did he hear me?"

"Yes. He heard you."

A smile broke out on her face. Her eyes sparkled. "Thank you, Kristy. I'm going to go play now." Jumping off her lap, she opened the door and was gone.

Smiling to herself, Kristy pondered the encounter as she looked in the mirror and adjusted her hair. "I wish I had the faith of that child. I'm going to go play now too." She laughed softly, then opened the door and made her way back toward the reception hall. Through the door of a side room, she recognized Billy's voice.

"Sam, what am I going to do? I can't stand girls like her."

Kristy stopped. The door was cracked enough she got a glimpse of Billy, standing just inside. "She reminds me of the adulterous woman in the Proverbs. 'Lips dripping with honey . . .'"

Sam laughed. "It's not that bad, Billy. She's just showing admiration. Most guys would be flattered. She's beautiful."

Billy snorted. "Well, I'm not flattered. Give me a little purity for a change."

Kristy froze.

Purity?

"I think she's the kind of girl that would lead a guy to destruction. She only awakens lust—"

Kristy's heart sank. She backed up from the door, grabbed her coat and headed for the parking lot.

Before she reached her car, Kristy lost it. How could she go from hope, to jealousy, to inspiration by a child's simple faith, to despair so quickly? Her emotions were all over the map.

She'd known it all along. Of course he wanted purity. That look during the wedding and before asking for a dance had drawn her in again. She was such a fool.

He was irritated with Marcel for cutting in on her. It was probably her he was talking about. But if Marcel wasn't pure enough, no way would she be.

But he knew some of her past. She had told him there were things she was ashamed of. He should have guessed she wasn't "pure." She had certainly warned him. So, why did he look at her like that? Was it admiration, longing and … desire in those dark gray eyes? He must know she was not pure.

And why did she care? He was not what she wanted either. Tears cascaded down her face, washing off any remaining make-up. She mopped them off with a napkin from the glove compartment and drew in a ragged breath.

She'd already given up on him.

It was over!

She had to get a grip!

"God, help me! I'm Cassie's maid of honor. I can't just disappear. I've got to go back in there."

She raised her eyes to the front door of the church. Through blurry vision, she saw two figures emerge, hand in hand, looking both ways. She sat up, focusing on the blurry figures through tears. They darted around the corner.

Was that Brian Potter and Hannah?

What was she doing with him?

What should *she* do?

Her eyes found the front door again. Someone else emerged. He looked both ways.

Oh no! It was Billy!

She tried to duck, but he had already seen her and was approaching the car. She cringed.

He rapped on the window. "Kristy!"

She opened the door.

"Are you all right? Everyone's wondering where you are. Cassie's about to throw her bouquet. I'm sure you'll want to be--" He stopped, studying her in the dimly lit car.

"You've been crying."

"Just give me a minute, okay?"

"Sure." Clearing his throat, he swallowed. "Uh ... Is there anything I can do?"

Suddenly, Kristy straightened. "I think maybe there is. Your little sister ... Would you check on her for me?" Motioning with her hand, she continued, "A few minutes ago she disappeared between the buildings with Brian Potter."

Billy's brow raised. "*Brian Potter?*"

"Yeah."

"Brian Potter and Hannah?"

"Yes, Billy ... They were holding hands."

His eyes widened. Turning abruptly, he jogged over to the building and disappeared around the corner.

✿ ❦ ✿

The doctor stood at James' bedside, dumbfounded. "What did you say?"

James looked down at his moving toes, smiling widely. "I said they prayed for me and Jesus healed me!"

The doctor wagged his head. "There was some chance that feeling would return, you know." He examined the chart in his hands, leafing through papers. "I'll recheck the records. There must be some mistake. Voice laced with skepticism, he peered over his glasses."

James met the doctor's eyes. "I don't care what your records say, I couldn't move my feet last week. I couldn't feel a thing below my waist. I know Jesus healed me."

Going over to close the door, the doctor returned and sat on the bed. "Okay. Tell me what happened."

"These guys have come to my room every day for the last few weeks, singing and commanding life into my legs and healing into my spine. The day before yesterday I felt the presence of God. Something went down my back-bone and into my legs. It was like fire. Then, yesterday, I started moving my feet! Today I felt sensation below my waist! I can feel it when I have to use the bathroom! It's not under control yet, but it's coming. I feel pain in my legs! It's wonderful! I never thought I'd be so happy to feel pain!"

The doctor rose, sighing and studying James' legs and feet. "You might be right. There is definitely a difference from last week. You can move!"

Tears streamed down James' cheeks. "I still can't believe God would do something like this for me."

HITTING THE WALL

Where can I go from your spirit? Where can I flee from your presence? Surely the darkness will hide me...

(King David)

Billy peered into the dark corridor between the church and the adjacent building. Two forms slipped deeper into the shadows.

"Hannah!"

No answer.

"Hannah! I know you're back there! Come out right now, or I'll get Dad."

Hannah slid into the soft light at the corner of the building and her chin tilted. "I needed some fresh air."

"In the dark? Who's with you?"

In her green formal, with a coat draping her shoulders, her head lowered. "No one."

Billy came close, lifted her chin and looked into her face. "I heard you left with Brian."

"What of it?" An insolent voice rang through the darkness and Brian emerged into the light to stand beside Hannah.

"We aren't doing anything wrong. Just talking."

Billy grabbed Hannah's arm and pulled her into the bright entry lights at the front door. "Then talk inside, where there's witnesses to your innocence."

She halted. "Billy, please don't tell Daddy."

Billy looked down at his little sister. Strands of curly blonde hair blew over smooth, fair cheeks in the evening's gentle breeze. Her small, upturned nose crinkled and her rosebud lips turned down in a worried frown.

Almost fourteen, she looked sixteen.

Or older.

She shivered and he knew it wasn't due to the temperature. Her brown eyes pleaded.

"Please, Billy."

"Okay. I'll make you a deal. If you tell him, I won't."

"Billy!"

"Come on. Cassie's about to throw her bouquet."

Heels clicked on the pavement and he looked back over his shoulder. Kristy had pulled herself together, but she didn't look happy. He opened the door, letting Kristy in first and then guiding Hannah inside.

Once inside, Hannah broke loose and fled. He turned to Kristy. "How long were they out there?"

"Not long."

He studied her. Heaviness and defeat hung in her posture and her soft features were hard with determination.

"Are you okay?"

She avoided his eyes. "I think so," she said, "I'll freshen up in the restroom."

"Don't be long. They're waiting."

"Bye! God bless! Have fun!"

The wedding party stood in front of the building, sending off the wildly decorated yellow Toyota. It was late. Billy turned to Kristy. "Will you be at church tomorrow?"

She cleared her throat. "Probably not."

He frowned, studying her averted face. "Okay. Just thought I'd ask."

"I've got to go help clean up." She turned and left, reentering the building.

Later, Billy caught a glimpse of Kristy heading for the door. Bewildered, he shook his head, twisted his lips and turned to his little sister. Preparing to leave, she put her arms in her coat sleeves, lifted her chin and bolted out the door.

He turned back.

Women!

"Joey, do you need a ride?"

❦❦❦❦❦

On the way to her lonely apartment, Kristy drove in silence. She parked the car, hung her head and the woeful silence engulfed her. Gathering an armload of wedding mementoes from the front seat and stifling tears, she made her way to the front door and entered, kicking it shut.

She already missed Cassie.

What was she going to do?

After spilling the stuff on the kitchen table, she grabbed her purse and headed for bed. Yanking off her satin formal, she threw on her pajamas, plugged in her phone, crawled in and switched off the light.

Curled on her side, she hugged herself a good while, then turned to her back and stared into darkness.

"Oh God, where are you? What should I do for the next few weeks? I can't visit the Watson's without Cassie. It's too uncomfortable. But I'm so lonely."

Who could you talk to?

Her chin quivered. "This sounds strange, but even after everything that's happened, it would probably be Billy. He's still a friend. I need a friend right now." Tears rolled down her face. She gave in, pulling the covers over her head.

Was she crazy?

She couldn't talk to Billy.

A telephone ring pierced the heavy air. Startled, Kristy bolted up to switch on the light, fumbled with a tissue and blew her nose. In the process, she knocked the blaring device off the stand. It rang again from the carpet. She dove off the bed, picked it up and flipped it open.

"Hello?" she said with forced cheerfulness, voice hoarse.

"Kristy, its Billy."

"Oh ..." She choked. "Hi, Billy." Clearing her throat, she sniffed, unplugged the phone and climbed back in bed.

"Have you been crying again?" he ventured.

She groaned and blew her nose.

"I was thinking about you. I know there's no one there with you."

"I'm okay."

"You don't *sound* okay."

She sniffled. "You're right. I'm not okay."

"You want to talk? ... Kristy?"

"No."

"I'm here for you, Kristy. If you ever need anything or just want to talk, call me, okay?"

She sighed. "Okay."

"Good. Please call."

"Thanks Billy."

"You're welcome, Beautiful ... Are you coming for Christmas? It's in only twelve days. Cassie and Jeff will be back by then."

"I don't know. I'll see."

"Don't spend it by yourself, Kristy. Will you promise me that?"

"Okay. I'll make sure I do something on Christmas."

"Are you sure you can't come to church tomorrow?"

"I'll see. I'm awfully tired."

"I don't buy that. You may be tired, but that isn't the reason you'd miss."

"You're right. ..." She sniffled. "Goodbye, Billy." Abruptly, she hung up.

The next morning Kristy awoke with a headache. She drug herself out of bed and gazed out the window at the gray sky. It was drizzling rain and a cold wind whistled through the trees. She went to the kitchen to get a glass of water. It was eight A.M. Sighing, she returned to bed and stared at the ceiling.

Christmas ...

She didn't fit here.

She was ... alone.

Where could she go?

Suddenly, she bounced from the bed and began stuffing clothing into a suitcase. "I'm going home. I'll surprise them. They're not perfect, but they *are* my family."

Late Sunday afternoon, Kristy pulled into the driveway next to her mother's car. She lugged her bag to the front door. It was unlocked, but a strange quiet greeted her.

"Mom?"

She had to be there. Her car was in the driveway.

"Mom? ... Are you home?"

Shuffling sounded from the back of the house. Puzzled, Kristy put down her bag and crept down the hall to the closed bedroom door. She knocked softly.

"Mom, are you in bed? It's Kristy. I decided to come home for Christmas break." She knocked again. "Mom?"

The knob turned. Cracking the door, her mother peered through. "Oh. Hi, Kristy." She laughed nervously. "What a surprise! I thought you weren't coming home for Christmas." Her cheery smile somehow seemed false.

Kristy examined her mother's mussed hair and bathrobe. "Aren't you dressed? Are you feeling okay?"

"No ... Uh ... I mean yes. I ... I'm fine." She forced a laugh again, smoothing a hand over her rumpled dark curls. "Just napping." She yawned, patting her mouth. "I'll be dressed in a jiffy. Do you think you could go to the store for milk? We're out." She still stood in the door, with it mostly closed.

Milk? Now?

"Uh ... sure. I guess so." She studied her mother's pasted on smile. "But now? Where's Toby?"

"I don't know. I think he's at a friend's house. Could you get the milk?"

Puzzled, Kristy nodded and turned away. Exiting the house, she noticed a strange black BMW parked directly across the street. She got in her car and headed for the store.

❦❦❦

Ben closed the shop door and started for the back of the house. He picked his way around frozen puddles and snow, lifted his eyes to the gray sky and zipped up his jacket against the wind. He wouldn't be surprised if there was another snowstorm headed their way. At the side of the barn, voices reached his ears through the thin wooden walls.

"I've waited long enough. I'm telling Dad."

Ben halted.

"Please, Billy."

"Why won't you tell him?"

"Because I know he won't let me see him anymore. He doesn't like him."

"I don't like him either. I don't like the way he's treating my baby sister. He shows no respect for her or her family."

"I'm not a baby! I'm almost fourteen! And you guys don't understand. He needs someone to talk to. He doesn't have anyone."

Ben stepped through the barn door, closing it behind him. "What is it you need to tell me, Hannah?"

She paled, then turned to Billy, brown eyes round.

Billy headed for the barn door, inching around him. "Uh, I think I'll be going now."

Ben blocked his way. "Just a minute, Billy. I want you to stay

116

until the story's out." He turned to his daughter. "Go ahead, Hannah."

She gulped. "Uh ..." Looking down, she bit her lip. "Brian and I were talking at the wedding."

"Talking? You and Brian Potter?" He glanced at Billy. "And why would your brother be concerned about that?"

Hannah continued to study the ground. "We were in the alley beside the church."

"Alone?"

She nodded.

"Hannah, look at me."

She raised her eyes.

"Daddy, we were only talking. It was loud in the building and he wanted to go somewhere private."

Billy piped in. "When the guy's holding your hand in a dark alley, I think you might get a clue that he has more in mind than talking. And he was defensive when I told you to come in."

"He wasn't holding my hand! ... Well, maybe a little on the way out, but he was just being friendly."

Ben sighed. "Billy, do you have anything more to say?"

"I don't think so, Dad. But I didn't like it." He turned to his sister. "It also worried me that Hannah wanted to keep it from you."

"Thank you, Billy. I'll take it from here."

Billy went for the door while Hannah dissolved into tears, burying her face in her hands.

"So why didn't you want to tell me about this, Hannah?"

She sniffled. "Be ... because I knew ... you wouldn't like it."

Ben paused. "Why wouldn't I like it?"

"Because you th ... think I'm ... too young to have a boyfriend ... and you ... you ... don't like him."

"It hasn't been that long since we talked about this. You *are* too young to have a boyfriend. And as far as me not liking him, it's his rebellious attitude I don't like. It would be best if you didn't even talk to him. I don't trust him. You're only thirteen and he—"

"I knew you'd say that! I knew it!" She turned and ran into the house, slamming the back door.

Ben looked to the sky. "Lord, help."

A scene from Hannah's childhood came to mind. At four years old, she had disobeyed him. She had followed a group of children into a forbidden vacant lot near the church, scattered with scrap metal and debris. He had specifically instructed her and Joey to stay out of there.

On the way home from church, she sat in the back seat, face sober and large brown eyes wide with dread. Rarely did he discipline her, leaving most of it to Linda. But this time he was going to take care of it, since he had given the order.

Hannah was banished to wait for him in her room. When he entered, she sat on the bed stiffly, back straight and brown eyes fearful. Approaching her gently, he asked, "Hannah, why did you disobey me?"

Hannah's large brown eyes filled with tears. She looked up at him, lower lip quivering.

"Be ... because, Daddy, I'm a sinner!" Burying her face in her hands, she wept.

I almost lost it.

Used to Cassie, who was in his face with her opinions, agenda and rebellion, he was totally unprepared and had to do a double-take.

After that, he thought he had her pegged. Gentle and sweet, he'd never seen her really rebel.

Until now.

Somehow, this seemed more dangerous than Cassie's outbursts.

What was happening?

Opening the back door, he removed his boots. He passed through the kitchen, where Linda was busily preparing lunch. Coming up behind her, he encircled her waist, pulled her close, and buried his face in her hair.

"You smell good."

She smiled and dropped the spoon on the counter. Pulling his arms tighter, she snuggled into him.

"Do you think you could get away and pray with me for a bit?" He whispered. "It's Hannah. I need help."

⸝⸱❦⸱⸜

Kristy couldn't sleep. She groaned.

Some homecoming.

Merry Christmas!

By the time she had arrived with the milk, the black BMW was gone, confirming her suspicions. But her mother would not admit to anything. Kristy confronted her, it turned into a screaming match and Toby entered the house in time to get caught in the middle of it.

By Wednesday evening, she and Toby had bought a Christmas tree and set it up. There were a few gifts to go under it, but Toby wasn't interested.

She took him to the mall, but he didn't last long. He was in a hurry to get back to his friends.

On the way home, she asked, "Toby, doesn't it upset you that Mom is so self-absorbed? She hasn't done anything to prepare for Christmas and it's only a week away! And she's sneaking around acting like a wayward teenager. She hides a boyfriend in her bedroom and then pretends it didn't happen. How long has she been doing this? It certainly wasn't happening last summer!"

"You don't understand, Kristy. Mom's been real crazy lately. It's best not to hassle her."

"What about *you*, Toby? You need a stable family and people who care for you."

He let out a harsh laugh. "You think I'm hoping for that? I'm almost seventeen. I don't even remember my father. Mom's always stressed out and angry. Sometimes I can hear her crying in her room. She's lonely and sad. In some ways I'm glad she has a boyfriend. At least I've seen her smile a few times in the last month. It's too bad she has to put up a front for you. You've never really accepted her for who she is. When you come home from college, all you can do is fight with her until you both blow a gasket. No, I'll never have a 'stable family,' whatever that is. Don't you think it's obvious that I have to take care of myself?"

Alone in bed that night, Kristy seethed with anger and frustration. She was livid. She couldn't stay here. She was better off in her apartment.

But she was so alone!

Would she always be alone? She didn't fit anywhere. After tossing and turning for two hours, she switched on the light and pulled out her Bible.

"Lord, please talk to me!"

She thumbed through it, eyes scanning the pages. An underlined red lettered verse caught her eye.

I will not leave you as orphans, but I will come to you.

"I feel like an orphan. Father, why do I always have to feel like an orphan? What can I do?"

೫ಖ ❦ ❦ಖ

James awakened to peaceful silence. Joy and hope flooded his heart.

He was going home today!

Swinging his feet over the side of the bed, he reached for his Bible. Stepping carefully to a chair, he leaned on his cane for support. His legs were gaining strength every day. The pain was subsiding and with help from physical therapy, he was walking! He had even regained control of his bladder! He opened his Bible, a gift from Barry, to a now familiar Psalm.

I love the Lord, for he heard my voice; he heard my cry for mercy. … The cords of death entangled me, the anguish of the grave came upon me; I was overcome by trouble and sorrow. Then I called on the name of the Lord: "O Lord, save me!" … Be at rest once more, O my soul, for the Lord has been good to you. For you, O lord, have delivered my soul from death … that I may walk before the Lord in the land of the living.

Tears trickled down his face. He was getting used to tears. "Why, God? Why did you do this for me? Why me? I turned my back on you years ago. I was angry. I blamed you for everything. But it was my fault the whole time. I did everything wrong. Even when I tried to do right, it all went wrong. I was a miserable failure. If it hadn't been for Barry's persistence, I don't know if I would've ever turned back to you and called to you for help. Why did you come to me? Why?"

Because I love you.

Joy swelled and he erupted in laughter.

FALLING APART

"You're leaving?"

Thursday morning Patricia Jones emerged from her bedroom to find Kristy lugging her bags down the hallway toward the front door.

"Yes. I'm leaving. You don't want me here."

Chin lifting, Patricia stiffened. "That's a fine thing to say. Don't blame this on me! You're sticky sweet one moment and then out of control the next! First, I hear that you're not coming home because you're spending Christmas with those ... those *people*. Then you show up unexpectedly and when I don't drop everything and cater to your expectations, you fly into a rage and accuse me of all sorts of stuff! Now you've got Toby's hopes up for a family Christmas and you're going out the door. Leaving it all to me!"

"When are you going to get some help, Kristy? Like I said, you're bipolar or something. You had an uncle like that. And your father—"

"I'm out of here," Kristy said. She slammed the door, threw the suitcase in her car, hopped in and headed for the freeway. Weaving through traffic, she sped out of town.

After an hour of driving, she settled in, staring silently at the cars ahead. No tears came to relieve the pain and anger. And the closer to Oregon, the more depressed she became.

What was she going to do for Christmas?

She had promised Billy.

After six hours of driving, she arrived at her apartment. Loneliness assaulted her when she unlocked the door. She lugged the bags in and flopped into bed, exhausted.

A few hours later, clad in pajamas, she drug herself out of bed, flipped on the television and began to eat. Cookies, stale potato chips, left-over ham and chocolate. Lots of chocolate.

Well into the next day, in the same pajamas and still parked in the front room, she was sick of television and movies, so flipped it off. Restlessness and emptiness fed her growing anger. Legs shaking and skin crawling, she paced in and out of the kitchen, opening and shutting the refrigerator. Attempts to pray brought no comfort or satisfaction. By evening, they were long abandoned, replaced by deep soul-sickness and disgust.

Disgust with her miserable existence.

She was pitiful.

Entering the bathroom, she looked at her frowning self, dark circles under her eyes and hair hanging clumped and tangled. Rage boiled within her and the ache in her heart increased. She threw up her hands.

This was ridiculous.

She had to get out of here!

She was done!

She couldn't do this *Christian* thing anymore. She found a number in her phone and dialed.

"Hey, what's going on tonight? ... Yeah, I'm around. ... Sure, that sounds fun. ... I'll be there. ... See ya soon."

Flipping the phone shut, she ripped off her pajamas, threw them in the corner and climbed in the shower.

She was going out!

Billy didn't want her to spend Christmas alone.

Well, fine! She would hang out with friends.

Of her own kind!

An hour later, Kristy examined herself in the full-length mirror. Eyes heavily penciled, face pale with make-up and lips painted dark, she looked like a different woman. Her brown hair hung straight, loose and ragged over pale shoulders. Long, dangling earrings hung from her ears. A strapless top, tight over her full bust, exposed her pale midriff. A very short, tight leather skirt hung low on her hips, her pale legs and thighs bare.

That's more like it.

Slipping her feet into high platform shoes, she reached for her black leather coat and headed out into the dark winter evening. Cold wind bit her legs and blew her hair as she climbed into the car.

She ignored it.

ε♥⟩-⟨♥ə

Not many came to the Prayer Room that Friday night. But Billy was there, stretched out on the carpet.

> *Salvation spring up from the ground,*
> *Lord, rend the heavens and come down,*
> *Seek the lost and heal the lame*
> *Jesus, bring glory to your name ...* [9]

"Where's Kristy?" he prayed.

She hadn't shown. He'd tried calling, but her phone kept going to voicemail.

Was she okay?

He prayed in the Spirit. ...

"Please, Lord, keep her safe. Give her a break-through, Jesus. You're the Savior."

Around midnight, Billy rose to leave. After pulling on his boots, he reached for his coat.

Outside, William Tell's Overture blared from his pocket. He pulled out his phone. "Billy here."

"Billy! I finally got you!"

"Kristy! Where are you? I've been trying to call you all week. You haven't even answered my texts."

Faint and muffled male laughter came through the phone.

"Kristy? Are you there?"

"Yeah. I'm here. I need some help. You said to call—"

"Where are you? What's wrong?"

"I'm at the Eastside. My car won't start."

"You're *where*? … Kristy?"

"It's okay. You don't have to help me. I just thought—"

"I'll be right there." He pocketed his phone and ran to his pickup.

The Eastside Tavern?

What was she doing at the Eastside?

And she didn't sound right. A little too … flippant?

Some men come to restore.

"God, I don't know how to *restore*. Help me."

Billy pulled up to the Eastside. There was a commotion in the corner of the parking lot, where a group was gathered. Straining his eyes in the dark, he made out the figure of a girl, standing by what looked like Kristy's green Pontiac. Three men stood around her, laughing and talking in loud voices. Two couples stood watching. Voices rose in jeering.

"It looks like you can't get out of here!" a male voice said.

"I need a jump! Would you please move your car?"

Was that her voice?

It didn't look like her.

"You're in a fix, aren't you?" Drunken laughter erupted and the guy standing beside her grabbed the front of her jacket with one hand. The other went up her skirt.

"Come on, give me a little—" He laughed.

She struggled and finally broke free. "Leave me alone!" A loud smack resounded through the night air.

The guy drew back. "Hey! That's not nice!" Male laughter rippled through the small crowd.

It *was* her.

Another dark form stepped forward and took hold of her other arm, "Hey, Bob, you're right. She's a feisty one!" Kristy pulled out of his grasp, shoving him away.

Billy stepped into the circle. "Leave the lady alone."

Tense silence fell on the group.

No one moved.

"*Lady?* What lady?"

"This lady." Billy's voice cut through the night air and he stepped up beside her.

After a short silence, they dispersed, snickering nervously.

Turning, Billy grabbed her arm. "Let's get out of here."

He led her towards his pick-up and opened it. "Get in."

"What about my car?"

"We can leave it here for the night. There's too many cars around to jump it now." He extended his hand. "Give me the keys and I'll lock it."

On the way to Kristy's apartment, both said nothing. Billy glanced at the young woman next to him. Ramrod straight and slightly quivering, she sat as if expecting the guillotine. The air reeked of alcohol and tobacco. Her bare white legs almost glowed in the dark, with knees turned toward the door, as far away from him as she could get. Otherwise, she was black. All black.

She had to be freezing. Whatever possessed her to wear that outfit?

"I can imagine," He muttered under his breath.

"What did you say?"

"Nothing." He pulled into the parking lot of the apartment, turned off the engine and turned to her. "Talk to me, Kristy."

She grabbed the door handle. "Not now."

"Yes." He gripped her arm. "Now."

"Let go of me. I'm cold and I'm going in."

"Then I'm going with you." He let go, hopped out of the pick-up, and followed her. Striding to the door, she stumbled in her high-heeled shoes and he reached out to steady her.

Those shoes had to be at least six inches high!

After regaining her balance, she pulled away.

Opening the door, she flipped on the lights and tore off her jacket. Billy stifled a gasp.

It was worse than he thought.

"Why are you dressed like that?"

Ice hard eyes met him, blazing with anger and something else he couldn't identify. "What do you think? I went to the bar with some friends … for a few drinks and some company." She turned away, sinking into the couch, folding her arms and crossing bare legs.

"Friends? Some *friends.*"

A harsh laugh spilled from her dark lips. "Why do you look at me like that? Get used to it. This is the real me. I suppose I look to you like the 'adulterous woman' in the Proverbs, lips dripping with honey."

"What are you talking about?"

"Billy, admit it. I'm not the girl of your dreams. I heard you talking with Sam at the wedding. You want *purity.* … Do I look pure? Trust me, I'm far from it." She kicked off her shoes, refolded her arms and stretched out on the couch, her back against a pillow.

Her bare feet twitched.

Trembled.

Silent, he studied her. The small bare feet, with the pink painted toenails, twitched with feeling, betraying her steely facade. They looked vulnerable. *Afraid.*

Looking again with his heart, rather than his eyes, he saw fear and yes, *desperation.* Now he could see the slight tremors in her hands, midriff and even her face. She trembled all over.

Removing his hat and jacket, he threw them near the door and crossed over to sit in an overstuffed chair.

"I don't believe this act. You're drunk. You don't know what you're saying."

She exploded. "I'm not drunk!" Gathering herself again, she turned to him, pasting on a wicked smile. "I only had enough to loosen up. Now you can find out the real truth about me!"

He looked away. "Like you know the real you."

"I am what you see! You're worried about the adulterous woman. Well I'm that and worse! I'm a slut—"

Billy sprung from his chair. "That's enough! You're not a *slut!* No matter what you've done, you're not what you're feeling right now. You are who God says you are. You're forgiven. You're pure. You're believing lies from the devil."

Kristy's painted eyes went wide and she leapt to her feet. Raised on her toes, she glared at him. "You have no idea what I'm talking about. You're so pure and undefiled—"

"Of course I know what you're talking about! I'm twenty-five years old, Kristy. You think I've never messed up?"

"You've never sinned like I've sinned." Her chin lifted, quivering.

"Would you quit holding that guilt and shame up like some sort of trophy? Don't give it so much honor and glory! Jesus conquered it! It's his!"

She screamed and a fist hit his chest. The next thing he knew she was pummeling him with both fists."

"You ruined me! You and Cassie ruined me! I hate you! I hate you both!"

Stunned, Billy grabbed both hands and held them away from him.

"Damn you! Let me go! You're such a know-it-all!" She fought him, kicking and clawing. "You religious, self-righteous pig! You have … no idea … what it's like … to be drug … through the dirt!"

He turned her around and pinned her against himself,

avoiding her flailing arms and legs.

"I don't fit anywhere! ... I don't belong anywhere!"

"What are you talking about?"

She continued flailing and kicking, trying to escape from his grasp.

"I'm the worst! I'm everything you hate! I've done the worst!"

He held on. "But you're forgiven."

Tears streamed down her face. "But I'm not pure, I'm dirty and ... miserable! I'm miserable!" She kicked his shins with bare heels.

She gasped. "And alone! ... I can't even go back to my old life! It's no fun anymore! And I can't ... be a Christian. I'm just like my mother, who I hate. I'm ruined! Let me go! ... Let ... me ... go!"

Billy finally wrestled her to the carpet and sat on her, holding her arms to the floor.

She finally gave up. He gazed into running, blackened eyes. The cold hardness was gone and in its place, devastation and defeat. A torrent of tears broke loose and she burst into violent sobbing. He let go.

Bare arms flew up to hide her face. Turning away from him and onto her side, she curled in a ball and her loose hair spilled on the floor in a silken brown mass.

He slowly stood and watched her weep on the carpet, curled in a fetal position with arms covering her tucked head. Deep sobs wracked her body.

Pain swelled in his chest and a lump grew in his throat as he absorbed the sight. The curled form that was Kristy, shaking and shuddering, soaking the carpet with her tears.

It was too much.

What could he do?

Moved with compassion, his eyes shut.

Lord help me!

He reached over to the back of the couch and retrieved a

throw. Kneeling beside her, he gently covered her exposed body, praying silently.

A box of tissue was on the nearby lamp table. He rose to his feet and placed it near the chair. Then he removed the throw, grabbed her hands and pulled her to her feet. She didn't resist, but complied passively, continuing to sob. Wrapping the throw around her, he sat on a chair and pulled her onto his lap.

Face hidden in her long hair, she shuddered and shook with sobs. He pressed her against his chest and held her firmly, willing strength and peace into her. Surrendering, she continued to cry, soaking the front of his shirt. When it seemed she was spent, he turned her face towards him and gently pulled her hair back. Her eyes remained tightly closed, refusing to look at him. Running his fingers through the damp strands, he stroked her cheek, saying nothing. Another wave of sobbing followed.

Would her anguish never end?

Dam that conversation with Sam.

Finally, after a long while, she stilled. From a box on the lamp table, he pulled out several tissues and offered them to her. Silently, he held her, watching her mop her swollen and blotchy face.

"Kristy, I'm sorry," he said. "I can see I hurt you with my comments to Sam. Of course I didn't know you were listening, but I really had no idea what I was talking about."

She glanced up. Briefly. More tears pooled in her red and swollen eyes. She nodded.

"Can you tell me what's been happening with you?"

She buried her face against him again. A muffled voice came through his shirt. "I went home."

"Home? When?"

"Sunday morning. I got there about four in the afternoon. I thought I would surprise them." She looked away and sniffled. "I didn't want to be alone. But I should've known better than to go there. I was more alone than ever. My mother wasn't exactly glad to see me.

"She was in the bedroom, 'napping,'"

Still swimming with tears, her eyes rolled. "Billy, she never admitted it, but she had a man in that bedroom. She was hiding him in her bedroom when I got there. She sent me away to get *milk*."

Wiping her eyes, she continued, voice hoarse. "Toby says I'm right. She has a boyfriend. Why can't she just admit it?" She paused.

"Go on."

"We had a big fight. Then I took Toby, got a Christmas tree and did a little shopping, but it just wasn't working for me to be there."

"Why did you go to the bar?"

She groaned and swiped away another tear. "I was lonely. And angry. I felt empty. I couldn't connect with God. Cassie's married and I couldn't go to you. So I got madder.

"I decided to go back to my old life. At least I had some fun back then." Choking, she continued, "But it didn't work. It wasn't like before. It wasn't any fun and they were terrible to me. Bob and his friends were there and he—"

"Do you really want to go back to that?"

"Not really, but I can't do this. I'm afraid—"

"Afraid of what?"

"That I'll never be accepted. You want purity. I've known it all along. And I'm not pure. I've done things that Christians hate. I've made horrible choices and I know I'll have to suffer for them. You know, reap what I've sown."

"Who told you that?"

She shrugged. "I don't know. It's in the Bible, isn't it? And Christians preach against people like me all the time. They have crusades against us. Like it was enjoyed, getting all messed up."

"What about Jesus? Do you feel that way about him?"

"No. Jesus loves me. He's forgiving."

"But Christians aren't?"

"That's been my experience."

"Do you really hate me?"

She sniffed. "Not really."

"So why did you beat on me?"

"I don't know. I was really angry and I couldn't hold it in any longer. It's stupid, isn't it?"

"No, it's not stupid. You've been hurt. Are you still angry?"

"Probably."

"Kristy, your heart needs to believe something different. Something has to change. Don't you think you've suffered enough? Can you be a child? Let someone help you? Trust again?"

A giggle erupted. "Well this is about as close to being a child as I've been for a long time. I threw a temper tantrum, crawled in your lap and bawled my eyes out. I haven't done that since I was little. With my father. Before he left.

"But I'm still afraid. Afraid to tell you what I've done."

"You keep saying that. Do you think it makes any difference to me what you've done? Or my family? You're a new creation in Christ, Kristy. We believe it. Don't you think it's about time you did? The only reason I would hate what you did is because it hurt you, hurt others, separated you from God and separates the two of us right now.

"You know, if you would let us know you, you might find the love and acceptance you're looking for. You're hiding the real you. You're letting the fear of rejection keep you from love."

She looked down. "I know."

Billy glanced at the clock on the wall. "Kristy, do you know it's one-thirty in the morning? I'm alone with a beautiful woman in her apartment. My mother wouldn't be happy. I don't think this is the time or the place for further discussion. I need to go home, but I'm not leaving you here alone."

He helped her off his lap and rose to his feet. "Go change your clothes and pack a bag. I'm taking you home. You can sleep in Cassie's bed."

She stiffened. "Uh … I don't know if I'm ready for that yet.

And besides, I don't want to be a bother."

Looking at her sideways, he studied her blanket-wrapped form, tear-stained face and mussed hair. Jaw set, her stubbornness was back.

He chuckled. "Okay, Kristy."

Falling to his knees, he took one of her hands and looked up at her in mock begging. "Will you do me the honor of accompanying me to the humble abode of my family?"

She giggled. "Are you sure it'll be all right?"

Rising to his feet, he smiled. "Of course it'll be all right. Both Mom and Dad have been asking about you. They'll be glad to know you're not alone and that you're okay. You're always welcome, remember? I heard Mom tell you—"

"Okay. I'll go get some things together." She turned to leave the room, clutching the blanket around her shoulders. Before going down the hallway, she turned back. "But Billy, don't tell them where you found me tonight. ... Please?"

"I wasn't planning on it. If you want them to know, you can tell them yourself."

"Not a chance."

SAFE AT LAST

How great is the love the Father has lavished on us, that we should become children of God! (Apostle John)

The peaceful sound of deep, regular breathing filled the pickup cab. Billy glanced at the snug figure, curled on the seat beside him. Asleep. Again.

He sure wasn't sleepy. He was wired. She was listening when he complained to Sam about Marcel? That wasn't fair. The last thing he wanted to do was drive her further away.

He was accustomed to living in a world of self-protection from women. After all, he might be manipulated. He knew that well from living with sisters. And chased brazenly in school, his skills were honed in running and avoiding drama. He hated drama. Still did.

But this drama might be worth it.

Kristy moaned in her sleep, turned in the seatbelt, and nestled her head into his shoulder.

Billy held his breath. Blowing it out slowly, he consciously relaxed. Visions of her scantily clad form, curled and sobbing on the floor filled his mind.

God's words at the wedding returned.

That's her.

Could he handle this?

You did well, Son.

"I did? It sure hurt like hell. What should I do now?" he whispered under his breath.

Do what you planned.

"Leave her? … If you say so."

He shrugged. "It shouldn't be a big deal. It's not like we're engaged or anything."

A short while later, Billy pulled up to the dark porch and parked.

"Kristy, we're here," he said. She stirred, but continued sleeping. He nudged her in the ribs. "Come on, Sleepyhead. Wake up! We're here."

She jumped and pulled back. "Sorry, Billy. I was just so tired after everything—"

"Don't be sorry. It's okay." He opened the door.

&a❧ ❧&a

When front door opened, Linda Watson woke with a start. Someone was entering the house.

She looked at the clock. Two-thirty in the morning? That must have been a long prayer meeting. Footsteps climbed the stairs and her brow wrinkled. Two sets of feet? What was up? Shrugging, she turned and snuggled against her sleeping husband.

She'd find out in the morning. She dozed.

A soft knock—then the squeaking of her bedroom door disrupted her sleep.

"Mom? Are you awake?"

She sat up. "What is it?"

"Could I talk to you?" Voice tight, Billy stood in the doorway.

Bolting from the bed, she reached for her robe. "Is something wrong?"

135

Head hanging, he started down the hall for the living room and wiped his face with his shirt sleeve.

She reached for his arm. "Honey, what happened?"

He flopped on the couch and buried his face in outstretched palms. "Mom, I brought Kristy home tonight. I couldn't leave her alone in that apartment. I put her in Cassie's room." His voice broke and drawing in a shuddering breath, he fought tears.

Surprised, Linda felt awkward. She sat on the couch and lay her hand on his shoulder. "Want to talk about it?"

He didn't answer. Instead, he stretched out on the couch, laid his head in her lap and cried.

She ran her fingers through his short, curly hair. "Is it Kristy, Honey?"

He nodded.

Swallowing, he wiped his face with his sleeve. "Mom ... I'm in over my head. I'm in love with her."

"I thought so. ... Did something happen tonight?"

"Yeah. You could say that. She needs something I can't give. Could you help?"

"I'm willing. I told her I was available anytime she needed to talk, but she—"

"I think she's ready, Mom. Offer again, okay? I'm going to take off for Spokane after the first of the year. To work for Uncle Dean, like I planned. Could you offer to let her stay here? She could commute to school this winter."

"Sure. Kristy's always a help around here. I'll offer. But are you okay?"

He sat up. "It was rough tonight, but yeah, I'm okay."

⸾⸙ ❧ ⸙⸾

Kristy woke late, to a sunny, cold December morning. She snuggled under the warm covers.

What time was it?

They must have been up for hours!

Memories rushed in from the night before. Pulling the covers over her head, she groaned. How could she face him?

136

But she had been at her worst and he had been so incredibly tender. Well, maybe not at first, but when it really counted, he was tender. Maybe he was safer than she thought.

Drawing in a long breath, she calmed.

She had survived. He knew more about her now than he did before.

She pulled the covers down and stared at the ceiling.

"Jesus, help. I'm scared. How am I going to be here without Cassie? It's awkward."

It's time, Kristy.

"Time?"

Time for your healing.

Kristy stared at the ceiling. "Lord, would you give me a scripture about this?" Turning to the bedside table, she saw a Bible, picked it up and leafed through it. Her eyes fell to I Peter 2.

... Like newborn babies, crave pure spiritual milk, so that by it you may grow up in your salvation.

"What is the pure spiritual milk?"

My love.

The warm feeling of Linda's embrace on Thanksgiving Day returned. "That was your love, wasn't it? ... Okay, Jesus. I'll trust you." She bounded out of bed and quickly dressed.

Approaching the kitchen, Kristy caught Linda drying a frying pan. She turned to her. "Good morning. Did you sleep well?"

Kristy smiled. "A little too well, I think. What time is it?"

"Ten o'clock. I didn't have the heart to wake you. I'm sure you needed the sleep."

"I suppose I did. Where is everybody?"

"The guys are out in the shop. Hannah's babysitting for the neighbors while they're Christmas shopping. Do you want anything to eat?"

"Sure. What do you have?"

Rummaging through the refrigerator, Linda produced a boiled egg and muffin. "Would you like some orange juice?"

"That sounds good. I'm hungry."

"Help yourself."

Kristy prepared herself a plate, poured some orange juice and sat at the table, while Linda continued to work in the kitchen. A few moments later, Linda pulled up a chair and joined her.

"How was your week?"

Kristy froze, glass of juice halfway to her mouth. Her sore eyes widened.

"Uh ... not so good."

"What happened?"

It was difficult at first, but Kristy made herself tell Linda about her feelings of loneliness and her trip home. Blushing, she alluded to her mother's perceived transgressions. "I was a bit of a mess the last few days."

"Sounds like your mother's very unhappy."

"Yeah. I think so ... There's a lot of hurt between us."

"What about your father?"

"I haven't seen him since I was eleven years old."

"You must feel really alone."

"I do."

"That's not good. Billy thought I should invite you to come and stay with us until you finish the school year. That would be fine with me and Ben, Kristy. We would love to have you. You're great help. You could commute to school. It isn't that far, you know. And you could save on rent."

Kristy stared at her. "Are you sure?"

Linda smiled and put a hand over Kristy's. "Of course I'm sure. As long as you pitch in as you have been, it would be great."

After talking and making plans with Linda, Kristy relaxed. Soon the back door opened and Billy entered.

He grinned. "Hey! You're up!"

"We need to get your car. Are you ready to go?"

"Anytime you are."

"While you're there," Linda said, "I'd like you to stop by the store and get a few groceries. I have a list." She glanced at Kristy.

"Also, go ahead and pick up some of Kristy's things. She's planning to stay awhile."

Billy's eyebrows rose. "Is that right, Kristy?"

"Yeah. It's the best offer I've had yet."

Beaming, Billy said, "Then let's get a move on. ... We've got work to do. If we have time, you can help me do a little Christmas shopping."

᪥᪥ ᪥ ᪥᪥

Long lay the earth,
In sin and error pining
Till he appeared
And the soul felt it's worth ...[10]

A warm hand covered Kristy's. She glanced upward to see Billy's smiling gray eyes watching her. Heart singing for joy, she returned his smile, grasped his hand and entwined her fingers in his. Pastor Evan rose and walked to the front of the church. It had been a wonderful pageant. The children acted out the Christmas story and Sam had led the congregation in singing carols.

Pastor Evan began:

"For to us a child is born, to us a son is given, and the government will be on his shoulders. ...

"Jesus was the Lord of glory. He left heaven and came as a little child. He made himself vulnerable and entrusted himself to a young woman and man. He became a child to enter the world and save us. We become children so we can enter the Kingdom of God...

"Jesus received from people. He allowed himself to be nursed and cared for as a little baby. He trusted God and believed that God would take care of him through us. He's asking us to put ourselves in that same type of position. ...

"We obey God by attaching ourselves to his

people, becoming a member of the body of Christ and trusting Jesus, through them, to bless us. When you connect to the body, that's submission. It will not be perfect, but it will nurture you. If you cut yourself off, there's no life. You can't expect to do well if you isolate.

"Jesus obeyed God by emptying himself. He's asking us to empty ourselves, let go of our pride and fear and join ourselves to his body. His Kingdom. He did this for the reward of gaining us. We do it for the reward of gaining him.

"Do you want to follow Jesus by emptying yourself and becoming a child? Only a child can enter the Kingdom."

Tears rolled down Kristy's cheeks. "Come with me, Kristy. Let's go up for prayer," Billy whispered.

Wiping her face, she nodded. They rose and started toward the front of the church.

⋙ ❦ ⋘

Kristy admired the gold necklace lying in her lap. The heart-shaped emblem was studded with a tiny imitation diamond. Smiling widely, she reaching over, laid her hand on top of his and squeezed.

"Thank you Billy."

Billy grinned, turned his hand and returned her squeeze. The two sat side by side on the couch, surrounded by paper and ribbon. Sounds of delight filled the room.

Having returned from their honeymoon, Cassie snuggled into Jeff's encircling arm on the love seat. Grandma Watson's twinkling brown eyes found Billy and Kristy across the room and she smiled.

Kristy turned to Hannah. No smile there.

Something was wrong.

Later that afternoon, Cassie shut the door to the bedroom and flopped on the bed beside her. "Oh, Kristy! It was so wonderful!" She leaned back and stared at the ceiling. "Hawaii was so warm and romantic!"

Kristy turned to her. "From the look in Jeff's eyes, I'd say that it was more than Hawaii that was warm and romantic."

Cassie laughed. "You're right. We had a wonderful time together." Wrapping her arms around her waist, she hugged herself. "I'm so happy."

Kristy laid next to her friend, turned and studied her. "You didn't fight?"

"Nothing major. It was our honeymoon!" Cassie's dreamy eyes glowed. "He was wonderful!"

Kristy turned to her back. Silence filled the room.

"Mom says you're staying here." Cassie said.

"Yeah. She invited me."

"I'm glad. I can't imagine you in that apartment by yourself. Are you looking for another roommate?"

"No. I moved out. I'm staying here till school's out."

"Really? Whose idea was that?"

"Billy's. But your mom said she was glad to have me."

"Well, if you need a place to land in the middle of the day, you can always come over to our apartment. And if the roads get bad, you can stay there ... We'll have to check our schedules, but we could probably have lunch together most days. Jeff doesn't usually come home for lunch."

Kristy smiled. "Sounds great. I'll count on it."

Cassie turned to Kristy. "I noticed you and Billy are getting along really well."

"How so?"

"Well, you were holding hands on the couch. That's a switch! And I noticed something in his eyes when he looks at you. It wasn't there a few weeks ago."

"Really?"

"Kristy, at the wedding you were still running scared. What happened?"

Kristy blushed. "Uh …"

"Tell me!"

Pursing her lips, Kristy began, "I went home after the wedding. … I was really depressed. I thought I'd go back for Christmas. It didn't work out and I was right back here a few days later and a total mess. I fell apart and Billy happened to be there to witness it. … It was bad."

Cassie giggled. "Sounds like a bonding experience to me."

"I guess. It was totally humiliating, but he handled it."

Suddenly, Cassie sobered. "Are you serious about him? You'd better decide fast. He is about you."

"You think so?"

Cassie grunted. "I know so. I know my brother. I've never seen him like this. I'd say he's way in love with you."

"Really?"

"I'm sure of it. … Well?"

"Well, what?" Kristy turned to see Cassie's brown eyes gleaming.

"Do you like him? … You know some of his habits and weaknesses. Do you trust him?"

Kristy sighed. "He's pretty tough on me sometimes, but I do trust him. That's not what concerns me."

Cassie frowned. "It's your past, isn't it? … Have you told him about your past?"

"I've hinted at it."

Rising, Cassie paced at the side of the bed, gesturing dramatically with her arms. "Kristy, it's time. You've got to tell him. Now. What are you waiting for?"

Kristy looked away. "Cassie, I haven't even told you."

Her friend halted. "Then try me. Do you think it's something that God's grace won't cover?" She lifted her chin. "Let me decide. Come on Kristy. Out with it."

§❦ ❧ ❦§

A young girl's blue eyes pleaded. "Daddy! I need you!" A little boy stood at her side, holding her hand, eyes round with questions. ...

James bolted up in bed and shook himself. Groaning, he lay back down. "That dream again. It's my kids. God! Are you telling me to go back? Why? I'm sure they hate me. I deserted them." Throwing back the blanket, he rose and paced at the foot of the bed. "They won't want me now. Patricia ran. I know her. She won't be happy to hear from me. She didn't even want my money to help support the kids. How can I do this? I barely support myself! I have nothing to offer them."

Who are you?

"What? Me? I'm nothing."

I'm in you.

He smiled. "I do have you. But will she listen?"

Trust me.

He gave in to the nudge toward his computer, pulled it out and turned it on.

"Let's see. ... Patricia Turner ..."

COMING CLEAN

*Praise the Lord, O my soul, and forget not all his bene-
fits—who forgives all your sins and heals all your
diseases; who redeems your life from the pit ...*

(King David)

An elbow nudged Kristy. Joey muttered, "Hey, could you pass me
another egg?" She complied.

Ben looked up from his breakfast and turned to Billy. "Hey,
do you think you can handle the feeding this morning? I've got
some errands to run in town. Joe can help."

Joey groaned. "I wanted to go with you, Dad. I wanted to get
some things."

"I'll help Billy," Kristy said.

Wide with surprise, all eyes turned to her.

Joey brightened. "That would work. What do you say, Billy?"

"Sure." Billy said, eyes twinkling.

Kristy looked away, setting her jaw. She had to tell him.
Cassie was right. It was his choice whether or not he could handle
it. He had handled her breakdown before Christmas. And Cassie

144

had survived her story yesterday. Maybe it would all work out like she said.

Billy and Kristy left the table, exiting out the back door. The two entered the barn in mutual silence and Billy bent to bust open a green bale of hay. "You got something on your mind?"

Clearing her throat, Kristy dove in. "I do." She watched as he fed the horses. "I need to tell you something before more time passes. If I don't tell you now, it won't be fair to either one of us."

"I've got something to tell you, too." He grinned, continuing to throw hay into the feeders.

"You do?"

"I do. You want me to go first?"

Kristy held her breath. "Sure."

"I'm going to leave for Spokane to work for my uncle after the holidays." He continued working, not meeting her eyes.

"For how long?"

"I'm not sure yet. A few ... months, maybe."

"A few *months?* Why?"

"I have planned to go for a while now. I went last winter."

She followed him out of the barn.

"You're sure about this?"

"Yeah, why not?"

He stopped. "What was it you wanted to say? I'm all ears."

Kristy looked down, hesitating.

He's going to leave?

She couldn't think about that now.

She had to tell him.

"Come on, let's get in the pickup. You can tell me there."

They opened the doors, Scruffy jumped in the back and they headed for the haystack.

It was time.

Before she lost her nerve.

"When I was in high school, I felt so alone. I guess I was desperate. Like I told you, I couldn't connect with my mother ... and I hadn't seen my father since I was eleven." Her voice choked, but she squared her shoulders. "There was this guy ... He was a mess too. We found each other—"

"And you fell in love."

Her lips twisted. "Not really. It was more mutual need and a lot of lust."

"Come on out, you can talk while I'm loading." He stopped near the haystack, opened the pickup door and exited. She followed.

She stood in silence, watching him heave the bales and stack them in the bed of the pickup. She resumed her story. "He was good to me for a while. But he wanted more than hugs and kisses, if you know what I mean."

Billy snorted. "I get the drift," he continued stacking the heavy bales, hopping in and out of the truck bed.

Her heart pounded. Was he brushing her off? He acted like he didn't want to hear what she had to say. *He* was the one who had insisted she get everything out in the open! She'd better spit this out before she talked herself out of it.

"One night, we went too far—"

Stopping, Billy turned to her, breathing hard. "You know, I knew this. You don't have to tell me."

"I do too!"

Looking away, he blew out a breath. "You're probably right. Wait till I get done loading."

When they re-entered the pickup, he turned to her. "Okay, go ahead."

"He hurt me. It wasn't a pleasant experience."

He let out a short, derisive breath. "What a jerk." He reached to turn the key in the ignition.

She reached out and touched his arm. "There's more."

He cranked the ignition. "Look, I'm not sure I want to hear it now. I need to feed."

She exploded. "Billy! Listen, will you? You told me to open up and I'm trying to do that. The cows can wait ten minutes! If I don't tell you now, we're both going to be sorry. Will you stop for a minute, shut up and hear me out?"

"Okay. ... Okay. I'm listening." He turned off the motor, removed the keys from the ignition, leaned back in the seat and toyed with them. "You have my full attention. Go ahead."

"That wasn't the only time we—"

"I get the picture."

"Billy!"

"I'm sorry, Kristy. It isn't easy for me to hear about some guy hurting you and using you in the worst way. But I'll try to behave." He removed his gloves and laid a warm hand on hers. "Continue."

She looked away. "He threatened to break it off with me if I didn't let him. And by that time he was my life. If my mother refused to let me see him, I would sneak out." She took a deep breath. "Three months later, I was pregnant. When I told him, he got mad and accused me of trying to trap him. Then he dumped me. I was seventeen and scared to death."

She looked up at him. Very still, he watched her, stone-faced and silent. But his thumb moved over the back of her hand, encouraging her.

Setting her jaw, she looked away and forced out the words. "I had to tell my mother. She freaked out. She wasn't willing to let me *ruin* my life and hers too. She couldn't be 'shamed again,' not after all she'd been through. She didn't want to lose her 'Christian' friends or her position in the church and financially, she couldn't handle it either.

"She took me to a ... clinic." Pulling her hand out of his, her voice broke. "It was horrible, Billy. I killed my own baby. It torments me. Was it a little girl? A little boy? And I bled a lot. I have never been ... the same since. I may not be able to have another."

Her face fell into her hands. "And there were ... other guys." She lifted her head, but looked out the window, unable to face him.

"After that whole ordeal, you'd think I would have known

better. But no." She shrugged. "Mom made me take birth control pills, so I guess I figured, why not? What difference did it make? But I felt dirty."

Head falling forward into her hands, she groaned. "I … I'll totally understand if you want nothing more to do with me. I know you want children. I ruined my chances for a good marriage and children to love. I'm sorry it took so long for me to tell you this stuff. … I should have told you before you brought me out here and all. "

A long silence followed. She was afraid to look at his face. She waited.

Finally, a warm hand rested on her shoulder. "Kristy, are you finished?"

She nodded.

"Could you look at me?" With one finger, he turned her face toward him. "I knew there was something like this. Even though I didn't know what for, I forgave you a while back. I'm sorry for putting you off. I'm glad you told me. Even if I didn't want to know. It hurts me too.

"It angers me to hear how badly you were hurt and the life that was ripped from you. And in a way … me. It shouldn't have happened. … And it hurts to know you gave yourself away so cheap. You're worth so much more than that." He paused. "I forgive you. But the real question is, will you forgive yourself?"

Through watery eyes, she found his. Deep compassion drew her in.

"I don't know. I keep thinking I should've stood up to my mother. But I was afraid. I felt guilty and so alone."

His arm went around her. "Scoot closer, will you?" She complied and he pulled her to his side, running the fingers of his other hand through the ends of her hair. "Have you told anyone else about this?"

She sniffled. "I told Cassie yesterday. She insisted I tell you. Right away. She said you could decide whether or not you could handle it."

He laid his chin on the top of her head and nestled her closer. "Cassie was right. I'm glad you told me. It wouldn't have been right for you to keep it from me any longer. Some things make sense now." He took her other hand in his, entwining his fingers with hers. "I'm sorry you've suffered so much."

In a congested voice, she continued, "It's hard for me to believe that I'm really forgiven. I keep thinking that I've failed and that no good man would want me now. That I'm evil."

"Evil? You're not evil. You were an innocent girl who was hurt and deceived, then dragged away for destruction. But God has rescued you and restored you. You're innocent—"

She pulled back. "If I'm so innocent, then why don't I feel innocent? It seems like I go from feeling guilty to feeling like a victim whose life has been ruined. I know it's not supposed to be true, but I feel it."

"You were a victim. You were abandoned, taught wrong things about God, taken advantage of by men, then encouraged to sin by your mother. But that is not *who* you are." Lifting their joined hands, he kissed her knuckles. "You are an innocent child of God. And a warrior.

"You'll overcome all this stuff. I hate the things the devil has done to you and the lies he tells you. You're not a victim. You're not weak. You're a fighter."

Teasing lit his eyes and he grinned down at her. "I bring out the fight in you. Don't I?"

Smiling, she nodded. "You're right. You do." She paused, looking down. "So are you okay with the possibility of not being able to have children? Ever since that time, except while on birth control, I've had only a few periods."

"Kristy, would you look at me?" Billy's gray eyes met hers. "I can't say that I'm okay with it, but I'll trust God. ... Do you want children?"

Nodding, she said, "Of course."

He broke into a smile. "I thought so. Will you believe with me for your healing?"

She stared at him.

Chuckling, he released her hand, put his arm around her, and kissed her forehead. "You need to talk to some older women about this and get some prayer and counsel, Kristy. They'll understand."

She winced. "I suppose you're right. But I told Cassie and you. Isn't that enough?"

"It's good enough for today." He sat up and pulled away, turning on the ignition. "How about going on a ride with me? There's not much going on around here today."

She scowled. "A ride? Last time I went on a ride—"

"Come on, Kristy. Get back on and try again. I really am sorry about how I handled that. I should've been proud that you took the initiative and tried another horse that day. You were brave. ... I was scared for you."

She smiled up at him. "I was scared for me too. But I guess I could try again, if you promise to be nice."

He laughed. "Don't worry. I'll be nice."

Linda opened the back door and filled the dog dish. "Here you go, Scruffy. That's a good dog." She stroked the border-collie's soft head as he devoured the food, wagging his tail. Laughter rang across the back yard and she lifted her eyes. Billy was helping Kristy onto Blackfoot. With a wide grin, he turned to mount Ginger and they galloped off through the snow-covered landscape.

She smiled. "Thank you Jesus."

Her eyes roved over the backyard to see Hannah sitting, forlorn, on the tire swing.

Linda heaved a sigh.

Crossing the yard, she laid a hand on her daughter's shoulder. "Honey, come into the house. I would like to visit with you. It's cold out here."

Nodding, Hannah stood and followed her mother.

In the living room, Linda sat on the sofa and patted the place beside her. "Hannah, what's wrong?"

Tears pooled in Hannah's brown eyes. "I don't know. ... It's just lonely around here. Joey's in high school and wrestling. He's got a group of friends and he's having fun. Cassie's married and gone. Billy has a girlfriend."

"What do you want to do? Do you want to play a sport or--"

Hannah bolted off the couch. "That's the problem! I don't know what I want or who I am! I'm just a ... nobody!" Sniffling, she turned to leave.

Linda grabbed of her arm. "Wait a minute, young lady. You're not leaving yet. Sit down." Hannah sunk back into the couch. "Now tell me how you feel."

Looking down, Hannah picked at her fingernails. "Lost. I feel lost. Cassie always knew what she wanted. She's beautiful and strong. She knew how to fight with Daddy for what she wanted. Not me. I don't even know what I want ... and Daddy ..." Her voice broke. "Daddy doesn't understand me. He and Cassie used to spend time together. They were close. I wanted that too." Tears rolled down her face and she swiped them away with one brush of her flannel cuff.

Linda's arm went around her. "Oh, Honey. Your Daddy loves you very much. You're different than Cassie, but no less special or important."

"I know." She sniffled. "But he ... he thinks I'm a baby. He won't really listen to me."

"He knows you're growing up, but you'll always be his baby. Do you think that's bad?"

"No. It's just that I'm almost fourteen. I want him to *listen* to me."

"From what I've seen, it's you that runs away crying. He doesn't take subtle hints and he doesn't want to treat you like a little child. He believes in you. You can stand up for yourself, you know, tell him how you feel."

"I don't like doing that. It scares me. Especially with Daddy."

"You can do it. I've seen you. You've been practicing on Joey for years."

Hannah smiled through her tears. "Okay, maybe I can try."

ꙮ ꙮ ꙮ

Billy pulled into the long driveway and parked, turning off the ignition. Leaning back in his seat, he frowned. "Lord, I've been having a great time with Kristy this last week. She's finally opened up and starting to trust me. Are you sure you want me to leave? I have a bad feeling about this."

Leaning his head forward, he rubbed his furrowed forehead and groaned. "She's clinging to me. In a way it feels good, but there's something about it that isn't right…"

ꙮ ꙮ ꙮ

"You're leaving?" Kristy's voice rose. "You can't leave!"

Billy marched down the hallway of the upstairs. It was evening and he was coming out of his bedroom with a duffle-bag. Linda emerged from the office in time to catch the exchange. Curious, she stepped out into the living room, listening to the raised voices in the upstairs hallway.

"Why didn't you tell me you were going to leave? This is too sudden. It's mean!"

"Look, Kristy, I did tell you. Remember? I'm sorry for the short notice, but I didn't want me to ruin your Christmas break by talk of leaving. I knew you didn't like it."

"That would've been better than this! You move me out of my apartment and get me settled in here. Then you … you desert me?"

"You'll be fine."

"I won't be fine. How can you say that? You're doing what every other guy has done to me. My father, and then my boyfriends—butter me up, get me feeling secure and then leave! … Billy, please!"

Linda strained to hear her son's response. "You need healing, Kristy. … I can't be your security."

"I knew it. You're backing away from me. I'm too wounded

for you, aren't I? … This is your way of letting me know you're moving on—"

"No, Kristy. It's not that at all. I'll be back."

She choked out a response. "Well, I just may not be here when you get back. … And I may not want you to find me. … If you leave now … consider it *over* between us!"

After a long pause, there was a muttered response. A door slammed shut. Linda looked up to see her son descending the stairs alone. He threw down his bag in the entryway. Looking at her, his gray eyes held a rare steeliness. A muscle twitched at the side of his jaw. "Mom, when's dinner? I'm leaving this evening."

Her eyebrows rose. "It seems not everyone's happy with this decision."

"You're right. But that's the way it has to be." He climbed the stairs again, returning with his guitar, a heavy coat and some work boots. He looked at her.

"I have to do this, Mom. I don't know when I'll be back, but I probably won't return for a couple months."

Dinner was tense. Billy sat across from Kristy, who with eyes downcast, silently picked at her food. Face set in grim lines and eyes red and swollen, she seethed. Determined, Billy set his jaw and remained silent. Hannah looked from one to the other, a worried frown on her face. Joey was the cheerful one. He talked excitedly about his wrestling team at high school and all their exploits. Linda and Ben exchanged meaningful glances, eyeing the two warring parties. A small smile played on Ben's lips and his brown eyes twinkled. "It will be okay," he mouthed to Linda.

After dinner Billy stood in the front entryway, saying goodbye to his family.

"Good bye, Billy. Stay safe," Linda said, and kissed him on the cheek.

Kristy was conspicuously absent from the circle.

Joey patted him on the back, embracing him roughly.

Ben hugged him for a moment, then pulled back and said,

"I'm proud of you, Son. We'll see you soon."

Billy hugged Hannah next, whispering into her ear. "You be good, little sis. No more sneaking into dark alleys—"

Hannah shoved him away.

He sighed, looking toward the stairway with a resigned smile. "I seem to have a way with women."

Ben chuckled. "Stand your ground, Son. It'll all turn out."

Nodding toward him, he headed out the front door and the family followed. He threw his luggage in the back of his pickup, climbed in, closed the door and waved goodbye.

❧ ❦ ❧

"Barry! I tried all the Patricia Turners I could find. Do you suppose she remarried?"

Barry Smith leaned back in his office chair, feet propped on the corner of the large wooden desk. "Could be. Or maybe she doesn't like the idea of being found. Have you tried her maiden name? What was it?"

"Jones."

He laughed. "That won't be easy! It's worse than Turner, but I'd give it a whirl."

Plopping down in the chair opposite his friend, James sighed. "I'm having second thoughts about all this. Do you think maybe I was imagining things—this business of God asking me to find my children?"

"Of course you're not imagining things. It sounds like God to me. He always wants to restore relationship."

James rose and went to gaze out the office window. "But what do I have to offer them? I remember feeling so inept at fathering when I was with them. I left most of the parenting to Pat. Now what are they going to feel about me appearing out of nowhere? I haven't paid any child support all this time or had any part in their lives. They'll be ashamed of me."

His boss studied him, eyes intense. "Are you going to continue to stay away because of what you have or haven't done? This is not about you, Jim. And it's not about money—or pride for that matter. I would venture to say your kids are crying out for you."

"You think so?"

"You told me your dream. What do you think? How would you feel if you were in their shoes? Would you be concerned about the past? Or money? Or pride? Haven't you ever felt alone, longing for a father? You have love to give. And wisdom to share, even if it's what not to do!"

James sighed. "You're right. ... I'll keep looking."

REVELATIONS

*Yet to all who received him, to those who believe in his
name, he gave the right to become children of God.*
(Apostle John)

Tears trickled down Kristy's face as she stood alone in the kitchen, peeling potatoes and quartering them for stew. One escaped off her nose and splashed on the cutting board. She sniffled and grabbed a paper towel to wipe her face. Pain swirled within her and ...

Emptiness.

She felt lost. And afraid.

"God, what's happening to me?"

It had been almost a week since Billy left and Kristy felt worse with each passing day. The anger had melted away. But anger was easier to deal with than this deep emptiness.

"I need you, Jesus. ... Help."

The front door slammed and someone entered the living room.

"Sit down, Joey! ... Now!" Ben's firm voice boomed.

She froze.

"What's the problem?" Ben asked.

"Nothing," Joey said.

"Nothing? Then why didn't you go to your history class today?"

A long silence. Finally she heard a moan, then Joey's voice. "I don't want to go back to that class. I hate that class! ..."

"You only have a few weeks left. If you drop it now, you'll get an F for the term. Do you want an F?"

"No. That's why I've hung in there, but I'm done. I'm quitting that stupid school!"

"Okay, Joe. ... What happened?"

"Nothing really. It's the teacher ... she just ... she just ..."

"I'm listening. ... She just ... what?"

"Dad, she has a thing against me. Every time I say something, she discounts it. It's not usually obvious. ... But the other day ... she was going off on Christianity and all the corruption in it and the bad stuff that has happened because of Christians. She kept looking at me. Finally, I had to say something. I tried, but it was weak... People laughed."

After a pause, Ben spoke up. "Why haven't you said anything? You've been in this teacher's classes since the beginning of the year. I had no idea you were fighting this kind of battle."

"I don't know, Dad. ... It wasn't so bad at first. Then when she started picking on me, I thought maybe it was my problem. I wanted to be strong—"

"You are strong." Ben's voice softened. "Let's pray about this, okay?" There was a long pause. "Father, you see what Joe's up against. Thank you that my son is recognized as a believer and that he's strong."

Kristy strained to hear, but could not make out the rest of the prayer. She moved to the refrigerator to get out the carrots. After removing a handful, she returned the rest to the crisper and closed the door softly.

"I'm proud of you, Son." He paused and Kristy heard a sniffle. "Would you like me to go talk to this teacher?"

"No!"

"Would you like me to talk to the principal? Or talk to the teacher with you?"

"Probably not ..."

"Is cutting class or quitting school the best way to handle this?"

"Probably not."

It was all Kristy could do to stand there. She wanted to run. But where to? She had to go through the living room to reach the privacy of her room.

"Kristy ... Are you all right?" Linda's voice pierced her consciousness, from over her shoulder. She hadn't heard her enter the kitchen.

"No." The little composure she had left dissolved and tears coursed down her cheeks. She sniffled and wiped them away with her sleeve, like a preschooler.

Linda enfolded her in a warm embrace. "Would you like to talk about it?"

Kristy shook her head.

"You want to go to your room for some privacy?"

She nodded.

Letting go, Linda directed her gently. "Go on, then. I'll take care of supper."

Kristy rushed out of the room and up the stairs. Firmly shutting the bedroom door behind her, she flopped on the bed and let the tears flow.

She couldn't stand this.

It was just too painful. She'd totally missed out. She'd never have a father. Toby would never have a father. Why did she have to watch this?

She had to get out of here.

❧❦❧

Linda threw the cut up onion into the stew, with excessive

force. She wanted to cry too. Kristy was going to run. She could feel it. Heart pounding, her stomach clenched.

"I can't reach her, Lord. I'm afraid she's going to run."

There's no fear in love.

"I know. ... What do you want me to do? She doesn't believe."

Believe for her.

"Okay. ... I will believe. I renounce this fear. She's going to make it. You love her and your love is greater than any rejection or grief.

"She's your child. Thank you for giving her what she needs.

"Lord, help me love her without strings. And without fear. Like you love her.

⸱⸱⸱

Kristy arrived home from school after dark. It was almost the end of the second week and she'd hit the ground running. Due to a heavy schedule, and a bad attitude about her living arrangements, she'd stayed late at the library, doing research for a paper.

She was grunting it out.

With little inspiration.

Parking by the porch, she entered the back door, shutting it softly and switching on the utility room light. Soft music played from the front room.

It was strange. Why was the house so dark? Maybe they were all out in the shop. A light was on out there.

Kicking off her shoes, she entered the darkened kitchen. She ambled over to the refrigerator and opened it, looking for something to eat. A soft giggle from the living room stopped her. Shutting the refrigerator softly, she crept to the doorway and peered into the adjoining room.

An intimate scene lay before her. Linda danced in Ben's arms, with the lights low, swaying to soft music. Both were in T-shirts and jeans with stocking feet. Ben kissed Linda's ear and chuckled.

Kristy stared.

The music switched, picking up tempo and Ben cranked it up. They laughed. Ben swung her around the room. They frolicked and played, continuing to laugh.

"They do that from time to time."

Kristy jumped. She turned to see Hannah slumped in a chair at the far corner of the dark kitchen. "Hannah! I didn't see you there."

Rising abruptly, Hannah knocked the chair to the floor. "No one sees me." She fled the room, heading for the stairs.

"Whoa," Kristy said to herself, returning to the refrigerator. "I guess I'm not the only one feeling sorry for myself."

⧫ ❦ ⧫

Kristy lay awake, unable to sleep. She had been a silent and almost ghostly boarder the last week. She'd hardly said a word to anyone in the family.

She was mad at everyone.

And everything.

Including God.

She sat up in bed and switched on the light. Grabbing her Bible from the bedside stand, she opened it to the book of Isaiah, to a passage she had read earlier.

I have chosen you and have not rejected you. So do not fear, for I am with you, do not be dismayed, for I am your God. I will strengthen you and help you; I will uphold you with my righteous right hand. ...

Agitated, she set it down, turned off the light and curled on her side. She groaned. Then she cried into her blankets, "I know you're saying something to me, Father! Help me to believe you love me and you're with me! I don't feel your love!"

She finally settled on her back, tears trickling down her face.

Sniffling, Kristy continued, "I'm sorry, Father. I'm angry. I'm dying inside. I can't do this anymore. It's killing me. I'm miserable again. I need you." She turned to pull a tissue out of the box on the headboard and blew her nose. "There must be a reason for me to be here."

After tossing and turning, she lay a long while staring into the darkness. Suddenly, a soft squeaking came from the other room. She sat up.

A door was opening. Slowly.

Soft footsteps crept through the hallway and down the stairs.

Was that the front door closing? It was past one o'clock!

Was that Hannah?

She bounded out of bed and crossed to the window. A full moon shone brightly on the snow-covered landscape and the wind howled through the trees.

Kristy sighed. "It must've been somebody going to the bathroom. I'm sure jumpy tonight."

Just as she was moving away from the window, she caught sight of a lone figure, creeping cautiously out into the driveway.

She moved back to the window and studied the figure in the moonlight, bundled against the cold night air.

Once in the driveway, the person hurried away from the house and the dog followed, wagging its tail. Bending to pat him, long curly hair fell out around the hood of the jacket.

It was Hannah for sure! After sending the dog back to the house, she looked around warily, then broke into a run towards the road.

Kristy scowled.

Where was she going?

She strained her eyes. Finally, lights flashed and a car moved away in the distance. Her heart pounded.

She grabbed her robe and made for the hallway. She had to tell Ben!

Linda woke to a soft knock on her bedroom door. It came again, louder. She rose abruptly, shaking herself out of a deep sleep. Jumping out of bed, she grabbed her robe. "Who is it?'

The door opened. "Linda! Come quick!" Kristy's voice was soft, but urgent. "It's Hannah!"

"What about Hannah?"

"She just took off! She got into someone's car at the end of the driveway!"

Linda frowned. "Are you sure?"

Kristy nodded.

"Ben! Wake up!"

Ben rolled over and groaned. Without looking up, he started to pull back the covers. Noting Kristy's presence, he sat up, suddenly alert. "What's up?"

"I saw Hannah leave the house just now," Kristy said. "I checked her room and she's gone! I thought I saw her get into someone's car at the end of the driveway."

Ben blinked. "Are you talking about Hannah?"

"Yes Honey. It's Hannah."

Suddenly alert, Ben jumped from the bed, grabbing his jeans. Kristy turned and left the room.

༄ ❧ ❧ ༄

Ben hurried out to his pickup.

"Lord ... help me find her!"

On the main road, he noticed a car parked along the side, not far from his driveway. He slowed down and pulled up behind it, shining his lights into the interior. Two heads popped up, then ducked, one with long, curly hair.

It was her!

Taking a deep breath, he paused to get a grip on his mounting anger. Stepping out into the night, he approached the passenger side of the vehicle.

He yanked on the door handle. It was locked. "Open up!" he said, rapping on the window.

Hannah jumped up and opened the door.

"Get in the pickup," he said. She slid out of the car and hurried to her father's vehicle.

Ben looked directly into the face of Brian Potter. "So it's you. How dare you sneak my daughter out of the house in the middle of the night?!"

Brian swallowed, eyes wide. "We just wanted a chance to

talk."

"Get out of here! And if I see you within a mile of this place, I'll call the police. You hear me?"

Looking down, he muttered, "I hear you."

Ben slammed the car door and returned to the pickup where Hannah hugged the passenger door, sniffling. The car sped off, just as he settled himself at the wheel.

"What do you have to say for yourself, young lady?" Jerking the transmission into reverse, he turned the pickup around.

"Uh ... I ..." she stammered, choking back tears.

"Well, you'd better start talking. I want some answers."

Sudden profuse sobbing came from the seat beside him. He glanced over to her bent form, her head buried in her hands.

Lord ... help!

Pulling up to the front of the house, he went around to the passenger door, opened it, and gathered Hannah into his arms. "Hey, Sweetie, don't cry ... Talk to me, will you?" She pulled free and ran into the house, slamming the front door.

He followed.

ๆ๑๑๑๑๑

Muffled weeping came from Hannah's room. Kristy listened from her bed as Ben made his way up the stairs. Cautiously, she crept out of bed and opened her door to the shared closet.

It was rude, but she couldn't resist.

Ben was in there now. What was he going to do? The stupid little fool! If it was her, she'd tan her hide! She was probably with that jerk, Brian Potter.

Ben spoke softly. "Hannah."

The weeping subsided.

"Let's deal with this situation first thing in the morning, okay?"

Hannah sniffled. "Okay."

Hinges squeaking, he left the room.

Deal with it in the morning?

Ben sat on the side of the bed, fully dressed, still in shock. "Linda, your daughter was in a car, parked by the side of the road, cuddling with Brian Potter." "I can't believe she did this."

"I can."

He faced his wife. "You can?"

Arms crossed, she was sitting up in bed. "Ben, she hasn't been happy. You said so yourself. It's her way of calling out for help."

He shook his head and began removing his boots. "I've tried talking to her. But she runs away crying."

Linda took hold of his arm. "You've got to be more persistent, Ben. And please don't yell."

"Why don't you deal with this? All I do is reduce her to tears. I can't talk to tears—"

"Don't let her tears intimidate you. She needs you right now!"

"What can I do for her? She's so sensitive—"

"Ben, she's not that sensitive. She's emotional and she's fearful. But she's growing into a strong woman. And she's rebelling! What are you going to do about your daughter? Back away from the fight?"

"What are *you* going to do? She's your daughter too. And you seem to understand her!"

Linda let go of his arm and sighed, falling back to lie flat. They both went silent, let the intensity of their discussion fade and laid deep in thought, staring at the softly lit ceiling.

She turned to face him. "This is not about me and her, Ben. It's about you and her. It was you that told her to stay away from Brian. If you back away and brush this off on me, you'll regret it. She'll perceive it as rejection. I've talked to her, Ben. It might be my fault this whole thing happened."

Ben's head shot up. "Your fault? How?"

"She was complaining about not feeling close to you. I told her to stand up to you. Tell you how she felt."

"She doesn't feel close to me? Really? Why hasn't she said anything? She hasn't told me how she feels."

"Honey, she's afraid. This might be the only way she can stand up to you. She says you don't listen to her. She thinks Cassie is much closer to you. She compares herself to Cassie all the time. In her mind, she always comes out the loser."

"Why haven't you told me this?"

"I've tried, Ben. But you wouldn't believe there really was a problem—"

"She's not like Cassie, but she's sweet. And she's wonderful-"

"I know you feel that way, Honey. Cassie was difficult. Hannah's been easier, but she doesn't tell you what she's feeling. She's more timid."

Ben was silent. Then he said, "Cassie and I clashed all the time. But we are close. Do you think I've neglected Hannah?"

"I don't know, Ben. But I know it's you she needs right now."

He sighed, running a hand through his hair. "You're right. And I haven't a clue what to do."

Lying back in the bed, Linda laid a hand on his arm. "You're going to have to trust the Holy Spirit to lead you, Honey. This could be an opportunity for a break-through for you both. He's never failed us yet. Let's pray, okay?"

❧❦❧

The next morning, Kristy woke to muffled voices coming from Hannah's room. The closet door was still partially open. She inched closer and opened it further. Hannah's closet door was open a crack.

She stepped into the closet, avoiding the squeaky floorboard in the middle.

"Hannah. What are you feeling?" came Ben's soft voice.

"I don't know. But Brian's really hurting. He told me he needed to talk to someone."

"I told you I didn't want you hanging out with him. Next thing I know, you're sneaking out to meet him in the middle of the night? What's gotten into you?"

"I don't know, but you don't care about him." Her voice escalated, choking with tears. "No one does!"

"You're not his psychologist," Ben said softly. "And he has you fooled. He doesn't want to talk. When I found you, he was kissing you, wasn't he?"

The crying stopped for a second. Hannah sniffled. "We didn't do anything bad Daddy! I told him 'no!'"

"I told you to stay away from him and you disobeyed me. I found you in his car. In the middle of the night. Lying on the seat with him. I call that bad, Hannah. "

"It's not what you think!"

"Hannah, you're fooling yourself and you know it. ...But this whole thing's not about Brian, is it? ... I think it's about you and me."

She sniffled.

"Do you have anything to say to me?"

Kristy strained her ears, but there was only silence. Finally, Hannah burst forth, "Nothing! ... I have nothing to say to you!"

"Okay, then ... I'll have to discipline you for this."

"Well, I'm too old to spank!"

"Oh really?"

"Of course I am. I'm fourteen years old!"

"You haven't blatantly disobeyed like this since you were a little girl. I spanked you then and it seemed to work."

"So you are going to spank me?"

"Maybe. Can you trust me?"

"But Daddy, you can't do that!"

"Okay then. You can sit here in your room until you're ready to trust me. Let me know when that is." The door squeaked.

"Daddy, don't leave!"

"You're ready then?"

"No!"

"Then let me know when you are." The door shut.

Kristy's blood boiled. The stupid girl! She didn't know how

lucky she was to have someone to protect her, love her, and discipline her!

Exiting the closet, she shut the door softly and returned to her bed. Sniffling, moaning and sighing came through the walls from the other room.

Suddenly, her own voice came back to haunt her.

I'm nobody's little girl! I'm twenty-one years old and I have paid my own way since I was sixteen!

She dropped back on the bed.

I'm busted!

Hannah wasn't a stupid girl.

She was just proud … like her. Proud, independent and stubborn. She would've said the same thing to her father when she was fourteen, if he'd been there. She was still doing it! She was doing it to her father in heaven.

"Oh, God, I need a Father. I need love and I need discipline. Father me! Please be my father. It's no wonder Billy hasn't even tried to call me. … I just wanted my own way. I was afraid. I pulled out all the stops. I really blew it! "

She leaned over to the bedside table, grabbed her Bible and opened it to a verse she had highlighted:

… the Lord disciplines the one he loves, and he chastens everyone he accepts as his son." Endure hardship as discipline; God is treating you as his children. For what children are not disciplined by their father?

"I want to receive discipline from you, Father. Would you help me?"

• • •

Linda stopped lacing her shoes and stared at her husband in disbelief. "So, are you going to *spank* her?"

"Maybe I should," Ben said, sitting on the edge of the bed.

"Ben, she's fourteen. She wants so much to be grown up. She already believes everybody thinks she's a baby. Especially you. Get her to talk! Connect with her!"

"I tried. She refuses."

"Then try again!"

"When I was going upstairs, God gave me an idea of how I might do that. I wasn't sure it was him, especially after our talk. Then she lifted that little chin of hers and told me she was too old to spank." He grinned. "Then I knew it was him."

His wife looked at him sideways. "I hope you know what you're doing."

"It was you that insisted she needed me to handle this. I think I heard from God. It may not be perfect, or the way you would do it, but can you trust me?"

෮ක ෧෮ක

Kristy opened her closet door and pulled out a sweater. The hinges on Hannah's bedroom door squeaked. She froze.

"You're ready?" It was Ben.

She knew she shouldn't listen.

But, she was curious.

Hannah sniffled. "Yeah … I'm ready."

"Okay then. Come here, Sweetie."

"But, Daddy, I'm too old for that!"

"You're wrong, Honey. You'll always be my little girl."

"Daddy! This is humiliating!"

A long silence …

"What are you doing?" Hannah said.

"I'm rubbing your back."

"I thought you were going to … Are you done?"

"I don't know. Am I done?"

Hannah sniffed. "Can I sit on the chair?"

"Sure."

"Why did you pull me over your lap? You knew I thought you were going to—"

"I wanted you to trust me. I am so pleased that you can still receive my love."

Hannah choked on a sob. "Daddy!"

"I'm your father. … I love you. … It hurts me when you won't come to me. I want to protect you. You're my little girl—"

"I'm not little!" Hannah's voice shook. "I'm fourteen!"

"I know. And I'm proud of you. You're mature for your age. You're responsible, capable, usually wise, and very smart."

"Then why do you keep calling me *little*? ... And why did you let me think you were going to spank me?"

"I wanted you to trust me. You know, receive from me. It was difficult, but you came to me. You do trust me."

She sniffled. "Yeah, I trust you."

"That means a lot to me. ... Someday I'll have to release you. But not yet.

"And you're right. You're not little anymore. I won't spank you. I don't want you to be afraid. I want you to receive my love and trust me. I only want to bless you.

"You are powerful. Your choices are powerful. And if you have questions, your Daddy is here to help you. I love my little girl ... Don't you still want to be my little girl?"

Hannah's soft voice choked. "Yeah ... I do."

"Then come and sit in my lap."

There was shuffling and a sniffle from Hannah.

"There, that's better," Ben said.

"Daddy, I'm really ... really sorry ... about last night."

Muffled crying sounded through the closet. Kristy strained to hear. After a long silence she heard Ben's soft voice. "Shh ... I forgive you Sweetheart. ... I'm sorry too."

Hannah's voice rang out. "What are *you* sorry for?"

"I'm sorry you don't know how beautiful and special you are ... and that you fell for some trick by a foolish and desperate boy. Would you forgive me for not doing my job?"

"What job?"

Ben chuckled. "Don't roll your eyes at me. My job is to convince you of your great beauty and worth. You are a lovely young woman, Hannah. You're my beautiful princess. Boys will swamp this place, trying to get your attention."

"You really think so? Are you teasing?"

"No. I'm dead serious. I wouldn't tease at a time like this. You know me better than that."

"Yeah, but are you sure you're not just trying to make me feel better?"

"Feel better? How do you feel?"

She sniffled again, voice congested. "Awkward … Clumsy … Stupid … Fat!"

"Hey, wait a minute! That's not true. Why would you feel that way?"

"Nothing fits me anymore. I already wear a bigger size than Cassie. And I'm shorter than her! … And my hair … it never does what I want it to. It's wild and sticks out all over. Terry says it looks like I stuck my finger in a light socket. Why can't it be smooth and straight like Kristy's?"

"Hannah, trust me. Your hair is gorgeous. I know it's a little hard for you to manage, but most women would kill for hair like yours, all thick, curly and silky. Boys like Terry admire you, but they're too young, insecure and awkward to express it well. And you're not fat. You're just changing, and changing fast—filling out in all the right places. … Just like a blooming, beautiful woman should. Don't compare yourself to Cassie. You are each amazing and beautiful."

"That's what Mom says, but I can't help it."

"Honey, you're built more like your mother. Don't you think she's pretty?"

"Yeah, but—"

"But? Hey! I think she's beautiful! She was beautiful enough to catch a handsome guy like me!"

Kristy closed the closet door softly and heaved a sigh. Crossing to the bed, she flopped on her back and stared at the ceiling.

She couldn't believe it. Hannah sneaks out in the middle of the night with a boy her father told her to stay away from and what does she get?

Cuddling?

And sweet reassurances and comfort?

"It's not right."

What would you want?

She sniffled. "But she—"

She humbled herself.

"She didn't have much choice. … But I guess I don't either."

She swallowed, grabbed a pillow and hugged it to ease the swelling pain.

"Oh Father. I miss my Daddy. I was a lot like Hannah. … I still am. I want to be important, beautiful. Grown up. I want to be loved. Why did he leave me? He could've kept me from getting into trouble. Being so foolish and desperate."

"I know I'm forgiven, but I have memories." She dabbed at rolling tears, paused and blew her nose.

She gathered all the used tissues, stood up, walked across the room and threw them in the trash can.

"Okay, I will believe! I'm done with this whining, sniveling and self-pity. You are a loving father and I expect you to bless me, heal me, and make me pure. I want it all. I trust you to discipline me tenderly."

She sighed and fell back on the bed, stretching out her arms. "I receive your love. I'll trust you. I'll obey you. I'll do anything. …"

"Billy. This is Kristy."

"Oh … Hi, Kristy, I'm glad you called."

Kristy swallowed. "I'm sorry it took me so long. Are you busy?" She sat on the bed.

"Not particularly."

"I just … wanted to say … I'm sorry. What I said to you before you left was wrong. Will you forgive me?"

Silence. "Uh … I forgive you."

A long pause.

He cleared his throat.

"How's school?"

"School's fine. Why?"

"I just wondered."

"How's work?"

"It's going well."

Another awkward silence.

"Well, I'd better get off the phone. Uncle Dean and I are on our way to a job. I'll talk to you later, okay?"

"Okay, bye."

"Goodbye, Kristy."

Kristy pushed the button on her cell phone. Was he trying to brush her off?

Well, at least she apologized.

But she had a bad feeling about this.

She took a cleansing breath.

"Father God, I'm going to trust you to take care of it. You're my Daddy."

HEARTS RESTORED

... the foolishness of God is wiser than man's wisdom.
(Apostle Paul)

"Daddy, can I help you feed this morning? It's my turn."

At the breakfast table, Hannah boldly sought an audience with her father. Wearing a wide smile, she glowed with renewed joy and eagerness.

Ben's eyes twinkled. "Is that okay with you, Linda?"

"I'll make do. Go ahead."

"Linda, did you need my help with anything this morning?" Kristy asked. "I'd be glad to help."

"Sure. That'll be great."

"Joe, you can feed the horses and then do a little shoveling in the barn," Ben said.

Joey scowled. "I should've known I'd get something like that if Hannah helped feed."

Ben gave him an affectionate pat on the back. "Hey. It all has to be done. This way you'll get done earlier. Didn't you have something you wanted to do in town this afternoon?"

"Yeah." Hope dawned on Joey's face. "You mean I can go?"

"If you get those stalls cleaned out, I don't see why not."

All three rose from the table and headed to the utility room, talking excitedly.

Kristy began gathering the dishes. "It's a beautiful day, isn't it?"

Curious, Linda looked at her. "You're sure happy this morning. What happened?"

Kristy laughed. "Just a little talk with Jesus."

Linda looked over her shoulder and smiled. "Well, don't make light of it. You're different today."

Kristy hummed a little tune. "What do you have planned?"

"Oh, laundry and cleaning, a little baking for tomorrow. That sort of thing."

"Sounds good."

ᔅᕉ ᕰ ᔆᔅᕉ

Linda studied Kristy while she dusted the furniture nearby. Tears streamed down her face. This morning must have been a brave attempt at cheerfulness. Since then, sorrow and silence had returned. There had to be unfinished business.

"Kristy, you're hurting. Want to talk?"

She turned to another table, lifted the lamp, and continued dusting. "I don't think it would do any good. I tried talking to Jesus and taking care of things and I felt better for a while, but here I am crying again! I'm such a mess!"

Choking, she dropped the dust rag and ran up the stairs.

Linda stared after her.

"Well, that went well."

Lord, help.

"What can I do?"

Follow her.

Linda climbed the stairs, knocked on Kristy's door, cracked it and peeked into the room. Dabbing her eyes with tissue, Kristy sat on the bed.

"Can I come in?"

"I guess so."

Kristy folded her legs and reached for another tissue.

"I think it would help to talk about it, Sweetie." Linda said as she sat on the edge of the bed. "The Bible says to bear each other's burdens and love each other. Will you let me love you?"

Tears brimmed in Kristy's blue eyes. "I don't think I know how ... to let someone love me."

Linda scooted closer, placed an arm around Kristy and leaned her head into her hair. "Father, Kristy's hurting. Give her your peace so she can receive love."

She waited, silent.

"Thank you, Jesus. ... Relax, Kristy. ... Let the walls down. ... Let the love in."

Kristy drew in a ragged breath. "Every time I hear Ben talking to Joey or Hannah lately, I want to cry," she said. "The pain is getting worse, but I'm compelled to listen. Last night when Hannah got home, I opened the closet door and listened ... I did the same thing this morning. It was wrong, but I was curious." She looked down. "It made it worse."

"Why did it make you sad?"

"I never had that. And I really needed it. Ben's so loving."

"Have you forgiven your father and mother?"

"I think so. But I can't help thinking that if my father had been there, I wouldn't have ..." She hesitated, swallowing.

"Wouldn't have what?"

"Messed up so bad ... Ruined my life. I guess I just missed out and it hurts to think about it. The longer I'm here, the more I hurt. It's killing me."

"Kristy, what you are believing is keeping you from freedom."

"What do you mean?"

"When we get hurt—and everybody does—we process it somehow. Without the grace and love of Jesus, we react in fear, shame, bitterness and self-protection. Often we draw wrong conclusions about ourselves and God. We believe lies. Lies corrupt our souls. Only Jesus can heal and deliver us. He is the truth. He sets us free."

"I *went* to Jesus."

"And Jesus led you here. To us."

"Do you think you can help me?"

Linda nodded. "I'd love to help."

Kristy stared at her. "Would you?"

"Sure … Can I ask you some questions?"

Kristy shrugged. "Go ahead."

"Do you believe you're abandoned and rejected?"

"Well, I was!"

"Do you expect to be betrayed?"

"Of course! I was! My father left me. He abandoned me to a mother who couldn't stand me! She has always rejected me!"

"I'm sorry. You were hurt. It never should have happened. But is this your identity? Is this the truth about who *God* is for you?"

Kristy stared at her. "I don't know."

"Have you believed your father God is like your natural father? Have you believed he loves you, but when the going gets tough, he'll throw you to the wolves?"

Understanding dawned in Kristy's wide blue eyes.

"Your father in heaven is good. He loves you. He has never rejected or abandoned you."

Kristy looked down. "You're right. I have believed lies." Her eyes filled. "Could you pray for me?"

"Of course."

A soft knock interrupted them.

Kristy stood. "Who's that?"

Ben spoke through the closed door. "Hey Kristy, is there anything for lunch around here? Where's Linda?"

"I'm in here, Ben. I'll be down in a minute." Linda turned to Kristy. "Hey … How about finishing this after lunch?"

Kristy nodded.

When Linda and Kristy entered the kitchen, Ben sat at the table with Hannah in his lap. Ben chuckled at something Hannah said, but lifting his eyes, he sobered.

It must have been Kristy's tear-stained face.

"Uh, you guys don't have to feed us. Hannah and I can handle it. I didn't realize … Maybe you should finish your talk."

"It's okay," Kristy said, opening the refrigerator.

Ben nudged Hannah from his lap and rose from his chair. "Can I help?"

Kristy sniffled, not looking at him. "Do you want to come and pray for me too?"

Puzzled, Ben froze, his gaze flying to Linda. "I thought I was offering to help with *lunch*."

Linda laughed softly. "I was just about to pray for Kristy." Turning to her, she asked, "Do you want Ben to help?"

Kristy shrugged. "It wouldn't hurt, would it?"

"Are you sure it won't make you uncomfortable? Two of us ganging up on you?"

Kristy let out a short, watery laugh. "I'm already way out of my comfort zone." She turned to Linda. "Do you think it would help to have him?"

"Maybe … Honey, do you have some time this afternoon?"

Ben smiled and nudged Hannah. "Can you spare your daddy for a while?"

She shrugged. "Sure, but don't be long. We have plans."

"How about getting the horses saddled while we talk and about one-thirty we'll take that ride?"

§❦❧❦§

"It hurts to see me with my children? Why?" Ben asked.

Kristy bit her lip. "I guess I'm jealous. I never had that. It makes me feel rejected and alone."

"Kristy, you're not alone. Most people struggle with some form of rejection or isolation," Ben said. "In fact, it was worse in the early church. Many were fatherless and orphans. Life was short and cheap. Violence and war were common. Disease was rampant. Immorality was the norm in a culture of idolatry. A good family, as we know it, was rare. The church met the need for family. Many great men and women of faith were born into very bad family circumstances. It was in the church they learned how to be brothers, sisters, sons, daughters, mothers and fathers. God wants to do the same today. Good relationship and bonding is a gift from God. It's the spirit of adoption."

"So what do I do? Adopt myself out?"

He chuckled. "Not exactly. You'll probably have many mothers and fathers throughout your lifetime. But it's important to find at least one for now and learn to become a child. Like Jesus did."

"How do I do that?"

Linda placed her hand on her arm. Her eyes shone with compassion. "Forgive your father for abandoning you. Then position yourself as a daughter and receive what you need from your father God and his people."

"Both my father and my mother abandoned me. He did it physically. She did it emotionally. I've forgiven them the best I can. But I'm still sad. Something's blocking me."

"Probably a cursed identity," Ben muttered.

"What?"

"Are you still looking to your mother and father to tell you who you are?"

After a moment of silence, Ben grabbed her hand and knelt in front of her, looking into her eyes. "I want to stand in for your father. ...Will you forgive me for abandoning you?"

Kristy's eyes widened. "What am I supposed to say?"

"I'm doing what your father can't do right now. Do you release him from the offense of leaving you and never returning?"

Kristy nodded, tears standing in her eyes.

"Then say, 'I forgive you, Dad.'"

"I forgive you, Dad."

Linda put an arm around her and looked into her eyes. "And I'll stand in for your mother. Would you forgive me, for abandoning and rejecting you?"

"Yes ... I forgive you, Mom," Kristy choked, voice breaking.

"Kristy, have you ever been baptized?" Linda asked.

Kristy looked up and nodded. "When I was nine. But then—"

"Do you know what it means?"

"I … I was accepting Jesus as my savior and repenting for my sins. I wanted to start over and be good so God would accept me."

"Baptism is a prophetic act," Linda said. "You wash away your old identity. You testify to the death of your old nature and the birth of a new nature. It's the putting on of a new identity and new way of thinking."

"I felt like a failure after I was baptized. I still couldn't do anything right. I couldn't be good."

"That wasn't exactly what it was about, Kristy. What you believe is powerful, so the prophetic act of baptism is a declaration that anchors you in a new belief system. Old beliefs are washed away and cleansed by identifying with Jesus' death. The slate is wiped clean."

"Is it okay to get baptized again?"

"Well, most of the scriptures about baptism are to reinterpret what you already did. You died with Christ in baptism, Kristy, and are raised to live a new life. You have taken refuge in Jesus. No more shame and condemnation. You are delivered from all your fears."

"But I need a fresh start. I haven't believed this. Is it okay to do it again?"

Arching her eyebrows, Linda looked at Ben. He shrugged.

"I don't see why not. Are you sure that's what you want?"

"When you mentioned baptism, my heart leapt. I think I need to do it again. Can we do it now? You have a pond. It's cool, but the sun is shining. I won't freeze."

"What do you think, Ben?" Linda said. "Could you and Hannah help before you go on your ride?"

Ben glanced at his watch. "I think we have time. Why not?" He stood. "I'll check with Hannah. You get my Bible and some towels."

Clad in shorts and t-shirt, Kristy stepped into the soft mud with Ben. The water was cold! She inched into the water, to her waist, shivering. The clouds had parted and there was no wind on the hillside that cool early spring day. The earth was holding its breath, watching her take this step. Linda, Hannah and Joey, beaming on the bank, witnessed the adoption ceremony. She was saying goodbye to her old identity.

"I baptize you in the name of Jesus Christ and wash the imprint of shame and fear away," Ben said. He dunked her in the cold water and she sprang up, soaking wet.

A deep peace washed over her. New excitement welled up from within. She was free! She lifted her wet arms and whooped.

Ben climbed out and pulled her to the bank while Linda read Galatians 3:26-29.

You are all children of God through faith in Christ Jesus, for all of you who were baptized into Christ have clothed yourselves with Christ … you are Abraham's seed, and heirs according to the promise.

"You are clean now, Kristy. Your face will never again be covered with shame," Linda said.

Hannah wrapped her in a towel and Ben placed his hand on her wet shoulder. "Father, thank you for sealing Kristy's new identity. Holy Spirit come and fill her."

"Thank you, Ben and Linda." She hugged them both, then reached for Hannah and Joey, soaking them wet with more hugs. "And you too!" They laughed again.

Wrapped in towels, she hurried to the house with them, shivering, but happy. Hannah started a song. They all joined in.

> *From my mother's womb, you have chosen me*
> *Love has called my name.*
> *I've been born again, into your family*
> *Your blood flows through my veins.*
> *I'm no longer a slave to fear,*

I am a child of God ... [11]

"Kristy," Linda said. "Do you have classes on Wednesday mornings?"

"Not this term. But I do on Wednesday afternoons."

"How about coming to a prayer group with me on Wednesdays? It's me, Dawn, Anne, Cindy and Karen. We'd love to have you."

"I'm not sure I could keep up with you guys. I don't know much."

"You don't have to. Jesus will take care of that. Just show up at Dawn's house at ten in the morning. You can go from there to school. It's on the way, you know."

Shrugging her shoulders, Kristy answered, "Why not?"

෯ ❧ ☙ ෯

After supper that evening, Kristy's phone rang. She fished it out of her pocket and saw it was Billy. Putting it to her ear, she headed for her room.

"Billy! It's so good to hear your voice!"

"Yeah. Me too."

She closed the door and sat on the bed.

"Where are you?" she asked, puzzled by his lackluster tone.

"At my uncle's."

"Are you alone?"

"Yeah. I'm alone."

She sighed. "How was your day?"

"Good."

"Look, Billy. You don't sound happy to talk to me. If you can't forgive me for being such a nitwit, tell me now."

He sighed. "It's not that."

"What is it then?"

"Kristy, don't get me wrong. I'm serious about you. But I don't know if I can live with someone who, when I try to obey God, attacks me with accusations and throws the hurt of all the other men in her life in my face."

"Obey God?'

"Yeah, Kristy. I felt like he wanted me to leave."

"Why didn't you say so?"

"That wouldn't have helped and you know it."

She paused. "You're probably right. But you won't forgive me?"

"I didn't say that."

"What are you saying?"

"I'm saying that I found out something about you. I need a wife who can fight with me for others. One who's on my team. Who trusts me to hear God. Someone who stands by me. Not someone who can't let go of her wounds and attacks me with her past. You've got to do something."

Hot tears rolled down Kristy's cheeks. "I—"

"Kristy, this is your chance. Get healing. God has promised it for you. I'm praying for you, but I'm going to give you some space. I'll call you once a week, okay?"

Kristy hung up the phone, confused. "Jesus, I thought I was healing. I just had a major breakthrough. He wouldn't even give me a chance to tell him about it. Why this? Why now?

"I can't prove to him I'm getting healed!"

❧ ❧ ❧

A week later, Billy's enthusiastic voice boomed in Kristy's ear. "How was your week?"

At least he wasn't flat and unemotional. Like last time.

"It's been great."

"Are you doing okay?"

"I'm doing great. … I'm feeling God's peace and He's speaking to me—"

"Really? What's he saying?"

"Uh …" Suddenly, Kristy didn't want to talk.

She'd been looking forward to telling him about her baptism. Hope and joy were increasing every day and she had enjoyed the prayer meeting with the women, but something held her back from sharing it. It wasn't going to be good enough for him.

Maybe she'd never be healed enough for him. She didn't like this. She wasn't some patient of his. Some project.

"Billy. This isn't going to work."

"What?"

"Me trying to convince you that I'm healing."

"I didn't mean—"

"That's what you said, wasn't it? You put conditions on your acceptance. I have to get healed or you won't have me! Well, healing comes to me because Jesus loves me. It can't be connected with pleasing you. I'm getting healed for me."

Silence.

"So what do you want from me?"

"I don't know, but I don't want to be your project."

"I never said that—"

"You didn't have to say it. I feel it."

"Kristy—"

"You … You said for me to get healing. If you really mean that, I think you'd better leave me alone for a while."

"… Okay. If that's what you want. I'll talk to you when I get home."

❦

Kristy strained to put one foot in front of the other. The trail was steep and treacherous, with no end in sight. Her father, mother and Toby had been with her in the beginning, but had disappeared and left her alone. She slipped. Panicked, she clawed the snow and ice.

Heart pounding, she awoke. Dim early morning sun shimmered through the blinds. For the last few weeks, her sleep had been laced with dreams about her father and mother, dreams about Toby and even dreams about Billy. A deep longing gnawed at her soul.

"Jesus, I have a new family. Please give me peace."

Emotions raged within her. Fear. Pain. Anger. Grief. Why was this happening to her? She was fine yesterday.

"Jesus … Help me." She closed her eyes and was suddenly in

another realm.

Someone held her hand and squeeze it. Even though she didn't see him, she knew it was Jesus.

Come with me, Kristy. I want to show you something.

She followed him into a hallway with many rooms.

These are the rooms in your soul.

He led her past open doors, with light shining in the windows. He smiled. Then they came to a closed door. He stopped.

I want you to open it, Kristy.

She became agitated. "No, Jesus. You open it. I can't."

You have to open it, because you closed it.

She hesitated, but finally reached out and turned the knob, hanging on tightly to his hand.

Jesus led her into the room. A frantic little girl, about five years old, ran around several file cabinets. The little girl had straight brown hair, in two pony tails, like her mother used to fix hers. She pulled out drawers and threw papers, scattering them on the floor. The room was so piled with papers, she could hardly get around them. "I know there's something here somewhere! Somewhere there's evidence. I can't be loved! I'm nothing! I'm worthless!"

She finally acknowledged their presence.

The girl's eyes should have been blue, but they were pure black and full of rage. Kristy held tight to the hand of Jesus.

She turned back to her frantic search. Kristy gasped. A gaping wound split the top of her head and extended down to the middle of her spine. Somehow, she knew the wound was self-inflicted. Large, fat maggots ate the rotting flesh. Nauseated, Kristy pulled back. She was going to vomit.

"Jesus! Get me out of here!"

Jesus reached out and took the little girl's hand. He pulled her toward him.

She faced Kristy.

No, my love. This is you. I want you to take her back.

"No!"

You can do it. I'm with you.

Peace enveloped her. She reached out her hand and laid it on the girl's arm. Kristy's other arm came around her and she pulled her close.

Then she woke, aware at once of pain throbbing down the back of her head and into her spine.

She felt strange.

"Lord, what's happening to me?"

Trust me.

"What should I do?"

Do what you were going to do. Go to prayer.

Slowly, she rose from the bed and began to dress.

❧ ❧ ❧

Gathered for prayer at Dawn's house, the six ladies had chatted excitedly, but Kristy didn't participate. Now they went around the room, praying for each other and Kristy amazed Linda. She prayed with a clear knowledge from the Holy Spirit and blessed each of them with words straight from the heart of God.

But something was wrong. Kristy was pale and drawn. She didn't look good. It was something Linda had felt all morning. She finally said something.

"Are you okay?"

Kristy grabbed Linda's hand. "No. I need help. Please pray for me." Kneeling down, she put Linda's hand on top of her head.

"Now."

"Alright," Linda said, turning to the others, "We need to pray for Kristy."

They gathered around her, but when Karen laid a hand on Kristy's shoulder, she paled. They each prayed in turn, but Karen remained silent. Finally, she said, "I don't know why I'm seeing this, but when I put my hand on your shoulder, I got a picture."

Kristy looked up. "What picture?"

"I see a gaping wound. It's really ugly. It goes from the top of your head to the middle of your—"

Kristy's head dropped to her hands. "Pray for me. It's real!"

"Real?"

"Jesus showed me this morning. I have a horrible headache. And my back—"

The ladies began to pray and declare, commanding healing. Finally, Karen heaved a sigh and smiled. "Now there's a light in the wound. It's being cleansed. A bright white lamb is there. It's the Lamb of God! He's closing the wound."

"The pain is gone!" Kristy said. "Thank you Jesus!" Smiling, she told them about her dream and the pain that followed.

&❧ ❧&

Kristy woke the next morning refreshed, heart overflowing with joy. "Something's changed in me, Father, I can feel it! Thank you so much! You're so good to me! Thank you! ... Thank you!"

"What happened when I was five years old? There are so many unanswered questions I have about my life. But thank you!"

"Please continue to heal me completely. I want everything you have to give. I want to be totally whole!"

Suddenly, she frowned. "Why did I tell Billy to leave me alone? I'm always messing up when it comes to him. I want to share this with him. I miss him!"

"Cassie! Are you home?" Kristy called as she opened the front door to her friend's apartment.

"I'm in the kitchen!"

"Cassie, you'll never believe what happened!" Kristy sank into a chair at the table and poured out her story.

Cassie's eyes lit with excitement. "That's awesome! I thought you looked different when you walked in." She rose from the table and opened the refrigerator. "Do you want a glass of tea?"

Kristy paused. "Cassie, did I tell you I told Billy not to call me while he was away?"

Still standing at the refrigerator, Cassie halted. "What? No! You haven't talked about him for a while. But I thought—"

Groaning, Kristy continued, "Maybe it's just my pride, but I couldn't bear him calling and checking to make sure I was healing. It just didn't feel right."

Cassie snorted. "I can imagine."

"Now I wonder …" Kristy stared out the window, a faraway look in her eyes. "It's been so long since I talked to him. I miss him."

Cassie reached over and grabbed her hand. "Don't worry, Kristy. Have confidence. You're following your heart. I don't think I could stand that kind of thing either. It seems to me Billy has taken too much of the upper hand."

Kristy crinkled her nose. "Upper hand? I don't know. Until recently, he was the one doing all the apologizing."

"Well, good for him. It's about time."

"I apologized last, though. And I'm not sure he's forgiven me. I told him before he left, we were done. I was desperate. I think I really hurt him. It's probably hard for him to let the whole thing go and believe in me again. He says God told him to leave."

Cassie smiled. "He'll handle it. You know, Kristy, for someone as 'messed up' as you say you are, you're so wise. And you're humble. I think you'd be great for my brother. In fact, you might even be stubborn enough to stand up to him!"

The two giggled, lifting their glasses of tea.

MORE HEALING

*God chose the foolish things of this world to confound
the wise.* *(Apostle Paul)*

Kristy sat in the circle of women. It was a bit awkward at first,
but now peace, comfort and unconditional love seeped into her
soul in this place. They prayed around the circle until Kristy's
turn came. At her request, they laid hands on her, praying quietly.
Gently, Dawn placed her hand on Kristy's lower abdomen and
looked into her eyes.

"Is it okay if I tell you what I'm getting?"

Kristy nodded.

"It feels like there's been violence in your womb. … Your
entire body, especially your womb and ovaries, seem to be
paralyzed with pent-up grief."

Linda's arm encircled her shoulders and pulled her close.

"I … had an abortion."

Dawn took her hand and continued, "God has forgiven you
and wants you to forgive yourself. He wants to totally restore you
and give you children."

Kristy lifted her eyes to the ladies surrounding her. Their eyes were filled with compassion.

"I break the curse of death and grief. Healing and peace, come in the name of Jesus." Dawn continued. "Papa is healing your womb and ovaries right now. Have you been having regular periods?"

Kristy stared at her. "No."

"You've been grieving, but you'll be different from this day forward. You will bear children. Children who bring you joy."

Tears gathered in Kristy's eyes. "I've always wanted children. I didn't ... believe I would ... ever have them. Not since..." The dam burst and Kristy sobbed into Linda's shoulder.

"I know the pain of this," Dawn said. "I have authority and faith for your healing, because I had an abortion when I was young. It just about destroyed me. But God healed my heart. He gave me three beautiful children and told me to bring healing to his broken daughters."

Kristy cried until she was spent.

&⁂&

"Of course this has evolved over millions and millions of years," the professor droned, his voice flat and obligatory.

Kristy rolled her eyes. This was painful. It made her mad. She thought biology would at least give her some hard facts to work with. But it seemed every class was painful drudgery. What was she going to do with a psychology degree anyway? Like a slave, she just did what others expected, not freely pursuing her own heart's desire. And what was that?

It was over. Finally. She slammed her books together in a pile and marched out of class. Opening her car door, she flopped the bundle on the passenger seat, slid behind the wheel, switched on worship music and headed for Cassie's. Before leaving the parking lot, she fished out her cell phone.

"Hey Cassie, do you want me to pick up anything from the store for lunch? Do you need anything?"

"Good, you're early. Just get here. I don't have much time

today."

Kristy smiled when she spied the spinach salad and tuna-fish sandwiches laid out on the table. "It looks beautiful! You spoil me."

"I know." A wide smile lit Cassie's face. "I enjoy having my own kitchen and especially a man to cook for. I've been inspired."

Later, Kristy looked up from her empty plate and pushed herself from the table. "Cassie, how do you tolerate school? I've about had it."

Her friend laughed. "I don't know that I do. I just learn what they think they know. Some things I want to learn. Some things I learn so I can finish my degree. It doesn't mean I have to believe them."

"Psychology classes are dreary. They're painful. After what I've experienced with God, the whole thing pales."

"Yeah. It seems to me the world is pretty good at defining the problem, but offers little hope for real healing."

"That's for sure," Kristy said. "My mother's been telling me for years she thought I was bipolar. It hurt me bad, but now I realize she was probably right. Jesus showed me that I fractured part of myself off. I became another person in order to function apart from the pain. He's healing me, though. I've received so much love and healing from the women at the prayer group."

"That's wonderful, Kristy. So what were you planning to do with a psychology degree?"

"I thought about counseling. But really, I think I was just trying to find answers and healing. Ever since I found Jesus I've had trouble studying, but especially this year. And lately, I feel like a slave to someone else's agenda. It's not mine anymore."

"So, what are you going to do about it?"

"Do? I thought I'd just tough it out or change majors, but now I'm toying with the idea of quitting school altogether."

"Really? What would you do then?"

Kristy shrugged. "I need to figure out who I am. You know, what I'm made for. What I want. I've thought about getting a job around here. I can't imagine going home." She rolled her eyes. "Last time I tried that, it was a disaster. What do you think I should do?"

"I don't know. Why don't you ask Mom or Dad? Sounds like a big decision."

"I suppose I could." Looking down, Kristy picked at her fingernails. "I need to have a plan. I really think I should move out from your parent's place."

"Why?"

She leaned back in her chair and folded her arms. "It's going to be awkward when Billy comes home. It's just a little too convenient with me there. If he wants me, he can pursue me. And if he decides against me, it would be better for us both if I wasn't there."

"Yeah. I can see your point."

"Would you pray with me about this?"

"Sure."

🙠 ❦ 🙢

Later, Kristy sat at the table, twirling a strand of her hair. "I need to ask you something."

"Go ahead." Linda said from the stove.

She blushed. "It's Billy."

"What's up?" She stopped stirring the soup and looked up.

"Did you know I broke it off between us right before he left for Spokane?"

"Yeah, I knew that, Sweetie."

"You did? Did he tell you?"

Linda smiled. "No, he didn't tell me, but I overheard the conversation. It was pretty tough. So what was your question?"

Kristy's eyes went wide. "You did?" She blushed, looking away. "Now that I think about it, I don't see how you couldn't have overheard. Anyway, I called him and apologized, but things are not the same between us."

"Didn't he forgive you?"

"He said he did, but also said he couldn't tolerate me

constantly attacking him with wounds from my past."

"Oh, I see."

Kristy swallowed. "So, I told him to leave me alone for a while."

"Why's that?"

"Because I didn't want to give him progress reports on my *healing* every week. I felt like I was trying to prove something to him. Besides, I don't believe I can guarantee I won't attack him again."

Linda thought a moment. "Well, I can understand that."

"Linda ... do you think I'm right for Billy? Do you think I might be too wounded? Could he ever be happy with someone like me? Because if he couldn't, maybe I shouldn't encourage him. Maybe when he gets home I should just tell him—"

"Hold on, Kristy. Let me tell you a story.

"When I met Ben, I was a lonely, hurt teenager. My parents had recently divorced and I'd been experimenting with drugs and alcohol. I went through many boyfriends."

Kristy stared. "Really? ... You?"

"Yes, me ... There was one guy in particular that I got very attached to. He broke my heart. I was devastated. I found Jesus not long after that and God restored me. Then I met Ben at church."

"He was strong in faith and handsome. It seemed he had everything together. His parents were both Christians and they had this beautiful ranch. I felt so inferior. He was so all-together and well off. It seemed he hadn't been through anything traumatic at all. I was intimidated, but I kept dating him. I felt safe. He respected me. It wasn't long until we fell in love."

Linda reached for Kristy's hand. "I soon realized that he'd been hurt too. No one escapes it. He helped me heal, but I was able to help him too. He needed me. He needed my love and comfort. It was tough at times and we had some intense confrontations, but we always had something to give each other. God was able to use my hurts and experiences. When you humble yourself before God, make yourself a little child, let him take away your pain and heal your wounds, those places where you were hurt can become some of your greatest strengths."

"You know the scripture that says: 'To whom much is given, much is required?' That scripture is talking about mercy. When God has given you lots of mercy and healed you of terrible wounds, you owe that same mercy to others. There's another scripture that says, 'He who has been forgiven much, loves much.' When you come out of great brokenness, you can be more aware of how much he has forgiven you."

"Kristy, have confidence. You'll continue to be dear to us even if you and Billy don't get together. And if you do, we'll gladly accept you as a much loved member of the family. But you shouldn't agree to it unless you feel you're equal to him." She laughed softly. "It needs to be a fair fight."

"Billy's strong. But there'll always be things you can do better because of your background and gifting. You'll be able to dish out love and mercy in very specific ways. Don't worry. If you get together, you'll stand strong beside him. You won't be a project."

Kristy bit her lip. "Thank you. I needed to hear that. ... I miss Billy. He's been good for me. But if he can't love me the way I am—"

"I don't think that's the problem. Have you prayed about this?"

Kristy nodded. "Yeah. But I don't seem to be getting anything but the words, 'Trust me.'"

Linda laughed. "That sounds like an answer to me. Leave it in your Daddy's hands, Kristy. I know this whole thing seems insurmountable to you, but it could all change in a day."

"Okay ... and Linda ... I have another question."

"Yes?"

"What would you think if I quit school? ... I can hardly stand it anymore."

"I've noticed you haven't been very positive about school lately. What do you want to do?"

Kristy wrinkled her nose. "I'm not sure. I don't know what I want to do with my life. I just know that attending school is almost unbearable for me."

"Ask God to reveal your heart's desire. He'll do that for you."

"In some things, I know my heart's desire. Is it okay to ask God for anything I want? I want miracles. Is that okay? Can I have faith for miracles?"

"You're God's child, Kristy. If we stay with and in Jesus, we can 'ask whatever we wish and it will be given to us.' Bold sons and daughters ask their father for big things, and believe for them."

Rising from the chair, Kristy hugged Linda tightly. "Oh Linda! I love you! You've done so much for me the last few weeks."

The front door slammed. "Mom! Daddy! Is anyone home?" It was Cassie.

Linda cracked the door, but continued to hold Kristy. "We're in the office! I'll be out in a minute!"

"Thank you, Linda."

"You're so worth it. Are we done here?"

Kristy smiled. "I think so."

Linda opened the door and led Kristy out of the room. "Cassie!" She embraced her warmly. "It's great to see you! What brings you out here tonight?" Holding her at arm's length, she studied her. "You've been crying ... Where's Jeff?"

"He didn't come with me. I think he's ... at home."

Cassie chewed on a quivering lower lip. "Is Daddy home?"

"He should be here shortly. He went to town for a meeting. Are you all right?"

Cassie nodded, sinking to the couch. "I think so. But I'm so mad I could spit. I need to talk to Daddy."

"Does Jeff know where you are?"

"Probably not. But he'll figure it out. Where else would I go?"

"What did you do, get mad and run out the door?"

Cassie's lips tightened. "Pretty much."

Linda planted her feet and crossed her arms over her chest. "All right, Cassie. Call him right now and tell him where you are. Right now, do you hear? It isn't fair to let him worry. And tell him you'll be home shortly."

"Mom, you don't know what he said to me!"

Linda glanced at Kristy, then over at Hannah and Joey, who slowly entered the living room, eyes wide and curious.

"Cassie ... be careful. Are you sure you want to talk about this in front of everyone? He's your husband! Do you want everyone involved in this and taking sides? Come with me." Linda grabbed her daughter's hand, pulled her from the couch, led her into the office and pushed her into a chair.

"Sit." She closed the door. "Now call him and tell him where you are."

Cassie lifted her chin and folded her arms. "I'm not ready to call him."

Linda stood her ground. "Then you're certainly not ready to talk to me or your father about your private business. March right back out the door and get in your car. You're married now. Go back and work things out with your husband."

"You won't even listen to me?"

"No, Cassie. Not before you call him. It's not fair to Jeff. "

"What about Daddy? I'll wait for him."

"Your father will support me in this. He won't discuss it. Not before you have at least called Jeff and told him where you are. While you're at it, you can ask permission to talk about this private matter with your parents."

"Mom!"

"If he doesn't agree, and you still think you need to talk to us, you can bring him back another day and we'll talk to you both."

"Mom, I just need to—"

"At your wedding I stood and promised before God that I would do anything in my power to support your marriage. I intend to keep that promise, as will your father. We will not come between you two."

Cassie blanched. "I wasn't intending—"

"I know you, Cassie. I know you love Jeff. I believe you're just having a normal, healthy disagreement. You're over-reacting. You need to pray about it, get another perspective, then go back and work it out."

Bursting into tears, Cassie said, "It's the first time we ... fought like this since months before our wedding. ... I don't think he trusts me ... or appreciates me."

The door creaked. Ben stepped into the room. "I heard you were here. ... What's wrong?"

She threw herself into his arms.

Over his daughter's shoulder, Ben arched a brow toward Linda.

She gave him a warning look.

"Where's Jeff?" he asked.

Her weeping intensified.

Linda refolded her arms and tapped her foot. "Jeff is home. He doesn't know where she is. I told her we won't listen to her account of their marital spat until she calls and tells him her whereabouts."

"Sounds wise to me."

"I also told her she can ask him for permission to discuss this with her parents."

"You have a wise mother," Ben said into his daughter's ear.

Cassie pulled back, turned and found a tissue. She blew her nose.

"Okay, I'll call him." She reached for her phone and pressed the speaker button.

"Hi Jeff."

"Cassie! Where are you?" There was a ring of panic in his voice.

"I went home."

Silence.

Cassie sniffled. "My mother insisted I call and tell you where

I was."

"Well, thank you," Jeff said, voice clipped and sarcastic. "That's considerate."

She rolled her swollen eyes. "Mom says I need to ask your permission before I can talk to them about our ... our discussion earlier."

"Really? ... Ask then."

Once more she rolled her eyes. "*Exalted* husband, will you grant me permission to talk to my parents about this private matter?"

He chuckled. "Can I trust you not to malign my character? Do you still think I'm an over-controlling chauvinist and don't trust you?"

"Well, do you still think I'm a spoiled brat, and may I quote, 'the most stubborn, obstinate woman you've ever met'?"

"I asked first."

"No and yes."

"Well that's an improvement."

"Your turn."

He paused. "No and ... not really."

"So you don't think I'm a spoiled brat?"

"I admit, that was harsh. I only said it because of your reaction to me when I confronted you. I got mad. But you're really good for me, Cassie."

Cassie didn't say anything, but let out a long sigh, a hint of a smile beginning to find its way to her tear-stained face.

"I love you, Cassie, and you're good for me."

The hurt and anger on her face were surrendering to hope.

Linda and Ben exchanged relieved smiles.

Cassie turned off the speaker phone. She turned to her waiting parents. Waving her hand, she motioned for them to leave the room.

Linda grabbed her husband's arm and led him out.

Later, emerging into the living room, Cassie wore a sheepish grin. She addressed her parents. "I'm sorry I involved you in all of this. It was just a big misunderstanding."

Linda looked up from her magazine. "Of course it was. You love each other and I have the utmost confidence you can work things out."

Ben chuckled, lowering the newspaper. "What do you think all that fighting you did before you married him was for? You should be pros at it by now. Do you want to tell us what happened?"

"Yeah. I guess I overdrew the account."

"Oh." Ben said.

Cassie's voice rose in defense. "From what he said, I thought there was money in there! It was a sweater I had my eye on for quite a while and it was on sale. Then I gassed up the car, like he told me to. He freaked out and yelled at me. He said I should *always* check with him before I go shopping, to make sure we have money. Especially at the end of the month. When I got mad, he threatened to have separate accounts. That hurt. We had words." Cassie reached for her coat.

Rising from the couch, Kristy set down her book. "I'll walk you to the car."

17

FAITH AND CHANGE

*I sought the Lord and he answered me; he delivered me
from all my fears.*   (King David)

Kristy climbed into the car with Cassie. "Are you guys all right?"

Cassie turned on the ignition and cranked up the heat. "What do you mean?"

"You and Jeff."

"Yeah, we're okay. He overreacts sometimes, but so do I." A smile tugged her lips. "Daddy says we're growing up together."

"Do you ever feel that Jeff's not your equal?"

"What?"

"You know, like you look down on him sometimes? Feel like he's your project?"

Cassie laughed. "Absolutely not! He's my husband!"

"I know he had a rough childhood. Is he ever intimidated because of his background?"

"Who Jeff? Intimidated by *me*? I would have never married someone I could intimidate. I also wouldn't have married anyone I felt couldn't rise up and be the man I need in a husband and a strong father to my children."

"I was just thinking about his wounds from childhood and all."

"Pooh! We all have wounds from childhood! I've seen some people take small wounds and camp on them, use them like trophies and never grow up. Others experience huge tragedies, forgive, get healing, and glorify God for his grace in their lives. It's all about whether you're willing to believe God for who he says you are and who he says he is." Looking at Kristy curiously, Cassie asked, "You're worried about Billy again, aren't you?"

"Billy's going to be home in a week. … I'm nervous."

Cassie leaned toward her. "Kristy, don't run scared."

"I'm not going to run. Not from Billy. I just need to know it's possible for me to be an equal partner."

Cassie laughed. "You aren't going to let this lie, are you? Okay, if there's anyone who's the project in our marriage, it's me. Jeff's had to fight to climb out of some bad mindsets. Because of that, he has a certain clarity in good ways of thinking that I am catching. We help each other, but many times he teaches *me*. He sometimes amazes me. Like just now. He apologized so easily. He truly is a humble man. To tell you the truth, I was a snot."

"You? I can't imagine that," Kristy said with a laugh.

"Seriously though, Kristy, be bold. Don't let Billy intimidate you. He hates that. You've got what it takes. Believe in who you are. Sometimes you worry too much about what things look like. Be free. Be bold. Even if it's wrong. It seems to me that people who live in fear never move or change. People who are bold in freedom make mistakes, but then they can repent and move on. They're able to grow and change faster."

"You're probably right. I've already had some pretty embarrassing experiences with Billy. They don't seem to have hurt our relationship."

※ ❦ ※

The next day, Kristy drove home from her psychology class with a heavy heart. This class either bored her or really got on her nerves. Today it was the latter. She was extremely irritated. And aching with cramps.

She smiled. There was a reason for this feeling. "I guess I forgot. It's been almost a year since I had a period. Father, thank you! You're so good!"

But it wasn't just cramps and irritation.

She wrinkled her nose. It was all she could do to attend class, let alone do the assignments. It was just more theories and diagnoses. They had no appeal.

Jesus had rocked her world. He was what she was looking for. His healing. His touch. His thinking. His presence. He was what she needed.

But her grades were suffering. With her present attitude, it was only going to get worse. But what could she do? Quit? She had over a year left and what was she going to do with a degree if she stuck it out? She certainly wasn't going on for her master's! She was going further into debt for something she didn't like. Could barely tolerate.

Her mother would throw a fit if she quit. What about her grants and scholarships? She could change her major, but she didn't have a clue what she wanted to do.

"The only thing I know, Lord, is I want *you*. I want to know you more! School's a distraction."

She drove with one hand on the steering wheel and twirled her hair with the opposite forefinger. It was a beautiful March day and spring break was fast approaching. Finishing the term with passing grades was heavy on her mind, but facing the classes for spring term filled her with dread.

"God? What should I do?"

What do you want to do?

"I don't know. I don't want to go to school right now, but I'm afraid to quit. What will everyone say? And what about my future?"

I will be with you.

෨ ❧ ❦ ෨

201

Early the next morning, Kristy woke to warm sunlight peeking through the blinds. The spring sun flooded the room when she opened them, warming her soul as well as her body. A song came to mind and she sang softly.

> *You are the everlasting God…*
> *You do not faint, you won't grow weary…*
> *You're the defender of the weak,*
> *You comfort those in need,*
> *You lift us up on wings like eagles.*
>
> *Strength will rise when we wait upon the Lord*
> *We will wait upon the Lord …* [12]

Flopping back on the bed, Kristy crossed her legs, pulled her Bible onto her lap and leafed through it. Her eyes fell to an underlined portion in the book of Luke.

The red-lettered words of Jesus.

"If you remain in me and my words remain in you, ask whatever you will and it will be given to you. …"

Sighing, she closed the Bible and laid it aside, falling to her knees beside the bed.

"Okay, Father. I'm with Jesus and in Jesus. I'm trusting in his love and his words. So it's time to ask. I want to be totally healed. Not for Billy, but for me. Because you love me. I don't want to feel afraid, alone, guilty or rejected any longer. Thank you for what you've done for me, but I want *all* you have for me."

Grabbing a notepad, she scribbled on the paper. "You promised you would restore my soul. You promised I could have righteousness, peace and joy in the Holy Spirit. Keep it coming, Lord."

"But, I want my Daddy back. He's not dead is he? If he's alive, would you tell him I miss him? Save him, Lord. I forgive him for leaving us. Please send him back." She scribbled down his name.

"I want you to save my mother too. Toby says she cries at night.

Touch her, Jesus. She thinks she knows all about you, but she's so lonely and empty. I forgive her for what she's done to me and for sneaking around and lying to me. Forgive her, Father. I'm sure she's hurting. Save her."

"I want Toby saved too. Please. Heal his wounds and restore his father to him. He needs a father. Tell Daddy to come back to us."

She dropped to her knees. "Lord, I want all the relationships in my family restored. You came to destroy the works of the devil. The devil has brought pain and destruction in my family. Destroy his work!"

"I'm just like Kelly in the church bathroom. I believe you're strong and that you're loving. I believe you love me and are listening to me. It feels like I'm asking for a lot, but I believe that you'll do it because you love me and because you love them."

"You said if I believe on you, I will be saved. Me and my household. Whatever it takes, Lord Jesus, save us!"

Sighing, she dropped to a sitting position on the floor, held her knees to her chest and rocked. "I'm not going to worry about this anymore, Daddy-God. I may remind you and remind myself that it's in your hands, but that's all." After a few minutes, she raised her hands. "Thank you Lord that you're going to take care of it all and even right now you're working on it. And just like Kelly, I'm going to 'go play now.'" She laughed.

"And about Billy ..." She rose and fell face forward on the bed, sinking her face into the pillows.

"I'm going to be bold," she heard her muffled voice say. Turning to her back, she continued, "No more worrying whether I'm good enough or healed enough for him. No more holding onto him like a security blanket. You are my security. You know I miss him. He's been good to me. He's strong and he's blessed. He'd be a good husband and a good father. But does he really love me, or is he falling in love with what I *could* be? He pushes me. It makes me feel like he doesn't accept me the way I am. I have no father to ask but you. You'll have to take care of me. If he won't have me, I trust you'll give me someone better!"

"Help me, Lord. I've decided to quit school. I haven't told anyone. Provide for me, Father. I'll need a job. Please have someone offer me a job here in Fishtrap. This is where I want to stay for now. And when I get enough money, I want to move from the Watson's. I love them, but I don't want to be here when Billy comes home. And he's coming home soon!"

꙰ ❧ ⸱ ❧ ꙰

"Hey. Can I sit here?" Derek Wheeler leaned over, grinning. Real friendly lately, he was eager to talk.

"Uh ... sure."

Dawn wheeled over to where Kristy and Hannah sat, now with Derek, waiting for church to begin. Her interruption was welcome. "Hey, Kristy, do you know anyone who could help Rhonda Barewood with her kids? She has little Justine and Raine, you know. They're heavy care, and she needs help."

"What kind of help does she need?"

"Constant help. Maybe live-in. Mandy's moving out and Rhonda's going back to school."

"Maybe *I* could help."

"You?"

"Yeah. Where is she?"

Before the day was over, Kristy had a job. And she was needed right away. As soon as finals were over, she planned to move in with Rhonda and start training as a care-giver. Room and board were provided and a little money to put in the bank.

"God, you're so good!" she said, as she descended the stairs to help fix dinner that evening.

"So you're leaving us?" Linda asked, peering across the table. Water pitcher in hand, she filled the glasses.

Kristy continued to lay out the plates and silverware, helping her set the table. "Yeah. I think it would be best."

Linda proceeded around the table. "Just because you're quitting school doesn't mean you have to move out. It would be fine for you to stay until you get your feet under you and figure out what you want."

"I know. You've been so good to me. But this way I won't feel pressure to make a decision for a while."

"I understand." She pursed her lips. "Have you talked to Billy lately?"

Kristy's head shot up. "No. Why?"

Shrugging her shoulders, Linda moved to the kitchen and returned with napkins and butter. "He phoned last night. He'll be here Thursday."

"I'll be gone by then."

Linda's blue eyes met hers. "I figured that. Are you sure you don't want to talk to him about this? He's expecting you to be here when he gets home. I get the feeling he's looking forward to it."

Kristy looked away. "You can tell him where I am. He can call me if he wants to talk."

Sighing, Linda shook her head. "Okay. If that's the way you want it.

"Dinner's ready!" she called over her shoulder.

"Okay. All loaded. We'll keep the rest of your stuff in the shed until you need it." Stepping up to the front porch to stand with Kristy, Ben slung his arm over her shoulder. "I hate to see you go. And I know Linda has sure appreciated your help."

Kristy smiled. "Thank you for everything you've done. You have no idea how you've helped me."

Ben's eyes twinkled. "It's been a pleasure to have you. I know someone who's not going to be happy when he comes home and finds you gone, but I have a feeling you know what you're doing."

Kristy's eyebrows rose. "You do?"

He laughed.

෨ ෨ ෨

Warm sun reflected off the white of Billy's newly washed pickup. Windows rolled down, he reveled in the cool breeze that played with the tips of his dark curly hair and the loose ends of his rolled denim shirt sleeves. Scanning the desert landscape, he rubbed the short scruff of his newly acquired beard.

A beautiful woman dominated his thoughts.

Long shining brown hair. Large vulnerable blue eyes. Wide smile. Smooth, fair skin and flawless complexion. Soft and feminine.

He pictured her again, wrapped in a blanket on his lap, sobbing.

He could almost feel her leaning against him in his pickup, sleeping peacefully.

Laughing at his side, they galloped the horses over the pasture road, heading for the creek.

Her sweet voice sang beside him in church.

Head bowed, she stood at church, receiving prayer.

Then she was in his arms, clinging to him for comfort.

He had it bad.

Coming to the top of the mountain, he scanned the Haywacah Valley. Snow-capped peaks surrounded a vast, green and brown checkered bowl, the city of Wallua Crossing nestled into the side of the mountain. The valley was just beginning to turn green, with soft, tender grass.

"The Valley of Peace," he murmured. "I love it here."

… I am going to do something in your days that you would not believe, even if you were told.

"It's that verse again. Why do you keep saying that to me? What does it mean?"

He sighed. God was calling him. Something was going to change. He could feel it. He had a bit of an idea, but wasn't entirely sure. "What do you want me to do next? Show me the way, Lord … and let that way include Kristy. You told me she was the one. I'm counting on it."

He didn't want to move ahead without her.

If he could help it.

It had been too long since he'd talked to her. For all he knew, she was still angry. She hadn't understood what he was saying in their last conversation.

He had hoped to have some contact with her while he was gone. At least a few phone calls. Sometimes he just didn't get it.

He recited a passage of scripture he'd memorized while in Spokane.

"My heart is not proud, O Lord.
My eyes are not haughty;
I do not concern myself with great matters
or things too wonderful for me.
But I have stilled and quieted my soul;
like a weaned child with its mother
Like a weaned child is my soul within me ...

"It's in your hands, Lord. It's all too wonderful for me. I am coming back and I don't have a clue what to expect. But I trust you. Mom says she's doing well. For both our sakes, let her put the past behind her."

꽃 🍃 🍃 꽃

"She moved?" Surprised, Billy stood in the upstairs hallway, peering into the unoccupied room.

Linda stood at his side, smiling and nodding. "Just yesterday. She's helping out at the Barewood's, with Justine and Raine. Rhonda needed help."

"What about school? How can she do that and continue in school?"

"She quit school."

"Quit school? Why didn't you tell me about this?"

"You never asked."

"I asked how she was doing."

"And like I told you, she's doing great."

Leaning on the door jamb with one stiff arm holding him, he scanned the room again with a worried scowl. "I have a bad feeling about this. Why would she move the day before I get home?"

Linda chuckled, turning to go down the hall. "That you'll have to ask her yourself."

ᔕ❦ ᔕ❦

"Kristy? What's going on?"

Kristy removed the cell phone from her ear and frowned at it. What a greeting after over two months! He sounded irritated. She returned it to her ear, heart pounding.

"Is this Billy?"

"Of course it's me. What's happening?"

"What do you mean?"

"Why did you move the day before I got home?"

"It just happened like that. They need me here. And I needed a job. Uh … It's a great deal for me. I prayed for a job and that's what God sent me."

"You refuse to talk to me the whole time I'm gone and then move out right before I get home? I get the feeling you're avoiding me. Are you trying to tell me something?"

Kristy paused. Her mind went blank. "I'm sorry, but this is a great deal for me. I really don't know what to say."

ᔕ❦ ᔕ❦

Ben sat in church next to his wife. He raised his arm to rest it on the back of her chair. Kristy and Hannah were on the other side of the church with Derek. Derek was quite friendly with Kristy lately and usually she showed signs of irritation. But not today.

Head turning, he saw Billy follow Jeff and Cassie in and head to their side to take seats nearby. Billy's eyes shot to where Kristy sat talking with Derek, his face grim.

I'm sure glad I'm not in his shoes.

Ben smiled down at Linda, who sighed. She liked him, but wasn't going to make it easy.

He chuckled. He was glad all this stuff was settled and behind him. He'd never want to go back. It hadn't been easy for him either. Like him, his older children had a stubborn streak that made it a bit difficult to hook up.

He looked over at Cassie and Jeff, who smiled at each other,

208

hands joined. But once the connection was made, it was solid.

It appeared Billy was eating his heart out watching her with Derek and making assumptions.

Just then, Sam Wallace approached Kristy and squatted beside her chair. They whispered something to each other and Kristy giggled. She rose and followed him out of the room.

When they stood to worship, Kristy appeared in front and began to sing with Sam strumming a guitar beside her, singing harmony and watching her closely. Amused, Ben smiled at his oldest son's stone face. He didn't know Sam and Kristy sang together. They sounded pretty good. Ben leaned back to relax, bobbing his foot to the music.

While she sang, Kristy's eyes drifted to meet Billy's unhappy gaze. Her voice quivered, but went firm, eyes traveling again to fix on the ceiling.

Pastor Evan walked to the front and read a scripture.

I pray that you, being rooted and established in love, may have power, together with all the saints, to grasp how wide and long and high and deep is the love of Christ, and to know this love ... that you may be filled to the measure of all the fullness of God.

"Later in this book, this is what Paul says, *Be imitators of God, therefore, as dearly loved children and live a life of love.*

"When we believe we are dearly loved children of the father, we imitate him. We can trust him in hard times. We can love others as he does. We can be bold. We can laugh with him. And we can overflow with hope, joy and peace, even when circumstances are difficult."

"It's all about the love of God. The power of God is his love. Miracles are his love. All healing is his love. All good things in our lives are expressions of his love.

"When I finally experienced God's love, I

was able to love myself. I was able to appreciate how God made *me*. My eyes were opened to see his love in his creation all around me and in the circumstances of my life. No longer was the Bible a rule book, but a book that revealed God's character and his love for me. I was able to see his love all through the scriptures. No longer was loving others merely obedience for me. It was my desire. A driving force. ..."

18

JUST BELIEVING

How much more will your father in heaven give good gifts to those who ask him!   (*Jesus Christ*)

Kristy pulled a clean T-shirt over Raine's wet head and reached for a comb. Dodging flailing hands, she combed her shining brown hair. Ten years old, Raine could not talk or walk, but she could grab. And she did. A lock of Kristy's long hair.

Gasping in pain, Kristy pried her strong fingers loose. While pulling her hair back in a ponytail, she turned to see the little girl grinning, bright eyes shining.

She laughed. "You little imp! You know what you're doing, don't you?"

There was something comforting about this place. She never knew that profoundly handicapped children could give so much back. They exuded quiet acceptance. She didn't have to explain or defend herself. They appreciated her attention and care. She could feel it.

They knew how to be children and were teaching her. She smiled. In some ways, they were caring for her heart, while she cared for their bodies.

… Their angels always behold the face of the Father.

For sure. They were in touch with angels.

And they were happy.

She frowned. She really thought Billy would be here by now, saying *something*. The phone "conversation" the other day was rough. And he hardly talked to her at church. He was upset with her. Maybe it was a mistake not to call him. But then, it was awkward.

She didn't know what to think.

Maybe she shouldn't think.

But she couldn't help it.

Did he expect everything to stay as he pleased and his neat little world to remain undisturbed while he was away for almost three months? He was the one who left. He didn't own her.

She lifted her chin. Well, if he was going to give up now, he wasn't the one for her.

Her phone rang. Expecting a call from Cassie, she pulled it out quickly and didn't look at the name. "Hello."

"Hello. Is this Kristy?"

It was a man. And it wasn't Billy. But his voice sounded familiar.

She stopped combing. "Yes, this is Kristy Turner. Who is this and how did you get my number?"

"This is your father."

Kristy felt the blood drain from her face. Her *father*?

"Is this some kind of joke?"

"No. It's me. James Turner. Your father."

Could this be happening? For real? It sounded like him.

"Where are you?"

"I'm in Seattle. Your brother gave me your phone number just this morning. I want to see you. Is that possible?"

"I don't know. Where's Toby?"

"He's here at the hospital. We're in the waiting room."

"The hospital?" Kristy asked, "What happened?"

"Honey, your mother's real sick. She came through surgery all right, but she's still not out of the woods. Toby, here, says you pray. Pray with me for your mother, okay? She needs our prayers right now."

Her mind went blank.

"Kristy? Are you there?"

Swallowing, she finally found her voice. "I'm here... How bad is she? How do you happen to be there?"

"I'm so sorry, Honey. There's so much I need to tell you. I think your mother's going to make it, but we all need your prayers. She had an appendectomy and developed an abscess. We almost lost her."

We?

"I need to see you soon. Maybe I could meet you at school somewhere?"

"I'm not in school anymore."

"You're not? Your mother said—"

"I haven't told her yet. I just quit last week. It might be best to keep it from her until she gets better."

"Whatever you say. Honey, ... why don't you call me when you've had a chance to think about all of this. I know it's a shock."

"That's for sure."

Kristy hung up the phone after promising to call him back later. She sat dumbfounded, staring at Rhonda, who had sensed her shock and disbelief. She had come to take over the dressing of the newly bathed and energetic Raine.

"Who was that?"

"You'll never guess."

୫ଭ ❥ ⧫୫ଭ

Billy pulled out on the highway and turned up the road toward Barewood's. It had been four days since he'd arrived home. It was time to talk.

He had wanted to take Kristy out for dinner on Sunday afternoon, but Joey planned a gathering to play basketball with his friends from church. Joey insisted he join them. It was enough of an excuse to put off talking to Kristy.

He was irritated.

She had looked good on Sunday, smiling and chatting with everyone. He sighed.

Mom was right. She was doing well.

She was even prettier than before. She was lighter somehow. And there was a peace about her that wasn't there before. She acted like she was okay. He frowned.

Completely okay.

And not eager to talk to him.

"Forgive me, Lord. But something about this whole thing really bugs me. I'm glad she's doing well, but—" He let out a frustrated groan, leaned back and rubbed his short beard.

It was late Tuesday morning and the gray clouds hung in the sky with the promise of rain. He was taking a risk. He probably should've called her and made sure this was an okay time to come and visit, but he was afraid he would be put off again.

And he had to see her. Today. He'd called the house Saturday and Rhonda told him she was busy all day in training to care for the girls. Rhonda said Kristy couldn't see him that day, but he could try late Tuesday morning. He hadn't set anything up, but wasn't going to give her a chance to refuse.

His gut twisted. What if she didn't want to see him? Maybe she didn't need him anymore. Didn't like him anymore.

She looked fine.

Just fine.

Words he read that morning came to mind.

Don't be afraid, just believe.

"Okay, Lord, you have all things in your hands concerning me. You told me she was the one for me. And she hasn't acted interested the last few months. She refused to even talk to me. I have no idea what's happening. But I believe I heard you. I'm going to trust you."

In the story he read that morning, from the gospel of Mark,

the guy knew his daughter was dead. It was a pretty hopeless situation, but he believed Jesus. He took his word for it. That was what he was going to do now.

He turned down the driveway to the Barewood's, a small acreage about five miles from town. A large green lawn stretched far into the back of the property, ending in a thick grove of pines and firs. Kristy's green Pontiac was parked in the driveway.

Hopping from his pickup, he jogged to the front door and knocked. Rhonda opened the door with a smile. "Well, well ... Billy. What brings you out here?" Her dark eyes twinkled.

"Is Kristy busy?"

Her face sobered. "Uh ... She's not here right now. She left about fifteen minutes ago."

"Where did she go? Her car's still here."

Rhonda's eyebrows rose. "It is? She must have taken a walk then."

"Is it okay if I look around?"

"Sure. Go ahead. She's probably not far away."

He scanned the area, then ambled out through the grass toward a grove of trees in the back yard. There was no sign of Kristy. He had just turned back to his pickup when he heard a soft moan. Curious, he crept back toward the trees and stepped into a small grassy clearing. The sound of sniffling and sighing drifted toward him.

There she was, lying on the grass, in a light jacket, jeans and boots. Curled in a ball, with head turned away, her loose hair spread out on the ground.

He crept closer.

"Oh, God! Why didn't she tell me she was sick? ... I haven't been in touch. I should've called. I haven't talked to her in so long. I was too busy worrying about the school thing and how to tell her. ... Help me. I don't know what to do." She paused.

"And *pray* for your mother?" She raised her voice. "If he believes, then why hasn't he contacted me? He really must not care about me." She tucked her head in her hands and there was a long pause.

"How can he just appear like this? I know I prayed for it, but now what am I supposed to feel? I'm not sure I want to see him. He deserted me!"

Billy stopped.

Have I been fooling myself?

He turned and tiptoed in the opposite direction.

Was she still upset about his leaving?

She had told him to leave her alone!

A low growl reached his ears. "And Billy! That nincompoop!"

He froze.

Voice choked and congested, she continued, "Why's he mad at me now? What did I do? Just when I need him most, he comes home all irritated, demanding explanations and getting jealous of Derek and Sam, of all people. He knows we're just friends." She sniffled and continued, shouting, "Well, if he wants me, he can come and get me! I'm not going to pander to his ego. I'm not some clinging vine that has to have a *man* to survive! Was I supposed to stay all packaged up at his parent's house for his convenience?"

Puzzled, Billy turned back and stared down at her curled form, her back to him, intense in prayer. Silently stepping forward, he dropped to his knees beside her, reached out and touched her hair.

"Kristy. I'm here."

She jumped, then froze. She didn't turn, but tucked her face deeper in loose hair.

He sat beside her, stretching out on the grass.

In one fluid motion, she flipped her hair back and lifted her gaze. Sniffling, she bit her lip.

"How long have you been here, listening?"

"Long enough."

She rose to her knees, launched herself onto his lap, threw her arms around his neck, and wept into the front of his shirt. Stunned, he held her close. He didn't dare speak.

What was wrong?

Well, at least she was reaching out to him instead of running the other direction.

Finally, she pulled herself together and looked at him, sniffling and wiping her face on the cuff of her flannel shirt—one he recognized from their hiking trip in the mountains.

"What took you so long?"

He grinned. "I'm a nincompoop."

"Oh, Billy, I missed you so much!" She threw her arms around him again.

"Why didn't you tell me?" He said into her ear.

She pulled back. "You didn't ask. Did you miss *me*?"

"Of course I missed you! I thought about you and prayed for you the entire time I was away."

"Then why the cold greeting on the phone?"

"I suppose that wasn't the best way to—"

She slapped his arm, swollen eyes flashing. "I guess not! After three months, you grab the phone and growl, 'Kristy, what's going on?'" Her voice returned to normal. "You were *irritated* with me. And before you even gave me a chance to explain!"

He twisted his lips. "I'm busted."

She pushed him down into the grass and climbed on top of his chest. "You big, overgrown lout! What do I see in you, anyway?"

He lay on his back, grinning at her. "I don't rightly know. What's a 'lout' anyway?"

"I don't know, but it seemed the right name to call you just then."

"Well, pretty lady, I'm mighty obliged that you see anything in me at' all. And I really like you there, sittin' on top o' me and all."

A small smile appeared on her tear-stained face, but she rolled her eyes, climbed off his chest and sat cross-legged next to him. She hung her head in her hands, hair falling forward. A long, pain-filled groan escaped.

Was she going to cry again?

He rose to sit beside her, leaning over and pulling a few strands back in order to peer into her hidden face. "Seriously, Kristy, I'm sorry. I was just so looking forward to seeing you. I guess I was surprised and hurt that you weren't there to greet me. I thought maybe you were giving me signals to back off again."

She sighed, lifting her face to gaze at the trees around them. Twirling a strand of hair around her forefinger, her eyes fixed straight ahead. "I guess I have a lot to learn. I thought you were having second thoughts about *me*. You never called—"

"You told me not to!"

Turning to him, she peered up at him through mussed hair, gaze turning mischievous. "You could have at least tried a few times, just to give me the chance to scold you. I didn't like your nagging me to 'get healed,' but at least then I would have been assured you were still interested."

Tackling her playfully, he pushed her to the grass. She shrieked, then laughed. Straddling her with his knees, he pinned her hands on either side of her head and looked into her teasing blue eyes. Smiling, he asked, "You know what the problem is between us?"

She met his gaze. "What?"

"I've never properly kissed you."

She went serious, blue eyes holding his. "Do you want to?"

His smile fled. "Of course. I've wanted to kiss you from the time I picked you up from the side of the road with that silly hairdo."

A soft smile tugged her lips. "Then what are you waiting for?"

He lowered his head, lips brushing over hers. She moaned and pulled him to her, returning his kiss with one of her own. Pulling her with him, he rolled to his back. She nestled into his shoulder. He kissed her again. "Kristy, I love you. Do you believe me?"

She chuckled into his ear. "I'm getting the idea."

He kissed her again. This time his soft lips explored her

eyelids, nose, each cheek and down her neck. Suddenly, he let go of her and straightened to sit. He ran a hand through his hair and cleared his throat. "I'd better behave, I'm sure Rhonda's wondering what's going on out here."

She sat up beside him, crossing her jean-clad legs.

After a long pause, he picked a long piece of grass and fingered it. "So ... are you still mad at me for leaving you? Is that why you moved out?"

Her gaze flew to his. "No. I apologized, remember? You told me God—"

"Then why were you shouting at God about me deserting you?"

"Deserting me?" Her brow creased and she tilted her head, puzzled. Then a light went on and her face cleared. "You shouldn't eavesdrop on people's conversations with God, Billy. I wasn't referring to you. I got a phone call this morning. It was my father! He wants to see me."

"Your father? Where is he?"

"He's at a hospital in Seattle with Toby. My mother's real sick. He thinks she'll be okay, but wants me to pray for her. I don't know what to think! How can he just appear after all these years and ask me to pray for my mother after he left us? And he wants to see me? I didn't know what to tell him."

"Wow! Have you been praying for him?"

She nodded. "Sure. I've been praying for them all. I asked God to save them and restore relationships in our family. The ladies at the prayer group have been praying for them too."

"Sounds like you asked for this."

"Billy, he's been gone ten years. I don't know him. I wasn't even sure he was alive. I didn't know how this was going to make me feel."

"Do you want your father back?"

"Well, yes, but—"

"It sounds like God's blessing his little girl. Receive it! You could at least hear his story."

"I guess, but I'm afraid."

"Of what?"

"The truth."

Reaching out his hand, he took hers, holding it firmly. He looked into her eyes. "There's nothing to be afraid of. You can only gain from something like this, Kristy. The truth will set you free. Even if it's difficult."

"Will you go with me to meet him?"

"Me?"

"Yes, you. I don't want to go alone."

"Of course I'll go. But under one condition."

"What's that?"

"You let me ask him for permission to date you."

Blushing, she looked down. "He doesn't even know me."

"Kristy, you didn't have a father to ask before. Now you do. And he's a praying man. That sounds good, don't you think? I want to honor him with that position in your life. You need your father."

"I do?"

"Of course you do. Some have to do without their father and God makes it up to them, but I think this will help you. It's an amazing answer to your prayers."

"But I've gone years without a father. God is my father now. How can he just appear and assume that role after all this time?"

"I don't know. If he's able to bless you at all, it will be up to you to forgive him and receive him. It's your Father-God's blessing. Restoration of family and relationships. He's all about that."

She flopped back on the grass. "Oh, Billy, you're so wise." She sighed. "I thought I had forgiven him. But this is a whole new level."

Looking down at her, he smiled. "I'm sure you can handle it. God's with you." He sobered. "Hey, fill me in on what's happening with you. You're different."

Rising back to a sitting position, she smiled. "Is that a good different?"

He grinned. "Let's just say you look great. You glow. And you have peace and confidence that wasn't there before. I don't know if I can put my finger on it, but—"

"I am different. It's been a series of miracles for me. I wanted so much to share them with you, but something kept me back. I wanted to be healed. But for me."

He folded his arms and scowled. "I have to admit, I feel left out. I want to know why you moved out of my parent's house and why you quit school. It seems everyone knows more about what's happening with you than me. Do Derek and Sam know about this? Every guy at church was making eyes at you."

"You have a very active imagination." She rolled her eyes and elbowed him in the ribs. "You certainly weren't. You were scowling at me all morning. You hardly said two words to me. And by the way, did you *worship* at all?"

"Okay, you're right. But can you tell me what's happened over the last few months?"

Rising to her feet, she put her hand to the backside of her jeans. "Let's head for the house and find some chairs. I don't know about you, but I'm getting wet rolling around in this damp grass. And it's starting to sprinkle."

Billy and Kristy moved to lawn chairs on Rhonda's deck. With feet propped on the same footstool as Billy, Kristy shared her many experiences. They talked freely while enjoying the spring sunshine peeking through parting clouds.

"That's awesome, Kristy. So what happened when you were five years old?"

"The only thing I can think of is my brother was born that year. Somehow that was a very painful experience for me. I felt rejected by my mother and my father started working a lot. And it seemed like he and Mom fought all the time."

"Hmm... Maybe that was it. Whatever it was, it must've caused you a lot of pain."

"I remember feeling very alone and ashamed of who I was."

"Maybe your father can help you fill in the gaps when you talk to him."

"Maybe."

"Okay, so why did you quit school and move out of my parent's house?"

She groaned. "I couldn't bear going to any more psychology classes. It all seemed so dry and laborious." Her voice rose in defense. "I just wasn't excited about it anymore, and I don't know what I want to do with my life, so why get a psychology degree?"

Grinning, he turned to her. "You don't have to defend yourself to me. I was just curious. I wondered what you would do with it anyway. But I did think you would make a good counselor."

"I thought so too, but now I'm not sure."

"So why'd you move? And right before I got home?"

Kristy looked away. "I prayed for a job. ... Barewoods offered me this position. It came with room and board."

Billy studied her. "I get the feeling you're not being totally straight with me."

She paused and met his eyes. "No, I'm not. Do you have to know everything?" Rolling her eyes, she looked away.

Was there a hint of hurt in his eyes? It was no use. She might as well tell him.

"Okay, I'll tell you. I wanted to leave before you got home. I didn't want to live there with you there too. Can't you see it's a bit too *convenient*? And it's awkward for me." Facing him squarely, she noted his tilted head and puzzled frown. "Look, Billy. I want to be pursued. I want to know you really want me before I totally give you my heart. Do you understand? I think your father did."

Brows shooting up, his eyes widened. "You discussed this with my father?"

"Not exactly. But he told me he thought he understood what

I was doing when I left. I got pretty close to your parents over the last few months. I would've stayed there, but for the fact that you were returning."

Throwing up his hands, he rose to his feet and walked to the other end of the deck. "Okay, I understand. You're right. It was convenient for me. I can see how it would be healthier for you to live somewhere else. Less awkward." Leaning his elbows on the railing, he gazed out over the pasture and paused. Then he turned to her with a sheepish grin, still leaning on the railing. "Even though I really enjoyed having you there. We were able to spend a lot of time together and we *were* well chaperoned."

"That's for sure. Every time we had an argument, we had an audience. That last one was the worst. I was mortified when I found out your mother overheard me threatening you and trying to keep you from leaving for Spokane."

"So it's not about being *pursued*. You're uncomfortable with my family."

She shook her head. "No. I love your family. After all the experiences I went through over the last few months with them, it probably wouldn't bother me for them to see us fight." Blue eyes searched his. "Billy, I truly want to be pursued."

He spread his hands. "It's a little late for that, don't you think? I've already fallen in love with you." He smiled slightly. "And from the way you kissed me, I think you must at least *like* me."

Chin lifting, she said, "That's not the point. I want to know you have chosen me and are willing to put out some effort to win me."

"I have put out effort. You told me to get lost several times and I'm still here!"

"I don't think you've made up your mind about me yet. It was *you* that said, and may I quote, 'I don't think I could live with someone who—'"

"Kristy, you don't know how many times I've gone over that conversation." Scowling, he beat a fist on the deck railing. His gray eyes pierced hers. "I didn't mean it like it sounded. I'm sorry! I was trying to make a point."

"You made a point, alright. I don't want to get hurt again. I want to make sure you love me enough to put up with me. Even though I believe God has healed me and I'm growing day by day, there are no guarantees that I'll be able to behave myself! Or be totally healed in *your* eyes. I might blow up again. You may decide I'm not mature enough to stand by you. You may want to go farther in life than I am able to go. Or maybe you won't like the *healed* me. How can I know that I wasn't just a person you were trying to help and now that I'm healing, you'll lose interest?"

He turned away, wagging his head and running his hand through his hair. "I doubt that very much." Sighing with resignation, his eyes again met hers.

"So how do you propose that I *pursue* you?"

Smiling mischievously, she rose to her feet. "That, my dear, is entirely up to you." She opened the glass door and tossing her hair over her shoulder, sashayed into the house.

He followed.

GOING HOME

*And he took the children in his arms, put his hands on
them and blessed them.*   *Matthew 10:16*

Kristy's words echoed in his mind as he drove home.

That, my dear, is entirely up to you.

Elbow resting on the pickup's open window, he drove his
pickup toward home.

She was sure getting sassy. But she was probably right. He
didn't know the healed Kristy. It was a bit more convenient when
she was intimidated.

He chuckled. But he liked this new Kristy just fine. Yes, just
fine. She was still herself, just more radiant and bold.

He could hardly believe how bold! She didn't even get
embarrassed when he spied on her conversation with God.

And she didn't pull away.

She threw herself into his arms!

She had really changed.

He winced. He had a feeling he was going to pay for his comments about her blowing up at him.

"And 'afraid she won't behave for me?' What's with that, Lord? That's not exactly what I meant. Oh well, we'll get through it. I love her!"

So, how could he *pursue* her?

Would taking her to a prayer meeting on Friday night count? He had a lot to do in the next few days. Spring was upon them and the planting wasn't finished. The cattle needed to be worked and turned out to pasture. And she had herself all booked up watching Justine and Raine.

He was going to have to make plans ahead of time to spend time with her. He'd never done this kind of thing before.

"Jesus, could you help me out?"

෧♥❧–❦෧♥

Alone in her room, after Justine and Raine were in bed, Kristy pulled out her phone. She hesitated.

"Well, here goes!"

"Hello, this is Kristy."

"Kristy! You called back!"

She gulped.

"Uh … yeah … I did. … How's Mom?"

"She's a little better. … Have you thought about getting together with me?"

"Yeah."

"Where do you want to meet?"

"Uh … When do you have in mind?"

"I was thinking right away, but with your mother being sick and all, I'm not sure. Maybe a little later, when we know for sure she's going to be okay. I hate to leave Toby right now."

"Where are you?"

"We're at your mother's house. I'm staying here with Toby until she gets out of the hospital."

"Is Toby there?"

"Not at the moment, but I expect him back shortly."

"Should I call Mom?"

"That would be good. She's kind of doped up, but I think

she'd appreciate a call."

"I'll call her then. Call me when she gets out of the hospital and we can make plans to meet somewhere."

"Whatever you say, Honey. And that'll give you more time to get used to the idea."

After flipping her phone shut, Kristy stared out the window. As if she was going to get "used to the idea."

She opened the phone again and punched in the hospital number her father had given her. It rang several times before she heard her mother's groggy voice.

"Hello."

"Mom! This is Kristy. I heard you were in the hospital."

"Yeah. I'm here."

"I'm sorry, Mom. How are you?"

"Not so good."

"… I'm praying for you."

"You do that."

Silence.

"I love you, Mom."

A sniffle. The choked voice continued, "I love you, too. … I gotta go, the nurse is here. … Bye."

"Goodbye."

Click.

Kristy looked at her phone. "She sounds afraid. Oh, God! Please bless my mother. Heal her and help her!"

The following night, Billy was preparing for bed, when his cell phone blared from the dresser. He reached for it.

"Billy here."

"Billy … It's Kristy."

Eyes darting over to Joey, he noted his deep, even breathing. "Hey, let me go to another room. I don't want to disturb Joey. He's out cold."

He stepped out the door and entered the guest room. "How are you?"

"Not so good."

"What's up?"

"I talked to my mother last night and she didn't sound good. She was afraid." Her voice broke. "Billy, I'm worried about her. My father says he doesn't want to meet me until she's better. He's staying at her house with Toby. Billy ... Would you pray with me?"

"Sure. Father, give Kristy peace. We believe her mother's in your hands and you love her. Thank you for working in this situation. Draw her to your heart through all this. Give her peace and heal her body. ..."

Kristy sniffled. "Thank you."

"Are you feeling better?"

"Yes ... that helped. I hardly slept last night."

"Why didn't you call?"

"You were just here ... I ... I don't know."

"Kristy. I want you to call if you get like that, okay? Don't suffer alone. I want to be there for you. Stand in faith with you."

"I was hoping *you* would call."

He paused. "All right then. Every night I'll call you about nine thirty. Just to check on you ... Unless we're out together, of course. That okay?"

"Sounds good."

He chuckled into the phone. "Will that count as points on the *pursuing* thing?"

She laughed. "Every time you call, it's worth at least one hundred points. A really good call could be as much as two hundred."

"How many points do I have to earn for you to consider yourself *pursued*?"

"Hundreds of thousands!"

"Wow! That sounds overwhelming. Got any other suggestions?"

"Romantic gestures and sweet words get real high scores."

He laughed. "Good night, beautiful lady. Sweet dreams. I'll fall asleep dreaming of your deep blue eyes and dazzling smile. ... You'll fill my thoughts. ...My heart yearns for you."

"Hey!" She laughed. "Be serious!"

"I'm dead serious."

"Go to bed."

෧෮❡෮❧෧෮

Friday night, Billy found himself at the Prayer Room with Kristy. They'd sung and worshiped freely, praising and dancing before the Lord. They'd been caught up in joy. He'd never seen Kristy laugh like that before. Now he lay face-down on the floor, enjoying the sweet presence of God. The music soothed him, the atmosphere thick with love.

> *I come ... like a child*
> *Lift my arms ... like a child*
> *Hold me ...*
> *Hold me ...* [13]

He raised his head and peeked around the room. People were scattered everywhere, in quiet meditation. He smiled. Pulling himself up, he sat cross-legged against the wall, studying Kristy. She was lying face-up, not far from him, eyes shut and arms extended in the air. Tears streamed down the sides of her face and into her shining brown hair.

Oh, God! She's beautiful.

She looked so vulnerable lying there, calling out to God. His heart tightened. She had really been hurt by her parents. And ... life.

Restore her.

His eyes roamed down her still form, clad in T-shirt and jeans, feet bare. He caught himself and shut his eyes, letting out a small groan. This could be torture.

How long did he have to *pursue* her?

"Father, you told me she was the one. I'm ready!" he whispered.

What's your hurry?

He chuckled. "You know me, I'm always in a hurry."

He closed his eyes and returned his focus to worship without reservation. Pure joy filled the room. Hungry for a touch from

229

God, he and Kristy joined in. They laughed again.

Later, he helped her out to the pickup, both still laughing. After settling her in, he went around to climb in the other side. Pulling out onto the highway, he headed for the Barewood's.

Both he and she were silent. Unwilling to interrupt her thoughts, he didn't break the full and easy quiet.

After parking at the Barewood's, he turned off the ignition. His arm rested on the back of the seat.

"Kristy ... What are you thinking?"

"I have to go."

"Go?"

"Yeah. I have to go see my mother and my father. ... I have to face this. I need to see Mom and I want to see my father. I want to know what's going on up there."

"Let's leave at ten o'clock tomorrow morning."

She turned to him in the darkness. "Let's? You mean you'd go to Seattle with me? Tomorrow?"

"Of course. Do you think I'd let you go there alone? I remember what happened last time. No way is that going to happen again, if I can help it. I told you I'd go with you to see your father. Remember?"

"Yeah, but I thought—"

"Don't you want my company?"

"Of course! But it's such short notice. Are you sure?"

"Of course I'm sure. Do you think you could find some place on the floor for me? I'll bring my sleeping bag."

She smiled. "I'm sure we can find a place for you to sleep at Mom's house. Maybe Toby's room."

"Can you get a few days off work?"

"I think so. Rhonda will be home this weekend and she knows what's happening. She even suggested I take a few days and go up there."

"Can you ask her tonight?"

She nodded. "Sure."

"Then call me. If it's okay with her. We'll leave in the

morning." He hopped out and came around to the other side.

Sliding out of the seat onto the gravel driveway, she shut the pickup door and threw her arms around his neck. Leaning back, she raised her head to look into his face, her laughter returning.

"Thanks, Billy. I can't believe you'd do this for me!"

He chuckled. "My pleasure." He pressed his lips against hers in a soft kiss.

Kristy chatted nervously about her family while Billy drove her car.

"I called each one and told them you were bringing me," she said. "My father was excited to see me. ... Mom was concerned, but who knows what's up with her. She might be just groggy and sick. But Toby surprised me. He sounded great ..."

For a long while, he didn't break the silence. Glancing sideways, he studied her pensive face, her jean-clad form, long fitted top and shining hair pulled back in a pony-tail.

Beautiful.

She shifted and fidgeted and her athletic shoes twitched. Occasionally she took a long, deep breath.

"You're really nervous about this, aren't you?"

She nodded.

"Are you nervous about me meeting your family?"

She nodded again and swallowed, eyes fixed on the highway. "My mother keeps referring to your family as 'those people.' I think she's jealous that I have such good friends. The funny thing is, I would've loved to be closer to her, but she wouldn't let me. There seems to be no pleasing her." She paused. "I don't know how she's going to be to you. She has no idea that I ... that I ..."

With a teasing smile, he turned to her. "That you what?"

"That I'm ... going out with you."

"She'll get used to it."

For several miles, they were silent again. He gazed at her curiously. "What are you thinking?"

She sighed. "I'm thinking about my father. Memories are

coming back. He was always so … stressed out. I don't think he's going to live up to my fantasies."

He laughed. "Join the human race, Kristy. No father lives up to our fantasies."

Tears pooled in her mournful blue eyes. Sniffling, she opened her purse to get a tissue. "Kristy, what about your fantasies?" he probed. "Tell me about the father you've always wanted."

"Oh, I don't know." Her voice choked and she blew her nose. "I always feel so inadequate. So needy. Like I'm never good enough and I'm not trying hard enough. I guess I just wanted a father to hold me in his arms and tell me I'm okay. Even special. That he loves me just the way I am." She paused.

"Go on."

"I wanted someone who's at peace, no matter what I do." She giggled. "Someone who's not controlling, but has himself totally under control. I wanted someone who is firm, yet loving."

A long pause followed and she sighed. "When I was young, I used to fantasize about a father who, when I rebelled or disobeyed, disciplined me, but not in anger. He would tell me what I did wrong, maybe punish me a little, but only enough to get through to me. Then he would hold me on his lap while I cried. Comfort me and tell me I was his special little girl. Tell me he loved me and was there to protect me. I sometimes still think like that. Still long for it." After a watery laugh, she looked at him sideways. "You must think I'm crazy."

"No … not at all. That's beautiful, Kristy."

"Really?"

"Yeah. What you described is what Papa God wants to be to you. He's that kind of father. Jesus is gentle like that. He came to show us the Father. You know that, don't you?"

"Yeah. He is love. What I want is love. But I'm sad that I didn't experience this in my childhood, if you know what I mean. And it's too late now."

He smiled, shrugging. "Oh, I wouldn't rule it clear out. My lap's available."

She let out a short laugh. "You're driving."

"You want me to stop?"

"No." Rolling her eyes, she shook her head.

"I can also tell you what you did wrong," he said.

"Billy! I was referring to my *fantasies*."

He laughed. "I'm teasing you." Rubbing his beard, he continued, "I suppose it's healthy to fantasize about a good father. Good fantasies can be fulfilled in your relationship with Papa God. They're a longing for him."

He paused. "But some people think a father should be something like Santa Clause, giving you whatever you want anytime you want. The truth is, even if you'd had a good father all this time, you'd have found out that relationship takes work. A good father isn't a vending machine that's controllable and predictable. And a father's discipline is seldom pleasant. It's tough to take and not very romantic."

She stiffened. "Romantic? You're the one who told me to share my fantasies. I can't help but have them. You wouldn't understand anyway, having had such a good father. You were lucky. He takes good care of his family and is always gentle."

"Now, wait! Even though I have a good father, don't put him on a pedestal. Do you think he was *always* gentle? When I rebelled or disobeyed, he would get hopping mad sometimes. Although he never seriously hurt me, sometimes I wondered!"

Her chin lifted. "You're a guy. And you're really stubborn. I overheard him disciplining Hannah and he was very gentle."

"That's Hannah. She's the baby."

"Well, I heard him confronting Joey and he was gentle with him, too."

"Joey? He yells at him all the time. He's not mean, but you should hear him sometimes when he's out working with him."

Finally, she paused, looking out the passenger window. Neither spoke for several moments. "So, is he still tough on you?"

"Not now, but it was rough when I was young. He was never around and when he was home, he was frustrated. He's changed a lot. According to him, it took a God encounter and some serious repentance to get where he is today. And he's still far from perfect. He'd be the first to admit it."

Surprised, she stared at him. "Can you tell me about it?"

"Sure. When I was little, Dad was really uptight about the ranch. He worked all the time. I hardly saw him. Mom was lonely and feeling neglected. They fought a lot."

"Really?"

"Yeah. It was tough back then."

"How did it all make you feel?"

He shrugged. "Oh, I don't know. I was lonely, I guess. Dad was always stressed out or in the office when he was home. The thing that bothered me the most was the fighting between him and Mom. I suppose it scared me. Or made me feel insecure."

"What happened? How did he change?"

"I'm not sure about all the details, but when Cassie was little something happened. It was like he woke up. He started being a father. I guess it was a few years later that they finally had a break-through in their marriage. Not long after that, Mom got pregnant with Joey. I was eleven when he was born."

"Wow … I can't even imagine that! They're so much in love."

"They've always loved each other. They just needed more peace and a certain deliverance from evil. Like all of us. Dad would tell you they were blessed with renewal in their marriage. He attributes it to a filling of God's spirit and a revelation of His love and grace."

"How do you think all this affects you now?"

"Now? Well, that's a heavy question. I suppose I could blame my insecurities on the hurts of my childhood. Maybe that's why I have a short temper sometimes or why I'm a bit of a workaholic, but I'd rather just move on. I have a great dad who loves me. I've forgiven him for the past."

Smiling slightly, she let out a small hiss. "Sounds like you have issues. Maybe you need to talk to some older men and get some prayer and counseling."

Winking at her, he smiled. "I'm not sure what kind of issues I have. I've heard you discover that sort of stuff when you get *married*. Right now I'm fine with who I am."

"Don't you think that attitude is a bit dangerous? You don't see any room for improvement now?"

He shrugged. "Of course there's room for improvement, but I can't prune my own tree. I have no idea what needs to be done. I'll either be too tough on myself, or too easy. I just go along and trust God to take care of it." He winked at her again. "*Children* make a mess if they try to fix themselves."

"So, you're going to save all the heavy-lifting for after you're married?" she teased. "Poor girl, I'll make sure to warn her—" Dodging a playful swat, she hugged the passenger door, laughing with him.

He sobered slightly. "One thing's for sure, I've lost a few rough edges since I met you. Don't you think?"

"If what I've seen in the last week is any indication of your state, I think you have a few yet to go!"

DADDY AND MOMMY

They stopped in front of her mother's small white house. A short and well-muscled man sat on the front step, with thinning brown hair and smiling eyes.

Kristy froze.

Looking straight ahead, she grabbed Billy's hand. "Billy, that's him! Does he see me? I can't make myself look at him."

"Relax, Kristy. It'll be okay."

The man rose from the step and approached the passenger window of the car, wearing a friendly grin. He stood outside the car and waited a few seconds. When Kristy didn't acknowledge his presence, he rapped on the window.

She finally turned to him. Twinkling blue eyes met hers. She rolled down the window.

A wide, even grin spread across his face and his eyes

moistened. "Hey, Kristy! Is that you, girl?"

She nodded.

His smile broadened. "Of course it's you. I'd recognize you anywhere, but now you're more beautiful than ever!"

Kristy wasn't about to move, so Billy pried her fingers loose from his hand and got out of the car, walking around to the other side. He extended his right hand. "Mr. Turner. I'm Billy Watson."

Lifting his eyes from his daughter, James straightened and grabbed Billy's hand.

"James Turner ... Thanks for driving her up, Billy." Then turning back, he lowered his head and said, "Come on, Kristy. Are you going to get out of the car and greet me proper-like?"

Billy opened the door, reached for her trembling hand and helped her out. Hand clinging to his, her eyes stared ahead, avoiding her father's.

"Mr. Turner. Give her a minute, okay?"

Stepping back, her father relaxed, eyes full of understanding. "Sure. She has all the time she needs. Come on in." Turning on his heel, he led them to the house.

Hanging back, Billy asked softly, "Are you okay?"

Nodding, she squeezed his hand and whispered, "I think so, but please stay with me."

"I'm not going anywhere. Try to relax, okay? The worst is over. He's your *father* and he's really glad to see you."

"I know. It's just—"

"Shh. ... Let's go in." Billy stepped up to the open door.

James stood aside, then followed them in. "Have a seat. Can I get you a glass of water or something?"

Billy accepted for them both. "Please." Hand on her waist, he directed her to a love-seat in the front room and they sat.

Later, Toby came crashing through the door with a bag of groceries. "Kristy! You're here!" He headed for the kitchen to dump the food on the table.

Kristy rose and greeted him with a hug. "Hi Toby!" He

looked much the same, maybe a bit taller, but wore a white T-shirt with a fish on it and a big smile.

A fish?

What was that all about? This is the first time she'd seen him in something besides black for over a year. And she'd never seen him look so happy.

Toby beamed. "I see you've met Dad."

"Yeah. We met."

He looked up. "This must be Billy. The farm boy you told me about."

Billy extended his hand and the two greeted each other, grinning. "Yeah, I'm the farm boy. Glad to meet you, Toby. Your sister's told me a lot about you."

"Oh, no." He smiled at Kristy. "She probably told you how ornery I am. How long have you been here?"

"Not long."

"Did Dad tell you he's been calling Mom for nearly two months?"

Kristy's eyes flew to her father's serene face. "Really?"

He nodded, an awkward silence filling the room.

Toby plunged ahead. "Come on, Dad. Tell her the whole story."

They sat down and listened to her father share the story of why he disappeared.

"... I decided to move back east rather than fight to see you kids. When I was a kid, my parents went through an ugly divorce and fought over me and my younger sister. I vowed I would never put my children through such an ordeal. And I figured I didn't have much to offer you anyway. I had lost my career. I couldn't even get a decent job. I wanted to start over and begin a new life, so I ran. It was wrong, but that's how I felt at the time."

He pulled out a picture from his wallet of Kristy and Toby at ten and five years old. "I've carried this around and prayed for you all these years," he said. "But I wasn't on very good terms with God most of that time."

He then shared about his car accident the summer before. "I almost died," he said. "When I awoke, I wanted to, but I had a friend who kept praying for me. Lying in that hospital bed paralyzed, I was angry and disillusioned. … Still running from God."

"But I couldn't run anymore. In fact, I couldn't walk at all. I had no feeling from the waist down and no hope of ever walking again. Then, a few months later, Jesus *healed* me! It was a miracle! Through that experience, I turned my life back over to him. God met me and for the first time in my life I was convinced that he loved me and had forgiven me. He convinced me to find you kids and face your mother. I wanted to ask for her forgiveness."

His voice choked with emotion. "I was responsible for much of your mother's pain. She was very lonely. We weren't getting along and I worked all the time. I was also responsible for much of our marriage problems, since I had pressured her to have sex before we were married. She became pregnant with you, Kristy, and her parents were horrified."

Kristy's eyes went wide. "You mean—"

"That's right, we were married a whole year later than we always told you. She suffered from a lot of shame because of that, especially from the church."

"She was working as a youth leader at the time. I was a new Christian. When our moral failure was discovered, they made her get up in front of the whole church and confess her sins. She did it alone, because I refused to return to church and go through that. I had a bad feeling about it. I must have been right, because it made things worse. I think they were scared others would do the same as we did. They were right. Many of the young people in that church did. There were leaders there that blamed your mother for starting the whole downfall. I don't think she ever really forgave me for all that."

"After we moved from there, she lived in fear. She made me promise I wouldn't tell a soul. But it never went away. It came between her and me and between her and you, Kristy."

His voice caught. "She told me that every time … she looked at you, she remembered … what she'd gone through while pregnant with you. She just couldn't shake it—"

"Please, stop!"

So this was why she felt the barrier with her mother.

Why she always felt so abandoned and alone.

Like she never should have been born.

Something gave way. She doubled over and buried her face in her hands. Intense weeping shook her body. Billy stroked her back.

Her father came to kneel before her. Tears streaming down his face, he took her hands in his.

"I'm sorry, Sweetie, it was never your fault. All of this. You were a beautiful and innocent little girl. Your mother and I loved you, and still do. I take full responsibility. Will you forgive me for what happened with your mother before you were born and for all the years of rejection, shame and conflict? Please forgive me for not finding you and telling you the truth about all of this. I need your forgiveness for deserting you. I've always loved you. It was my fear that kept me away. My fear and my own pain and hopelessness."

Suddenly Kristy dove from the love-seat and fell into his waiting arms. They knelt there, holding each other, weeping.

Toby and Billy watched in awe. Billy rose and wiped away a few tears of his own. He crossed over to Toby. "Hey, why don't you show me around or something? I think these two have business to finish in private."

Toby smiled nervously, eyes moist. "Sure. Sounds good to me." He led Billy out of the room.

"Daddy … I … forgive you." Kristy said into his ear.

"Thank you, Honey. Let me get you a tissue." He pulled back, rose to his feet and left the room, returning with a roll of toilet paper. "Here. It's the best I could find around here. You want to sit awhile and visit?"

Back on the love-seat, she gave him a watery smile. "Sure."

He sat beside her, leaned back and took her hand. "Tell me about yourself," he said.

꧁ ꩜ ꧂

An hour later, Billy and Toby returned to find father and daughter seated, holding hands and conversing easily. They sat on the couch opposite them.

"What's been going on around here? How did you happen to be here now?" Kristy asked.

"I've been calling for over two months from Florida, trying to make contact with you or Toby. Your mother wouldn't tell me where you were and she wasn't too keen on reestablishing contact. She kept putting me off. I kept trying and I guess I stressed her out." He let out a short laugh. "That's what she said anyway. I found out later that she was diagnosed with appendicitis and went in for surgery about three weeks ago."

"I got a phone call from her early last week saying she was back in the hospital and very sick. She was frightened and worried about Toby. She said there was no one to take care of him if she were to die." He turned to her brother.

Toby nodded. "I was home alone at the time. And staying with friends. I guess she had a high fever and was freaking out."

"I was packed and ready to go. I hopped on the first plane I could find and flew to Seattle."

"How's Mom now?" Kristy asked.

Her father and Toby looked at each other. They didn't respond.

"Well?"

"Uh … She's not improving like they expected. I'm not sure what the trouble is. It's like she's depressed or something."

Kristy rose from the couch. "I'm going to visit her."

"I'm not sure that's a good idea, Kristy," Toby said.

"Why not?"

"She said to tell you not to come," her father said.

"What?"

"She said to tell you she's too sick to see you and that it would only upset her." Toby said. "Why do you think I didn't call and tell you she was sick?"

"That's a bunch of bull. I came all the way up here and I'm going to see my mother!" Kristy said. She stood and looked at the clock. "It's five thirty. We'll be back in a couple of hours. You guys can make dinner. I can't eat until I see her anyway."

James chuckled and shrugged. "Okay. See what you can do."

Kristy grabbed Billy's hand. "Well, come on. Let's go!"

〜⟩⟨〜

Billy drove, smiling at the irate woman letting off steam beside him.

"I know why she doesn't want to see me. She's ashamed! Dad comes up here and blows the lid off everything she's been hiding for all these years and she can't handle it! Well I'm not going to sit back and watch her wither away. She's my mother! I'm just relieved to know the truth!" Kristy leaned forward in the passenger seat of the car, eyes wide with passion and hands flailing in the air as she talked.

"She's hid in shame and guilt long enough. Does she think I don't know she's been struggling all these years? She keeps trying to cover everything up. Everyone knows something is wrong. One sin leads to another until she's convinced it's all too much for God! I, for one, am going to tell her what I know and let her know I forgive her. If I forgive her, God surely does! She must know this much after all those years of church!"

"You go, girl! Are you sure you know what you're doing?"

"Are you kidding? Of course I don't know what I'm doing! But my heart says I have to go see her and tell her I love and forgive her. I have to tell her that God loves her and her sin isn't too much for him. He bore the shame and she doesn't have to. Dad repented! She can too!"

〜⟩⟨〜

A conversation was going on in the room, so Kristy opened the door slowly and spotted her mother sitting up in the bed, face pale, thin and drawn. An I.V. pump clicked in the antiseptic-filled air. At the side of the bed, a meal lay untouched. The pastor's wife sat near, talking.

She knocked softly, the door partially open.

Her mother's eyes darted toward the door and widened. She went even paler, but forced a smile. "Kristy!"

Kristy entered, Billy at her heels. "I had to come, Mom." She crossed over and kissed her lightly on the cheek.

Turning to introduce Billy, Kristy said. "Mom … Mrs. Stuck. This is Billy Watson. He came with me to meet you."

Her mother gave him a weak smile.

Billy approached the bed and took her hand. "I'm pleased to meet you Mrs. Jones." He turned to the other woman. "And you, Mrs. Stuck."

The pastor's wife rose from her chair.

Her mother shifted in the bed. "You don't need to go, Jan. It's fine."

Mrs. Stuck sat back down and laughed nervously. "Well, I can't stay too much longer. But, like I was telling you, it's really too bad you're having so much trouble getting well. Life is rough. So many people getting sick with stuff I've never heard of before! I think there's got to be more toxins in our food. All those chemicals they use now-a-days, you know."

"Things are getting worse and worse every day. We all know that this world is going to hell in a handbasket. And God knows I'm tired. I would just as soon go to heaven and leave this place behind. But I'm still here. God knows there's still more people for me to beat into heaven before I die. That reminds me, I need to visit Tom Smith before I go. He's real bad and I'm sure he isn't saved."

"Also, there's another woman from church that I need to visit, who was just diagnosed with multiple sclerosis. She says somebody prayed for her and God healed her, but she looks the same to me. I think it's the medication. You've got to watch out, you know. There's so much deception anymore. People chasing after miracles. She could get her hopes up and then really get hurt. God has a reason for everything. Once I knew a guy ..."

Billy looked over at Kristy, his eyes shooting questions. She approached the bed, interrupting Mrs. Stuck's monologue.

"Mom, I need to talk with you about something. It won't take long."

"Oh. ... Of course you do. I'll be running along." Grabbing her purse, Mrs. Stuck headed for the door. "I'll try to come by tomorrow, Pat... Bye!" Waving, she was gone.

Billy followed her to the door and turned. "I'll be down the hall. In the waiting room."

Kristy went to the door and before shutting it, whispered, "Pray, Billy. I need you to pray."

Nodding, he tipped his hat and left.

Crossing over, Kristy sat on the side of the bed, close to her mother.

Scooting to the other side of the bed, her mother folded her arms across her middle and cleared her throat. She avoided Kristy's eyes. "This is not the time to bring up anything too intense."

Kristy didn't waver. "Mom, I love you. Whatever happens and whatever has happened, I still love you."

Her mother laid very still, staring straight ahead. Finally, she took a long, deep breath, but didn't respond.

"I know what happened before I was born. Daddy told me. I always wondered if there was something wrong with me, Mom—and why you always seemed so distant." Her voice choked. "I'm so relieved to know the truth. I'm so sorry about what you had to go through and how you were treated. I don't believe that was God's heart for you at all."

For once, her mother didn't argue. She sat in the same position, eyes daring to meet Kristy's for a short moment and then darting away, filling with tears.

Kristy plowed on. "It sounds like everyone around you was afraid. They were afraid of your failure and they were afraid of your sin. God isn't. He forgave us. Jesus proved it on the cross. He is love."

"I know, Mom. He's been loving me. And healing me. I've been so miserable and afraid. Now I'm forgiven and free! I, for one, am not here to punish you. I forgive you, Mom. I love you and forgive you. If I can forgive you—and you know me—the daughter who has fought with you all these years—then surely you can believe your father in heaven forgives you!"

Her mother bit her lip. "But you have no idea—"

"Mom. I know. You were a leader. You blew it. Then you were shamed. You were never restored. The shame and guilt has followed you all these years and tormented you. You've heard sermons condemning people like you. You kept trying to hide, trying to be good, go to church and make up for it, but it would never work. You were more and more miserable every day."

Hiding her face in her hands, her mother begged, "Stop! It's too late for me, Kristy. You know what I did to you. I made you get that abortion." Tears fell through her hands.

"And I never loved you like you deserved. I lied to you so many times." She groaned. "I couldn't tell you about your birth. I was too ashamed. Then I lied to you about your father. If he wouldn't forgive me for what I did, I knew you wouldn't! It was his best friend!"

Kristy laid her hand on her mother's shoulder. "Mom, I forgive you." Her voice caught. "I forgive you for everything."

Sobbing softly, her mother continued. "Then I did it again, Kristy. Last Christmas there was another."

"I know, Mom." Her voice choked. "I forgive you and Jesus forgives you. He loves you. He's the Savior." Tears dripped off Kristy's chin, falling on the bed sheets.

"I knew. I knew it was wrong. There was no excuse. I just couldn't help myself. I was a church leader. I was raised in the church. Why couldn't I stay pure? Why couldn't I? I know others fail and God forgives them, but I'm—"

"You're just like the others, Mom. You wanted to be loved

like everyone else. God knows. You're no better than them and no worse. You need love and forgiveness the same as they do. He loves you. He forgave the woman caught in adultery. You're just the same as her. Just receive forgiveness. And forgive yourself."

Her mother stilled, then lifted her head. "Do you really think there's hope for me? I always thought I was different than those kind of people."

"Of course there's hope, Mom. You're no different than anyone else. We're all failures and need God's mercy and love. Pride, doubt and fear are the only things that have kept you from being restored."

Dabbing her eyes with a tissue from the bedside table, her mother sniffled, then continued in a congested voice. "Well, I don't have much to be proud of now. I've blown it in every way possible. And doubt? How could I doubt now?" She gave a short laugh. "First your father comes and tells me he wants my forgiveness for all those years ago. Then he tells me he'll take full responsibility for all that went wrong between us and all that has gone wrong since. He doesn't know what he's saying. But if that isn't a miracle, then I don't know what is!"

Her mother looked at her. "Now you're here, after I told you to stay away. Telling me you love me and forgive me, after all you found out today. No. I can't doubt anymore. Maybe God does care about me."

"And what do I have to fear now? Everyone in my family knows what I've done. My church doesn't know, but I don't care what they think anymore. I'm tired of being stressed out and if something doesn't change, I don't want to live anymore!"

"Can I pray with you, Mom?"

She nodded and reached for Kristy's hand. "Please."

"Father. You heard my mother confess her sins. She needs you. She needs a savior. Jesus, be her savior and be her healer. I know you love her. Let her feel your love. ..."

෫෧ ෨ ෫෫෧

Billy entered the hospital room cautiously. The two teary-eyed women had their heads huddled together. He spoke softly. "Kristy, it's time to go. It's seven forty-five. Your father's expecting us for dinner. I don't know about you, but I'm hungry."

Kristy lifted her head, a joyous smile on her face. "Billy, how can you think about *food* at a time like this?"

He grinned, looking from Kristy to her smiling mother. Patricia's eyes and nose were red, but she seemed lighter, more alive and less pale.

Something was different.

"I'm sorry for interrupting you with such a mundane request, but I don't have to *think* about it. My stomach is chewing on my backbone and I'm out of gas. I'm about to fall over."

Both women laughed. Kristy rose and kissed her mother goodbye, still holding her hand. "Mom, we need to go. We'll come and see you tomorrow. Maybe you can get to know Billy better then."

Patricia smiled. "I think I'd like that."

Billy tipped his hat and smiled.

TROUBLE WITH THE KNIGHT

As a mother comforts her child, so will I comfort you ... (Isaiah)

The next morning, Billy walked into the living room where James sat in an overstuffed chair, reading. Billy cleared his throat. "Uh ... Mr. Turner, I need to ask you something."

James glanced over the top of his glasses, took them off and put down the book. "Go ahead, then. Shoot."

Billy laughed nervously and sat on the chair opposite him. He leaned back and crossed his ankle over his knee. "I want permission to date your daughter."

Brows raising, James smiled. "It looks like you're already doing so. From the way you two look at each other, I'd say it's a little late for permission."

Billy smiled. "You're right. We're fairly close. We've known each other since last spring, but we didn't start spending time together until fall. You weren't around then, but now that you are, I think it's important to have your blessing."

Her father leaned back in his chair. "You do? Well then, let's see. ... I can see you're a believer. What are your intentions?"

"Intentions?" Billy leaned forward, elbows on his knees. "I'm still *pursuing* her right now, by her request. When the time is right, I plan to ask her to marry me."

James's eyebrows shot up. "Oh? So this is not just permission to date her. You're asking for her hand in marriage?"

Billy grinned. "Pretty much. I'm in love with her."

"I see. ... Does she feel the same?"

"I don't know, but I think so."

James cleared his throat. "Do you have a job?"

"I work for my dad on our family's ranch. I also do some construction work for my uncle."

"Ranching? Do you think she would be happy as a farm wife? She's always lived in the city. And is she still afraid of horses?"

"Not anymore. I've been giving her riding lessons."

"Really? I thought maybe she'd outgrow that. When she was a little girl, I made the mistake of taking her out to a friend's ranch. I wasn't with her when there was a mishap. As far as I know, she's been afraid of horses ever since. It's good to know she's over it, but she probably doesn't have a clue about the demands of farming or ranching. Do you think she has any idea what she's getting into?"

Billy stiffened. "I don't know, but I think so. She spent some time with us this last year."

"That's good." He paused. "Are you in debt?"

"No. I've got some money saved and a few investments."

"What do you have for an education?"

"A college degree in business administration."

James looked down at the newspaper in his lap. "It's pretty hard for me to evaluate whether you and her are right for each other, after so short a time. I can't say. But you do seem to be a responsible sort of guy. And from what little I've seen, you treat her with respect. Go ahead and keep dating her. But keep me posted, okay?"

"Posted on what?" Kristy asked, entering the room.

"He wants to know how the two of us get along after we

leave."

Kristy looked back and forth between the two men. Noting their serious expressions, she frowned. "What were you two talking about?"

Her father laughed. "Don't worry. It was all good. Hey, are you three going to head over to the hospital this morning?"

Billy rose. "I think that would be good. We have to get back on the road this afternoon. Both of us need to be at work tomorrow."

Patricia sat on a chair when they entered her hospital room, her I. V. out. "Kristy! The doctor says my blood work is much better this morning. They're sending me home!"

Crossing over to her, Kristy sat on another chair and reached for her mother's hand. "That's wonderful, Mom. Does Dad know?"

Patricia's face fell. "No ... I haven't told him yet."

Toby pulled out his phone. "Don't worry, Mom. I'll call and tell him. I'm sure he can find someplace else to stay until he leaves for home."

"No, wait!" Patricia reached out her hand. "Give me that phone. I'll call and tell him. He's welcome to stay for as long as he wants. ... While I'm recovering."

Open-mouthed, her son and daughter stared.

She brought it to her ear and glanced up. "What? Don't look so shocked. He's your father. And I could use the help."

Wagging her head, Kristy said, "Whatever you say, Mom."

A few hours later, sunshine peeked through the clouds onto the rugged, evergreen landscape of Snoqualmie Pass. Kristy and Billy were on their way home.

"Billy, I just can't believe it. My father's saved! My mother's saved! God's healing her too. I prayed for her last night, right before you came in the room, and she got better! Isn't that awesome? They've both repented and Toby's well on his way to believing too. I never imagined God would do this so fast. Can you believe it?"

Billy turned his head and gave her a smile. "It is pretty incredible."

She smiled. "It is, isn't it? I'm so happy. My father *loves* me. He's in my life again. I know he's not perfect, but he loves me! That feels so good to know. He admitted he was wrong. He asked for my forgiveness. I never imagined that could happen. And Billy, my mother loves me! She asked my forgiveness! She cares!"

"Yeah. It's pretty cool."

She grabbed Billy's hand. "Oh, Billy. Thank you so much for coming with me. Thank you so much for your support. I couldn't have done it without you. You were there for me when I needed you. You've been there for me so many times in the last year."

He gave a little bow of his head. "You're most welcome. It was my pleasure."

She laughed, swatting his thigh. "Quit the formal act. Do you know you're my knight in shining armor?"

"I am?"

"You are." Kristy went silent, smiling to herself as she watched him drive. Dark curls teased the back of his collar, tempting her fingers. His neatly trimmed beard gave him a rugged outdoorsman appeal. One strong, tanned arm stretched out on the seat behind her and the other remained on the steering wheel.

She recalled her mother's recent words.

"I'm surprised at how handsome he is. And he's so polite. He really seems to be a nice, strong young man. When you said he was a farm boy, I didn't expect this! I think you really snagged a good one, Kristy. Don't let him get away!"

Kristy's smile broadened.

Studying him, she sobered. He seemed so serious and thoughtful this afternoon. And it had been too long since he'd kissed her. If it wasn't for the fact that he was driving, she would jump into his arms and bring him out of that heavy mood. He seemed … reserved this afternoon. Oh well, she couldn't expect him to be as excited as she was about all of this, could she? He was probably just tired. It had all been so intense. Yawning, she adjusted her position, eyelids heavy.

Billy glanced at her. "Hey. You had a full and emotional day yesterday. There's a pillow in the back if you want to take a nap. I'll be all right. I'll wake you if I get sleepy, okay?"

She yawned again. "Are you sure?"

"Of course." He turned back to her with a dazzling smile. "What are knights in shining armor for, anyway?"

δ⚬❥❥❦δ⚬

The sun glared on the road ahead and Billy reached for his sunglasses. Out of the corner of his eye, he studied his companion. Her head rested against the passenger door and her chest rose and fell in a slow, even rhythm. He smiled at the sight.

The words of Mrs. Stuck in the hospital room came back to haunt him.

You've got to watch out, you know. There's so much deception anymore.

No wonder she had such a hard time finding God. Watch out for deception? He let out a harsh laugh. Deception? From what he'd seen, most Christians were already deceived. They followed a form of godliness without power. Well, he wasn't settling for hopeless religion. He wanted God's Spirit, his presence *and* his power! Power for radical salvation, healing and deliverance.

Deep, heavy breathing came from the seat next to him and he turned to look again. The lines of Kristy's face were peaceful in sleep. Long, dark lashes lay on smooth, pink cheeks. Snuggling into the pillow, she let out a contented sigh.

So young. So vulnerable.

He snorted. Those looks could fool. From the way she went after her mother last night, she was as bold as a lioness.

And that with her own mother!

The bright spring sun and the hum of the engine caused his thoughts to wander to the words of Kristy's father. Not for the first time that afternoon.

Do you have a job? Are you in debt? What do you have for an education?

Billy shifted uncomfortably. There was something about that whole conversation that disturbed him. Really disturbed him. He scowled.

Suddenly, his lips thinned. He sighed, slamming his palm on the steering wheel. When he decided to ask her father for permission to date Kristy, he had no idea he would give him the third degree! So much for his desire to be right and proper.

Of course he had a job!

Did he think he was a bum?

And he didn't give him any credit for helping her get free of her fear of horses. That wasn't easy! He snorted. *Grow* out of it? That didn't happen. He had no idea what they went through.

How could he appear out of nowhere and then hassle him about his ability to provide for her? Like he had provided for her and protected her. He hadn't been there to protect her from the jerks that hurt her!

That whole conversation bugged him.

Had her father noticed?

Probably not.

I just kept smiling away, like I did that kind of thing every day— asking deadbeat fathers for permission to date their daughters.

Maybe he should have said something. But he was glad he didn't. It was best James didn't know he had upset him.

❦

Billy was strangely quiet. All she could get were grunts and one words responses. No smiles. No opinions. No lectures. Something was definitely wrong. He was not his normal light-hearted self. Now two hours from home, Kristy was getting curious.

Fully dark now, they stopped at a Burger King. Kristy sat across from him and quit trying to make conversation. He didn't even notice, but devoured his hamburger in silence, looking out the window.

"Billy, are you okay?" she asked.

He shook himself from his brooding thoughts, leaned back in the chair and stretched out under the small table, fingers fiddling with his paper cup. He looked up.

"What?"

"I asked if you were okay. You've hardly said a word since I woke up and you don't look happy."

"Oh, it's nothing. I'm just tired."

"Nothing?" She pursed her lips. "I don't buy that. I'm not allowed to hold things back, but you are? I don't think so. What's bothering you?"

He rolled his eyes. "Okay. There is something bothering me, but I didn't want to ruin your joy about the happenings in your family. I'll work it out. It's my problem."

"Be the macho man and work it out on your own? That's your solution? Okay, then, good luck!" Rising from her chair, she grabbed her purse and headed out the door to the car.

"Kristy, wait!"

After unlocking the door, she opened it and climbed in the driver's seat. He went around to the passenger door, opened it, and leaned over to peer at her. "Are you sure you don't want me to drive?"

"Positive. Get in."

Five minutes passed in heavy silence as they headed back down the freeway. Billy sighed from the seat beside her. "Kristy, don't get all huffy. I'm just not ready to tell you what's on my mind. It has nothing to do with you. It has to do with your father."

Her gaze flew to him. "You're bothered by my father? Why?"

Wincing, he looked out the passenger window. "It was something he said."

"Really? I thought you guys were getting along well."

"We were. I just … Can we discuss this another time? After I've had a chance to think about it and pray about it?"

She took a long breath, letting it out slowly. "You know,

you've helped me through a lot of stuff. Am I not allowed to help you? That hurts."

Billy grimaced. "Look, I promise I'll discuss it with you soon. Can you come with me to prayer on Friday night?"

"You're not going to talk to me about this until *Friday night*? That's a whole week! A whole week to brood?"

"I'll call you every night, like I have. ... We'll see."

They had just arrived back at the Barewood's from the Friday night prayer meeting, when Kristy said, "Okay, Billy, out with it."

He chuckled, pulling the keys from the ignition and leaning back in his seat. Both were distracted at prayer and the air was thick between them. Conversations over the phone were stilted throughout the week and Kristy was done waiting. Things were no better.

"You're still not okay. I can tell. I want to know what's eating at you."

Billy played with the keys, exhaling in resignation. "I asked your Dad for permission to date you."

"You did? Did he refuse or something?"

"No. He said go ahead. And keep him posted."

"What's so bad about that?"

A long silence ensued.

"Billy?"

He answered softly, looking out the window. "He gave me the third degree. He wanted to know if I had a job, if I was in debt, what kind of education I had—"

She laughed. "So? What did you expect?"

"I don't know what I expected. It just bugged me. He acted so protective. But he's been gone! You've been anything but protected. All kinds of jerks have gone out with you without such inquisitions and you've been hurt real bad—"

Chin lifting, her blue eyes flashed. "And finally, a decent guy like you comes along and my father doesn't understand that he's supposed to bow down and kiss your feet. He doesn't understand that he should be grateful that finally you have come along to rescue his *defiled* daughter and bless me with your presence. He didn't give you the proper *respect*, did he?"

"Wait, Kristy—"

"It's true, isn't it? You were the one who wanted to ask his permission to date me. You said I needed a father and I needed his blessing. Silly me! To actually believe you meant what you said! But you didn't really want him to do his job, did you? It was all a formality to make you look good. You thought he should recognize how lucky he was to have someone like you interested in me. After all, I'm damaged goods. I should be an easy catch for you. Someone who can remind you of how clean and good you are in comparison. You know ... you're stuck up and you're proud!" She opened the pickup door.

"Kristy!"

"It's true. ... Isn't it?"

He stared at her.

Slamming the door, she turned and ran into the house.

"Hey, girl! How are you?"

"Dad! I'm so glad you called."

"What's up?"

"I need to talk!" Kristy scampered out the sliding glass door to the Barewood's back deck, cell phone in her ear. This was the second time in the past week she had talked to her father, but this time she was bursting with frustration. And indignation.

"Are you okay?"

She sniffled. "No. I'm *not* okay. ... It's Billy."

"Billy? It's still not better?"

"No. It's worse!"

"What happened?"

"Oh, Daddy! Remember I told you there was something bothering him about his visit with you? He finally told me. He was offended that you put him through such an *inquisition*."

He paused. "Really? What did he expect?"

"I don't know. He's been good to me, but I'm starting to see another side to him. He's proud! He thinks he's better than other people. He thinks I'm wounded and he's trying to use me to make himself look good!"

"Now wait a minute, Honey. Don't you think you're being a bit hard on him? He seems like a good, decent kid. Every young man struggles with pride."

Unable to hold back any longer, Kristy burst into tears. In a choked voice, she continued, "Well, this time it was bad. We had a fight. ... He really aggravates me sometimes. ... He hasn't called or talked to me ... since."

"When was that?"

"Last night."

"Honey, give him time. It'll be okay."

⟡

Billy turned the tractor around a corner. The sun was going down, but the lights beamed ahead, showing him the way. Kristy's words rang in his thoughts.

"You didn't really want him to do his job, did you? He didn't give you the proper respect, did he? ... After all I'm damaged goods! His defiled daughter ... I should be an easy catch for you. You're stuck up and you're proud!"

"Oh, my God! I'm busted. She's right. It's so easy to preach at her about the right thing to do and the proper ways to act. 'Be a child,' I tell her, but when it comes to actually doing it, I'm worse than her. ... I did have a bad attitude about her father."

"What should I do?"

He frowned. "There was a reason I didn't want to tell her why I was bothered. I wanted to deal with it on my own. But no, I had to blab the whole thing and now she's mad. Here we go again. Will I ever get past having to go to her with my tail between my legs, apologizing for sticking my foot in my mouth?"

"Lord, why do I get the feeling you're laughing?"

⟡

Sitting on the aisle next to Hannah, Kristy waited for church to begin. Billy approached and squatted beside her. She stiffened.

"Can we talk?"

She didn't look at him. "You didn't call me last night."

"I know. I thought it'd be better to wait and talk to you in person. Mom said I could invite you to come for lunch. We could take a walk afterward."

She looked down at her clenched hands. "I suppose I could do that."

"Good." Rising to his feet, he returned to sit with Jeff and Cassie.

Billy lifted his voice. He missed singing. He needed it. Something about worship helped to put everything in proper perspective.

Pastor Evan walked to the front and opened his Bible.

"Turn with me to Luke chapter nine, verse forty-seven." He read aloud.

> *"Jesus, knowing their thoughts, took a little child and had him stand beside him. Then he said to them, 'Whoever welcomes this little child in my name welcomes me; and whoever welcomes me welcomes the one who sent me. For it is the one who is least among you all who is the greatest."*

He moved from the podium and came close to the front row. "Dawn, would you bring up Gavin?"

Dawn brought her little grandson to the front and set him on his feet. He looked to be about two years old. Pastor Evan squatted down beside him. The little boy wrapped his arms around Dawn's leg.

"Is it okay if I tell these people what a wonderful example you are to us?"

Gavin nodded, eyes big.

Pastor Evan stood.

"It's not whoever has the most wisdom, the

most powerful gifting, the best record of behavior, or has been a Christian the longest that's the greatest among us. No, Jesus says it's the *least* among us who is the greatest. It's the one who's most like this little child—and the one who receives the little child. When we welcome the least, we welcome God himself."

"We all want to be significant. We want to think well of ourselves and have others think well of us. God doesn't have a problem with that. A child is like that."

"But in a loving home, a little child receives love apart from his performance or position. He realizes his significance and value because of his parent's love. He doesn't get offended when others don't recognize how great he is. He's happy to be just who he is. ..."

Billy heaved a sigh, leaned back in his chair and folded his arms across his chest.

DADDY HELPS

The wolf will live with the lamb. ... and a little child will
lead them.   *(Isaiah)*

Kristy pulled her green Pontiac into the Watson's driveway. The sun was shining that Sunday afternoon and the air was unseasonably warm. Eyes roaming the wooded landscape, she noted the new grass on the hillside. At the side of the barn, she parked her car, opened the door and inhaled the fresh spring air.

It smelled good ... Pleasant ... Peaceful ... Like she remembered.

Hannah ran to meet her, a broad smile lighting her face. "Kristy! You came for lunch! I've missed you around here!" She enfolded her in a warm embrace. Turning, her arm remained around Kristy's waist as she led her to the house.

"Hey! Come out and take a ride with me after dinner, okay? The horses need the exercise. Cassie hasn't been out here much. She and Jeff were here last week, but are busy with something else today."

When they reached the porch, a pickup door slammed and

Kristy turned to see Billy approach from the driveway. "We'll see, Hannah. Billy invited me, so I think he'll want to lay claim to me. At least for a while."

"Oh." Hannah's face fell, eyes traveling to Billy's. "I suppose he'll monopolize you the whole afternoon."

"We do have a few things to discuss," Billy said, eyes finding Kristy's.

After lunch, Billy and Kristy left the house and ambled up the hill. Dressed in a light jacket and jeans, her hands remained in her pockets and a cool breeze blew long strands of hair across her pensive face. Neither spoke.

When they reached the pond, Billy sat on the log and patted the space beside him. Leaning back on a tree trunk, he stretched out his long legs.

"You were right, you know. I *am* proud. I knew it was wrong for me to get offended at your father, but I did."

She sat beside him, saying nothing.

"I didn't want to tell you. I was trying to get over it on my own. I knew it would upset you. I didn't want to tell anybody. It wasn't until after you reacted that I realized just how bad my attitude was. Do you really think you're 'damaged goods?' Kristy, I don't feel that way at all. And do you think I'm a snob? Do you think you are 'defiled' and should be an 'easy catch'? Someone to help me 'look good?'"

"Not really. I'm sorry, Billy. I guess I'm a bit defensive. I want you to love my father. And treat us both as if none of this had ever happened. Treat us as healthy, whole individuals. You told me you wanted to do that. But you didn't. It was like throwing my past and my father's in my face."

He heaved a sigh, folded his arms and stared out into the trees. "So much for being your knight in shining armor."

She smiled at him. "Oh, you're a knight all right. But it would help if you took off your armor once in a while so I could see who you are and what you're feeling."

He turned to her, eyes twinkling. "How can I be a knight without my armor? I kinda like it. But I'll try to take it off for you. It might stink under there, but you're worth it.

"So do you think you can forgive me? I had to go and spoil your new joy with a bad attitude."

"I forgive you. Will you forgive me for calling you a snob?"

"Of course. I don't seem to practice what I preach, do I?"

"Sometimes not. But you have some good wisdom to share. My father liked you, you know."

"He did?"

"Yeah. I told him you got offended with his inquisition and he defended you."

He straightened. "You what?"

"I told him you were offended. Don't worry, Billy, he said—"

"Don't worry? You tell your father I'm offended after I've just met him and you don't want me to *worry*?"

"Yes. I had to tell someone! It was kind of traumatic."

He groaned. "Kristy that was a personal conversation between the two of us. If I had known you were going to tell him, I wouldn't have said anything."

"He's my father! We used to be close. He asked how I was and I told him. I shared the problem with him and he helped me get a little perspective." Her chin lifted. "I'm glad I told him. I haven't had a father or mother to talk to in a long time. Was I supposed to clam up because of your pride? Excuse me, but I didn't think of that!"

He looked away. Did she have any consideration for his feelings? Would she go to her daddy with every little disagreement?

"Well, now that I know what you'll do with personal information, I'll try to remember next time we have a private conversation."

Kristy's eyes widened. She rose from the log and faced him, lower lip quivering. "This just may be the last *private* conversation we'll ever have! You can't trust me to protect your pride and I can't trust you to be ..." Voice trembling, a tear escaped down her cheek. "... transparent and humble enough not to get offended! Good-bye, Billy!" Wiping her face with a shirt sleeve, she turned and ran, down the path and back to the house.

Hands clenched in his pockets, he ambled to the edge of the trees, where he could view the ranch compound. She emerged from the house, got in her car and sped away. Grimacing, he picked up a stick and threw it as far as he could, growling in frustration.

Returning to the log, he buried his face in his hands. For a long while, he sat, eyes closed and head buried. Churning. Finally, he lifted his gaze, leaned back against a tree trunk and studied the smooth, still pond, surrounded by pines and firs. He rubbed his beard. The wind had stopped and the stillness was only occasionally interrupted by a small bug, skimming across the pond's smooth, glassy surface.

He leads me beside quiet waters. He restores my soul.

"Isn't my soul supposed to be like that? All quiet, still and peaceful, with only minor interruptions to the tranquility? Kristy sure gets me riled, Lord. You told me to go for it. And I did. Now I'm in love with her. ... But this isn't easy. I tried to apologize and I only made it worse!"

Why am I so bothered?

"I guess I didn't know she would expose me like that. I've always been a private person."

What are you hiding?

"I don't know. ... I guess I did hassle her about this very thing last summer. ... She wouldn't have gotten this far if she kept everything to herself. I've been proud of how she's opened up and received from people. ...

You're laughing again, aren't you? ... It's not funny. Is this going to work? ... That was a rough exchange. Not exactly romantic. So much for trying to apologize. What do I do now?"

Get help.

෧෩෨෪෧෨

Hannah was saddling Ginger when Billy opened the barn door. "You still want some company on that ride?"

Her flashing brown eyes rose to his. "I'm not sure I want to ride with you. What did you do to Kristy? She left crying!"

He reached for the saddle, carried it over to Blackfoot's stall and threw it on his back. "We had words. It was my fault, of course."

Her voice sounded from behind him. "Of course it was your fault. Kristy's sweet. Why don't you just ask her to marry you and get this over with? You're in love with her, aren't you?"

"Yeah. But it's complicated."

"Oh phooey! It's not that complicated! You two are madly in love and we all have to watch while you play cat and mouse, each unsure about the other's affections. Just tell her she's everything you ever wanted in a woman and you need her desperately. Then she marries you and you live happily ever after. Of course, you may have a few spats, but at least when you're married you have to face each other every day and work it out in privacy. Now you wait days and even months being upset while you torture yourselves and everyone watching!"

He let out a short laugh. "You have this whole thing figured out, don't you?"

She smiled. "You learn a lot watching an older sister and brother with their romantic relationships. You and Cassie are a lot alike. Both stubborn and proud."

Billy led Blackfoot out of the barn and Hannah followed with Ginger. He mounted. "And I suppose you're not proud?"

She mounted. "Of course I'm not. I'm the baby, remember? I'm humble. I have to be to survive around here." Laughing, she took off galloping. "I'll race you to the creek!"

Billy looked up, smiling crookedly. "Lord, is this your idea of help?"

🙟❦🙝

Laughter from the front room greeted Hannah and Billy when they came in the back door an hour later. They had company. Grandma and Grandpa Watson. Hannah removed her dirty boots and ran for it, stocking feet sliding on the kitchen linoleum. "Grandma! Grandpa! I didn't know you were coming!"

"Oh, we just got restless and decided to go for a Sunday afternoon drive to visit our favorite people." Grandpa said, hugging her tightly, eyes filled with mischief.

"Hey! How's my number one grandson?" Grandma asked from across the room when Billy appeared.

He went to embrace her. "Good."

After hugging his grandfather also, he sat on the couch, leaning back and sighing.

"He's not that good," Hannah said. "He just had a fight with his girlfriend." She rolled her eyes. "It seems there's a lot of that around here lately."

"Did she dump you?" Grandpa asked.

Billy blushed beneath his tan. "Maybe."

"Maybe? You mean you don't know?"

Ben spoke up. "Hey, Dad. Give the guy a break."

"It's kind of complicated," Billy said.

"Yeah. I know. Matters of the heart aren't easy. I remember when I was dating your grandmother. She had a way of always keeping me off balance. Still does."

"And you are *so* balanced," Grandma interjected, smiling. She picked up her knitting from the bag beside her and began working the soft yarn with needles.

Grandpa chuckled. "See what I mean? She keeps me humble."

"That's a woman's job, isn't it?" Linda said. She stood and stretched. "Would anyone like a cup of tea?"

§❧ ❧-❦§❧

"Dad, do you have a minute?"

The two were left alone in the living room after Grandma and Grandpa left. Billy put down his guitar and looked up. "Could we talk?"

Ben laid down his newspaper. "Sure, Son. What's up?"

"It's Kristy. I think I really blew it."

"I noticed she was crying when she left. What happened?"

"It's a long story."

"I've got time."

After Billy forced himself to share the story with his father, he sat back. "So what do you think?"

Ben smiled. "You've met your match in Kristy. She's not going to let you go on with business as usual."

"Business as usual?"

Laughing, Ben continued, "You've always been one to 'play your cards close to your chest,' if you know what I mean. I was the same way. She'll draw you out. You'll have to get to know yourself."

Billy snorted. "I'm not sure I want to know myself."

"Trust me. It's a good thing. And by the way, Billy. Was it *me* that taught you to be ashamed?"

"Ashamed?"

"Yeah. Ashamed of your feelings. So you were offended. Do you have to hide it or justify it? Admit it. Deal with it boldly. I would venture to say if you had admitted it from the beginning, you would've fared better. You might've even been able to laugh about it together. Shame doesn't look good on you, Son. And you have nothing to be ashamed of. You're a child of the King."

Billy leaned forward with elbows on his knees. He sighed, staring at the fireplace.

"Sounds like you're stuck."

"Yeah. Looks pretty hopeless to me."

"Hopeless? I wouldn't say that. But I have a question."

"What?"

"Why was your fuse so short with Kristy this afternoon?"

"I don't know."

"Make a stab at it. What did you feel?"

"Anger."

"Well, that could be. That emotion feels safe. Even powerful.

I would venture to say you were feeling something else when she told you she talked about you to her father."

"What?"

"Probably fear."

Billy sat in thoughtful silence.

"You're right."

"You'd get farther if you told her what you felt instead of biting her head off. Try something like, 'That scares me.'"

"That sounds vulnerable."

"How can you have *intimacy* without being vulnerable?"

Rubbing his beard thoughtfully, Billy's eyes found his father's. He smiled crookedly. "Yeah. But that doesn't mean I like it."

Ben snorted. "Get used to it."

"So what should I do now? I told her I wanted her to fight with me. But now I'm not sure I like it."

"How about fighting different? Learn how to fight for connection. Share your feelings without judgments or threats."

"Feelings? I guess I'm not too good at that. I'd rather give advice when she shares hers. Up to now she's liked my advice and claims she listens to me, but I guess I don't follow it myself. All along I've been encouraging her to open up, not be ashamed and be a child again. Then she nailed me on it." He sat back, raising his voice an octave. "Silly me! To actually believe you meant what you said!"

Ben chuckled. "You've got a tough one there. She'll keep you in touch with reality."

"Yeah, yeah, I know. This is all well and good, but I don't know what to do now. She's hopping mad. And has probably lost patience with me."

"Relax. I doubt it's all that bad. From what I know of her, she's not one to give up easily." Ben paused and tilted his head, peering at Billy curiously.

"You've had a pretty level head about this whole thing with her and her father. For the most part, I'm proud of how you've handled yourself. But I'm curious. Doesn't it seem a *noble* thing for him to look out for his daughter like that? It doesn't sound offensive to me. If it were one of my daughters—"

"I know!" Billy sprung to his feet and paced the carpet. "It's just …"

"Just what?" Ben said, leaning back and studying his son.

"He abandoned her! She's really suffered from it! And she's been unprotected. Guys have really hurt her."

"And you've suffered because of it. And you may suffer more."

"Me?"

"Yes. You."

"Oh. I suppose you're right."

"Will you forgive him? That's what Kristy had to do."

Billy sank to the couch.

"And how about Kristy? Have you forgiven *her*? You don't act like it. Why else are you so defensive, self-protecting, and untrusting?"

Billy remained silent.

"And another thing you could do, Son. Renounce your judgments of her parents. You have no idea what you would've done in their shoes. Honor them. Bless them. Trust me, I learned the hard way about this. They're her parents. Honor them and you'll both be blessed. Things just work that way if you want grace to flow."

Billy swallowed. "Do you think it's too late?"

"Nah. There's plenty of grace if you humble yourself. Snapping at her is getting you nowhere. It doesn't help to just feel bad about it. Or say you're sorry. She needs to see you've changed. And you can't change yourself. None of us can. You need God's grace. So humble yourself. Ask for it."

"Is that what you did?"

"That's right. I still do it."

"Could you pray for me?"

"Sure."

Kristy was on the deck again, alone. It was Tuesday, two days since she visited the ranch. Tears rolled down her cheeks and she angrily swiped them away.

"He hasn't called me and there's no way I'm calling him!"

Was her heart going to be broken again?

This was worse than ever.

She tried to protect herself against this stuff, but here she was again, eating her heart out over some guy. She was in love with the jerk and he wasn't going to call.

Her words came back to her.

This just may be the last private conversation we'll ever have!

"Why did I threaten him and run?" She grabbed another tissue, dabbed her tears and added it to the filling wastebasket she had brought out just for this purpose. She sniffled. "Why do I do that?"

Is this your 'armor?'

"But look what he does to me!"

Love endures all things.

Kristy blew her nose. "I'm enduring, all right. And *suffering* long."

Her phone blared from her pocket. She retrieved it, taking a quick look at the caller I.D.

Dad.

"Hello."

"Hey, my girl! How are you today?"

"Not so good," she said, voice dull.

"Do you have a cold or something?"

"Or something."

"What's wrong?"

"Billy."

There was a long pause.

"You're fighting again, aren't you? Want to tell me about it?"

"Last time I told you ..." She paused. "Oh, Daddy! I don't know what to do. He hasn't called in two days. I went to his house for dinner and he tried to apologize, but then I had to go and tell him that I talked to you and you knew he was offended. He got mad again. He said I betrayed his confidence. I just didn't think! I needed someone to talk to. I thought that was what fathers were for. He's the one who encouraged me to accept you back in my life and totally forgive you. He's the one who told me I needed a father and needed his blessing. But it's all gone so wrong. Oh, Daddy! I ended up leaving mad after threatening to never talk to him again!"

"Hmm ... Are you in love with him?"

Sniffling, she paused, then choked out, "Yes ... I do love him. He's helped me through so much even when I was really mean to him.

"I was hurting and ashamed of what I had done, and I told him. He was so gentle and accepting. He says he loves me and for the most part, I believe him. I've been worried that he might consider me a project, but lately he's been the one with the attitude!"

"Is this the man you want to marry?"

"Marry? He hasn't asked."

"What if he did? What would you say?"

"Uh ... yes! I'd say yes, even if he's being a jerk right now. He's the first guy I've met that I can trust. He *listens* to me. He loses his cool every once in a while, but he always comes back and apologizes."

"He's decent and stable, Daddy. He has a good heart and would be a good provider and father. He's a man of faith. I can't think of anyone else I would rather marry. But don't worry, there isn't much chance of him asking. We can't even carry on a conversation without yelling at each other!"

He chuckled. "You'll work it out."

"I wish I had your confidence, Dad. That reminds me, how are you and Mom getting along, living under the same roof and all?"

He laughed. "Fine. Actually, real fine. She's doing well and I expect to be leaving here soon. But I think I'll move to Seattle, to be closer to Toby. He says he wants me here."

The next day, Billy finally called.

"Hi, Kristy."

"Hi."

"I've missed you."

Kristy's heart rose in her chest and tears threatened. "Me too."

"I'm sorry. It was all my fault. You're right. It's *me* that needs to change. I couldn't bring myself to call you before now. Every time we talk, I blow it. Do you think you can forgive me?"

"Yes. I forgive you. And I'm sorry for threatening you."

"Threatening me? Did you threaten me?"

"Yeah. I said I thought it might be the last private conversation we would ever have, remember?"

He chuckled. "Oh that. I deserved it."

"I shouldn't have said it. I didn't mean it." She choked. "You mean a lot to me. Will you forgive me?"

"Of course. Do you think you could sing with me the Sunday after next? I'm leading worship again."

"That's fine. But Billy, I can't come to the ranch that Saturday and practice. I have to work and my father's coming to town that evening. He wants to take me out to dinner."

Billy paused. "How about practicing with me the Friday night before?"

"That would be fine."

"By the way, you can tell your father anything you want to about me. He's your father. I'm okay with it. I was afraid. And offended. You can tell him I'm an unreasonable jerk if you want to. I was one."

"I might."

He laughed. "Okay then. I'll try to behave myself from now on. Kristy?"

"Huh?"

"I love you."

"I love you too. ..."

"I'll call you tomorrow, okay?"

"Okay."

Kristy flipped her phone shut and sighed.

She could have called him first.

And should have.

THE KNIGHT SHINES AGAIN

How beautiful your sandaled feet, O princess daughter!
Song of Songs 7:1

"You look beautiful, Sweetie!" James Turner stood at the Barewood's front door, dressed in a dark suit. Twinkling eyes admired Kristy from head to foot. She had dressed to please him in a solid blue dress that clung to her curves and brought out the sapphire blue in her eyes.

She embraced him and lifted her cheek for a kiss. "You look handsome yourself, Dad."

"Thank you. I'm taking out my special girl." He smiled, wiggling bushy eyebrows.

He opened the passenger side of the car and she got in. Then he went around to the driver's side. "I hope I'm not interrupting your weekend. I know that special guy of yours will be missing you."

Her face fell. "I doubt it."

His eyebrows shot upward. "Oh?"

"He apologized to me, but we haven't gone out much. When

I was there last night to practice worship, he wasn't talkative. It's like he's holding back, afraid to bring up certain subjects. He hugged me, even kissed me, but made it clear he wanted me to go home early last night. It was ten o'clock! On *Friday* night!"

He turned the key in the ignition and took off for the highway. "That's too bad. He's probably busy or something."

"Yeah." She rolled her eyes. "Or behind on his sleep. And he didn't call me every evening last week like he said he would."

Her voice choked. "Things just aren't the same, Daddy. He seems distant." A tear escaped and she groaned, grabbing a tissue from her purse. "I told myself I wouldn't do this."

Her father smiled and placed an arm around her shoulders. "It's okay. You can cry all you want. I don't mind."

They arrived at the chosen restaurant, a cozy place in downtown Wallua Crossing. The hostess seated them at a private table and her father pulled out a chair for her.

Taking up the menu, he sat and scanned the restaurant. After a pause, he said, "Hey, look who's here!"

"Kristy turned around and gasped. "Billy? What are you doing here?"

Billy sat at a table behind them, dressed in a black suit. He rose and came to them, a sheepish grin playing on his lips. "I came to eat with a special girl."

Kristy froze.

A special girl?

Dizziness washed over her. No wonder he'd been distant. And it didn't even bother him! She looked away.

"Hey, why don't you join us? There's a *special girl* here with me." Her father said. "You don't mind, do you, Kristy?"

She stiffened, looking first to her father, then Billy. Her eyes returned to her father, pleading.

Daddy! Don't!

He ignored her and motioned to Billy. "Sit down. We'd love to have you join us."

Billy hesitated. "I need to check on something first." He

turned and left.

Eyes wide, she turned to her father with tight lips. "Daddy! What are you doing? It looks like he's here with someone else. This is horrible!" Grabbing her purse and coat, she rose. "I lost my appetite. I can't stay."

He took hold of her arm. "Wait, Honey! Don't leave."

She halted. Maybe it was his sister. Or … his mother. But why would he tease her like this when things were already so strained between them? She'd had enough!

"Come on. Trust me. Sit down."

Lips compressed, she willed herself to sit. For her father.

Billy emerged from the kitchen carrying a large bouquet of red roses. He set them in the middle of the table and Kristy's eyes went wide.

A waiter appeared, carrying his guitar. He pulled up a chair, saying nothing. After setting the guitar near Billy's seat, the waiter smiled, bowed and left them.

She squirmed in her chair. "Uh … Who are those for?"

"You."

She stared at him. "Me?"

"Yes, you. You're the special girl."

"You mean you were waiting here for *me*?"

He nodded, his grin returning. "Yep."

"But why?"

Billy exchanged a conspiratorial look with her father. He smiled, reached for his guitar and put the strap over his shoulder. Strumming a chord, he began to sing.

> *Like a river flows surely to the sea*
> *Darling so it goes, some things are meant to be.*
> *Take my hand, take my whole life too,*
> *For I can't help falling in love with you …*[14]

In a public restaurant? This was so unlike him.

Why was he doing this?

And why did her father look so smug?

He knew!

She squirmed.

They were making a spectacle. The people at the surrounding tables stared, enthralled with the scene. They smiled, whispering to one another.

The song ended and Billy sat.

Her father rose and cleared his throat. "I think I'll visit the restroom. I'll be back in a minute." He turned and departed.

"Why are you here?" Kristy whispered.

"Because I have a question for you."

He stood, then descended to one knee. "I know this is a surprise. And I've been a jerk lately. But I've been busy—"

"Billy—"

"Shh!" He smiled crookedly. "Listen for once, will you? I'm in the middle of something serious." He reached into his shirt pocket and produced a sparkling ring. She gasped.

His grin widened. Then he sobered. "I need you desperately, Kirsten Turner. You are very good for me. In fact, you're everything I've ever wanted in a woman and I'm madly in love with you. Will you be my wife?"

Mouth hanging open, she stared at him.

Chuckling interrupted them. "Are you going to answer the poor guy?"

Her father.

He stood at the table behind her, apparently having never left for the restroom. Stepping forward, he laid a hand on Billy's shoulder and smiled broadly. "I want you to know you have my blessing. I'm all for it."

She paused, eyes traveling from Billy's questioning gaze to her father's smiling face. Suddenly, she laughed and jumped into Billy's arms.

"Yes! ... Yes, I'll marry you!"

He rose to his feet and lifted her off the floor. Cheering erupted around them and they turned their heads. Everyone in the restaurant was on their feet, clapping. Billy and Kristy's lips met in a passionate kiss.

"You planned this *together*?" Kristy cut her steak, still trying to absorb the shock.

Her father had bowed out, saying he would see them at church in the morning. He wanted to be there when they announced their engagement, but thought they should celebrate alone.

She flashed her ring. "It's beautiful!"

Billy nodded and smiled. "I thought you'd like it. … Your father's staying out at the ranch tonight. He's a great guy, Kristy. He'll be a great father-in-law."

"What happened between you? I want to know from the beginning."

He laughed. "Of course you do." Chewing his steak, his gray eyes twinkled. "I was despondent that day up at the pond, when you went storming off. I did a little of that 'heavy lifting' you told me about. I went to Jesus. He told me to get help. So I went riding with my little sister." Grinning, he continued, "She gave me great advice."

"Hannah?"

"Yeah. She said I should tell you I need you desperately and you're everything I ever wanted in a woman. It worked!" She slapped his arm and he chuckled. "Probably because it's the truth. She insisted we were madly in love and something about getting this whole thing over with because we were torturing everybody who had to watch us fight."

She laughed.

"When we got back from the ride, I had a talk with Dad."

"You told him about our fight?'

"Why not? I figured I needed help. To rub off a few more 'rough edges.'"

Smiling, she nodded, urging him on. "Sounds good. Go on."

"I told him everything. He asked some questions and gave me some counsel. I guess he struggled with similar stuff in the past. We prayed together and asked for God's grace. I still didn't feel like I was ready to call you."

"Why not?"

"My track record with making apologies hasn't been good lately."

She blushed. "Then what happened?'

"The next day, your dad called."

"My father called *you*?"

"Yep. He'd heard about our spat from you. He said he was sorry for causing trouble between us and said you were really upset. He apologized and said he shouldn't have been so hard on me. Then he said I was a great guy and he thought I was good for you. He said something about how he wasn't used to this father stuff and I needed to cut him some slack."

"Really?"

Billy smiled. "Yep. Then he asked if I still wanted to marry you."

"He what?"

Grinning, he continued. "When we were in Seattle, I told him I planned on asking you to marry me. I told him I'd keep him posted, which I didn't. I got offended. He's a great guy, Kristy. He didn't have to apologize. It was *my* fault! It was humbling for me to tell him I forgave him for grilling me, when I was being such a snob. If you were my daughter, I would've done the same. I'm sure it would've been worse!" He paused.

She smiled. "I want to know the rest of the story. Finish."

He sighed, then smiled. "Then he encouraged me to go ahead and ask you to marry me. I balked. I didn't think you were ready. I thought you might say 'no' after the way I'd treated you. He reassured me you were more ready than I thought. He insisted that if there was more commitment between us, we might get along better. You know, solve our disagreements faster. He thought there would be less insecurity. By the second phone call, he'd talked me into it. That afternoon I called you and apologized. From that point on he and I were planning this."

He motioned with his arm toward the flowers. "By the way,

do you like the flowers?"

"Of course I like the flowers! They're beautiful! I thought you would never forgive me for telling my father you were offended. Even after you said it was your fault, you seemed distant. You didn't call much, and when you did, you hardly talked. I was worried. Last night it seemed you couldn't get rid of me fast enough. Come on, Billy, sending me home at ten o'clock on Friday night? What was I supposed to think?

"When we came in here tonight and I saw you, I was afraid you were here with someone else. Maybe Marcel."

"Marcel? Are you crazy?" He paused, searching her face. He sighed. "Kristy, I'm sorry. I haven't paid much attention to you this last week. I had to get the ring and stuff. Plus I was getting to know your father and keeping a big secret. We'd agreed to make it all a surprise. And there was work, of course. I told you we were working cattle, remember?"

He smiled sheepishly. "Sorry about last night. He told me he would call at ten. I did kind of rush you out the door. I didn't know you were suffering like that."

"Dad did! That stinker!" She laughed softly. "I still feel bad. I betrayed your confidence. I always was such a blabbermouth. I cried a lot last week."

His hand reached over and covered hers. "Really? I'm sorry. I'll have to make it up to you. I love you, Kristy. There's no one else for me. You're perfect. Mom and Dad think so too. They say you won't let me get away with anything. You'll keep me in touch with reality. I need you, Kristy. I need you just the way you are. You're not too wounded. You fight rather well." He grinned. "Too well, in fact. And you're not a blabbermouth. You're beautiful, smart, humble and sweet. Like Hannah says, everything I would ever want in a woman. And I love to sing with you!" He paused.

"Have I *pursued* you enough?"

She smiled shyly. "Enough for now, but don't ever stop. I like it."

He grinned. "I won't. I want you to feel special. You're

special, to me, Kristy. And I want you to feel it."

Tears pooled in her eyes and he squeezed her hand.

Billy put down his guitar after leading worship and pulled Kristy close. He looked out over the congregation and said, "I'm proud to say that Kristy has agreed to marry me."

Cheering erupted.

"I want to introduce my future father-in-law too. Will you stand, James?" He motioned with his hand. "This is James Turner. And I must say, I couldn't have caught her without his help."

Everyone laughed.

Letting go of a beaming Kristy, he picked up the guitar and strummed. The drum rolled and he grinned. "Let's sing one more song."

> We will dance on the streets that are golden,
> The glorious bride and the great Son of Man
> From every tongue and tribe and nation
> We'll join in the song of the Lamb ...[15]

He set aside the guitar and Sam took over. Noting Kristy's startled gaze, he whispered in her ear. "Come and dance with me." Then, taking her hand, he led her off the stage, wrapped his arm around her waist and began waltzing with her in front of the church.

He motioned to the congregation. "Come and join us. Will you?"

Couples came to the front and waltzed to the music.

At the end of the song, Pastor Evan came forward with a group of men, including James and Ben. "Stay up here for a minute, you two. We want to bless you."

They circled them, prayed for them, and blessed them. Then Billy and Kristy settled into a couple of chairs near the front. Smiling, their hearts continued to sing.

Pastor Evan opened his Bible and read:

> "Jesus said: 'Truly I tell you, unless you change and

become like little children, you will never enter the kingdom of heaven. Therefore, whoever takes the lowly position of this child is the greatest in the kingdom of heaven.

"I used to think that I only did this once when I accepted Jesus. After that, I could carry on as I did before, proving myself by performance and position. But Jesus was talking about a lifestyle. He was talking about a position close to our father in heaven. An intimate relationship. There's nothing like being his son or daughter.

"God called me to repent and not only from sin. I repented *unto* glory. I fell short of the glory. Stepping into my place as much loved son is returning to the glory of God for which I was created. ...

"Who will join with me to become a son or a daughter? Or upgrade their position as a son or daughter? Who will pledge to be the Father's beloved child and come close to him on a daily basis, practicing his presence? If this is your desire, come forward and we'll pray together."

Billy and Kristy looked at each other and nodded. They rose to their feet, along with several others. When they reached the Pastor, he smiled and laid a hand on each of their shoulders. They bowed their heads. "Father, thank you for this young couple that have planned a future together."

He paused. Then declared, "Your father has a bright future for you, Billy and Kristy. I see you in the glory of God, joyfully moving in power." He took each one's hand and continued, "I see people saved, delivered and healed through your hands. Let that power be released to you this day, because you have stepped into your places, Son and Daughter of the King. I command every demonic power to bow to your anointing and calling! Let this child-likeness and this *glory* change the world!"

CHILDREN AT LAST

How beautiful you are and how pleasing, Oh love with your delights! ... Come, my love, let us go to the country-side .... Song of Songs 7:6, 11

Kristy drove the highway, singing to a C.D. Billy gave her. A bright July day, the sun was high in the sky. Hot air blew through the open windows of the car, but she didn't mind the lack of air conditioning. Not today.

She surveyed the wooded mountains on the hazy horizon, eyes falling to the lush, green hay fields and golden fields of wheat. The clear blue sky was scattered with soft white clouds, floating overhead. Her heart soared and she paused.

"The sky is so beautiful, Father!"

A loud drum roll came from the C.D. Another dancing song.

"Billy loves to dance." She laughed. "I'm so blessed. It's wonderful to be loved. I'm not talking about Billy, either—or my father—or my mother. You're such a wonderful Father! I never dreamed I could be so happy. And now I'm going to be married!"

She pictured Billy grinning, gray eyes twinkling, tipping his cowboy hat in her direction. "I never thought I'd marry a farm boy—or cowboy—or whatever he is." She giggled.

"You're full of surprises, God."

The car lurched, then sputtered. "What? Not again. I don't even have my cell phone with me!"

A few minutes later, Kristy sat along the highway, stranded. She squinted into the sun, hand shading her eyes. She looked down at her bright yellow tank top, denim shorts and cheap flip-flops.

It was a long way to a house for help. Especially in flip flops. Billy was right. They weren't practical. But they were comfortable on a blazing hot day like this one. Sighing, she flopped down on the front seat, shed the flip-flops and dangled bare feet out the open driver's window. Perspiration beaded on her forehead and she wiped it away.

She didn't even have water!

Now what?

"Father, send someone. I think I'll finish this CD before I decide what to do." Surrendering to her predicament, she resumed singing along to the loud, happy music.

჎ᕑ ᕑ჎ᕑ

On his way home from an errand in town, Billy spotted the old green Pontiac parked at the side of the highway. Two familiar bare feet bobbed out the driver's window.

"What the—?" He burst out laughing. "I'd recognize those feet anywhere. I wonder what's wrong this time."

He pulled up behind the car and got out. The sound of Kristy's uninhibited singing rang through the air.

> *I could sing unending songs*
> *Of how you saved my soul*
> *I could dance a thousand miles*
> *Because of your great love*
> *My heart is bursting, Lord*
> *Because of all you've done*
> *Of how you've changed my life*
> *And wiped away my past ...*[16]

He whistled loudly.

She continued to sing, oblivious to his presence.

At the open driver's window, he grabbed a foot.

Startled, Kristy yanked her foot out of his grasp, and sat up. "Oh, Billy! Thank God! You about gave me a heart attack! How'd you find me?"

He smiled, teasing. "I couldn't miss you. This green bomb and those cute little feet would give you away anywhere. What's wrong?"

"I don't know. It just quit."

At the front of the car, he said, "Pop the hood."

After a few minutes, he slammed it shut and came to her window, wagging his head. Leaning on the car door, he smiled. "I haven't the slightest idea what's wrong. Come with me." He opened her door, took hold of her arm and led her toward his pickup.

She looked over her shoulder, "What about my car?"

"We'll get it later. Right now I have something else in mind." He brought her alongside his pickup and opened the door. "Hop in." Smiling, she complied.

Rambling down the highway, he took an unexpected turn on a gravel road.

"Where are you taking me?" Kristy asked.

He turned to her, a mischievous smile on his face. "I'm kidnaping you. Haven't you figured that out yet? I couldn't resist a beautiful woman stranded on the side of the road!"

"But they're expecting me at Barewood's. They'll be worried!"

Pulling out his phone, he handed it to her. "Here. Call. Tell them you were kidnaped and won't be back for a few hours."

She made the call, then peered at him, blue eyes questioning and playful.

"I'm thirsty. Got any water?"

"Sure." He handed her a dirty plastic jug, warmed by the sun.

She wrinkled her nose. "If I wasn't so thirsty, I'd throw up at the sight of this."

"It's wet."

She drank.

໑❧ ❧໑

"Here we are."

Billy pulled up to a grassy spot near a sparkling creek, shaded by aspens and willows. He stopped. "Let's go have a look." He jumped out of the pickup.

She caught up to him and turning, he smiled. "This is a pretty spot, don't you think?"

"It is."

He pointed. "There's even a picnic table."

Suddenly, he scooped her up in his arms, holding her close.

She gasped, then squealed. "Billy! What are you doing?"

He squeezed her to his chest firmly, smiling wickedly. "Holding you."

Squirming, she pushed against him. "Put me down!"

"Okay." He returned her to her feet.

He walked over to the picnic table and sat, pulling her onto his lap. Removing his ball cap, he laid it on the table. Then he returned his arm to encircle her waist and held her close.

"Is that better?"

"A little." She let out a long breath.

His gray eyes danced. "What do you feel?"

"Out of control … small … a little squishy …"

His eyebrows rose. "Squishy?"

She laughed. "Yeah. My heart's getting squishy."

A smile tugged the corners of his lips. "Good … Just sit here a minute more."

They sat in silence. Wind in the trees, flowing water and chirping birds gave them concert.

"What are you feeling now?"

She snuggled close. "Wanted … Protected … Loved."

Eyes locking on hers, he lowered his head and let his lips brush over hers. He chuckled softly and rubbed his nose on hers. "That's what I was shooting for. Do you feel like your father's much-loved child yet?"

She smiled. "I'm getting there."

Suddenly, she bounced off his lap and stood. "Okay. What can I do to help you feel like His much-loved child?"

He laughed. "That's a hard one."

Pouncing on him, she pulled him off the seat and onto the grass where she sat on him and tickled his ribs. But he just grinned. Unmoved.

She made faces at him.

No response.

"This is unfair! There's got to be something I can do!"

A teasing smile appeared on his face. He wriggled his eyebrows and said, "I can think of something that would make me feel loved ... But we better not go there."

She leapt to her feet. "Oh, Billy! Stop it!" Grabbing his hand, she pulled him to his feet, dragged him down to the creek bank and shoved him on a large rock beside the clear running water.

"Now take off your boots and roll up your pant legs. We're going wading."

Into the water they went, sliding on the slippery rocks, holding onto each other for balance. When they were up to their knees in the running water, Billy lurched, pretending to fall.

She startled, then shoved him playfully. He lost his balance and landed waist deep in the water.

"Burr ... it's cold!"

But he remained there, jeans under the moving water and T-shirt half submerged, peering at her with half a smile from under dark lashes, beaded with water.

Suddenly, he grabbed her ankle.

Kristy squealed. He pulled her down beside him and she gasped. The water was ice cold! But soon she recovered. She splashed and dunked him and he returned the favor. They wrestled and played in the cold water, laughing and splashing.

Later, they drug themselves to the grassy plot above, flopped down and lay in the warm sunshine, side by side. Soaked and mud-smeared they caught their breath, still laughing. Billy turned to her, propped on one elbow.

"You started it."

Kristy rose and sat cross-legged. She undid her mussed pony-tail and redid it, pulling wet strands of hair from her face. "What are you feeling now?"

"Happy."

She smiled. "Good. Do you feel like a kid yet?"

He gave her a crooked smile. "I'm getting there. Its hard work, but somebody has to do it."

Giggling, she bent and kissed his wet forehead.

§♦♦§♦

Hey Barry,

I'm still here in Seattle. I think I'll move here. I'll find something to do for work. Maybe even sell cars!

Like I told you, it's going well with the kids. Toby and I are spending a lot of time together. He's a great kid! He was angry with me at first, and still is, but its cracking. I'm so glad I came back!

Pat's doing real well. Something good has truly happened with her and God! She's back to work and really appreciates the help with Toby. We're getting along great. We'll see what happens.

And Kristy, she's engaged and very happy. But then I already told you about all that. I didn't realize how much she truly needed my blessing and to know I love her. Thank you for all your prayers—and for being there for me. My life has been restored!

Your friend and brother,
James Turner

You restored me to health
and let me live ...
In your love you kept me
from the pit of destruction ...
The living, the living—
they praise you ...
Fathers tell their children
about your faithfulness.
Isaiah 38:16-19

And His name shall be called,
Wonderful,
Counselor,
The Mighty God,
The Everlasting Father,
The Prince of Peace.
Of the increase of
His government and
His peace,
there will be no end.
Isaiah 9:6b-7a

Author's note:

Learning to be a child has been a life-long journey for me. I am still discovering the power and joy of being childlike. God made us to be joyful, fearless and free children, letting all anxiety go. It's the inner healing of father and mother wounds that paves the way to becoming childlike. God bless you on that journey of restoration and forgiveness of others and self. May the power of God flow in you, around you and through you as you become a child. Receive God's love and let your heart be restored!

Hearts Return

It takes a father

Jeff Carson is doing well until he falls in love with Cassie Watson. Convinced he's not good enough, he pulls away, sliding into old patterns and habits.

When Jeff withdraws, Cassie decides to fight. What is his problem?

Ben is alarmed. Jeff has won his daughters heart, but he's struggling. Ben wants to help, but he couldn't help Jeff's father. Will Cassie be okay?

In a story where God has a voice, an imperfect father restores identity and brings peace in the midst of turmoil.

JEFF LOSES HOPE FOR HIS FUTURE, ISOLATES AND SINKS INTO DESPAIR. IS HE DOOMED? OR WILL FAITH AND HOPE PREVAIL?

Valley of Peace / Book 1
ISBN 978-0-9822707-0-7

Look for Book Three in the "Valley of Peace" Series.

Hearts Revealed

It takes a friend

David Boone has given up on meeting the high standards of his family's religion. But he knows it is the only true way. Then he meets Hannah Watson. She's crazy! Is this what knowing Jesus is like? Intrigued, he is attracted, but could he be that free? What would his family think?

Hannah Watson is being stalked. David, her employer, repeatedly rescues her. Impressed by his chivalry, she welcomes his help and friendship. But he thinks she's clueless. And is he hiding something?

David and Hannah find answers in another relational adventure by Cheryl Hug.

Cheryl Hug and her husband of forty years, live in Eastern Oregon. They have seven children and fifteen grand-children. Experiencing God's love is changing her life, marriage and family. Her passion is for people to know the One who restores all things.

1. David Ruis "You're Worthy of My Praise " (Shade Tree Music, 1991)
2. Matt Redmond "Undignified" (Thankyou Music, 1995)
3. Billy J. Foote "You Are My King" (worshiptogether.com songs,1996)
4. David Ruis "Let Your Glory Fall" (Mercy/Vineyard Publishing, 1992)
5. Holland Davis, Mark McCoy, Rick Harchol "Healing Word" (Mercy/Vineyard Publisher 1995)
6. Terry Butler "Your Deep Deep Love" (Mercy/Vineyard Publishing 1996)
7. Jared Anderson "Rescue" (Vertical Worship Songs 2003)
8. Brian Doerkson "Faithful One" (Mercy/Vineyard Publishing, 1989)
9. Charlie Hall "Salvation" (Thankyou Music, 2000)
10. Adolphe Charles Adame, Bart Millard John Sullivan Dwight, Pete Kipley, Placide Cappeau "O Holy Night" (Public Domain, 1847)
11. Brian Johnson, Joel Case, Jonathan David Helser "No Longer Slaves" (Bethel Music Publishing, 2014)
12. Brenton Brown, Ken Riley "Everlasting God" (Thankyou Music, 2005)
13. John Barnett "Hold Me" (Mercy/Vineyard Publishing, 1995)
14. Hugo Peretti, Luigi Creatore, George Weiss "Can't Help Falling in Love" (Gladys Music, 1961)
15. David Ruis "We Will Dance" (Mercy/Vineyard Publishing, 1993)
16. Martin Smith "Happy Song" (Curious? Music UK, 1994)